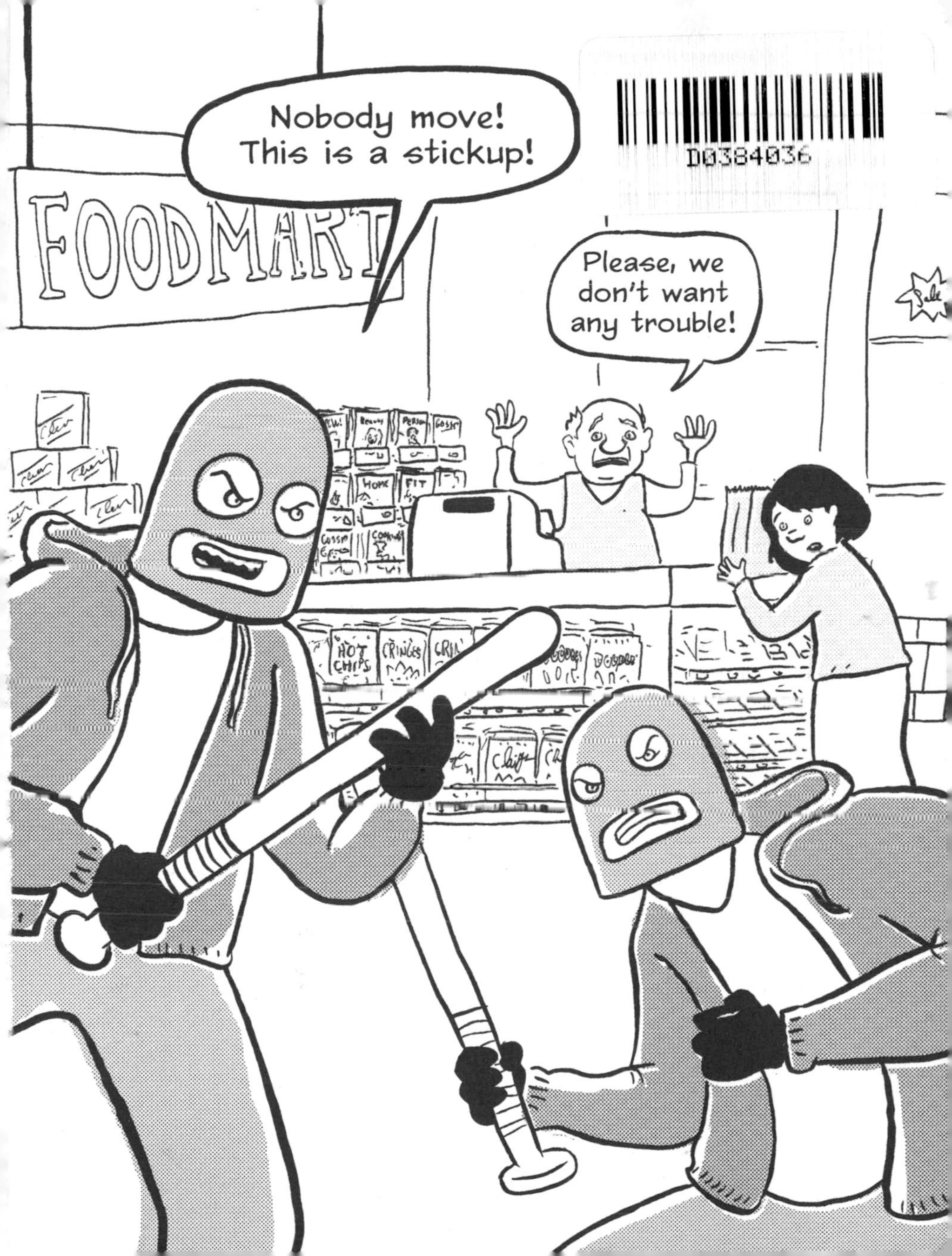
Nobody move! This is a stickup!
Please, we don't want any trouble!
FOODMART

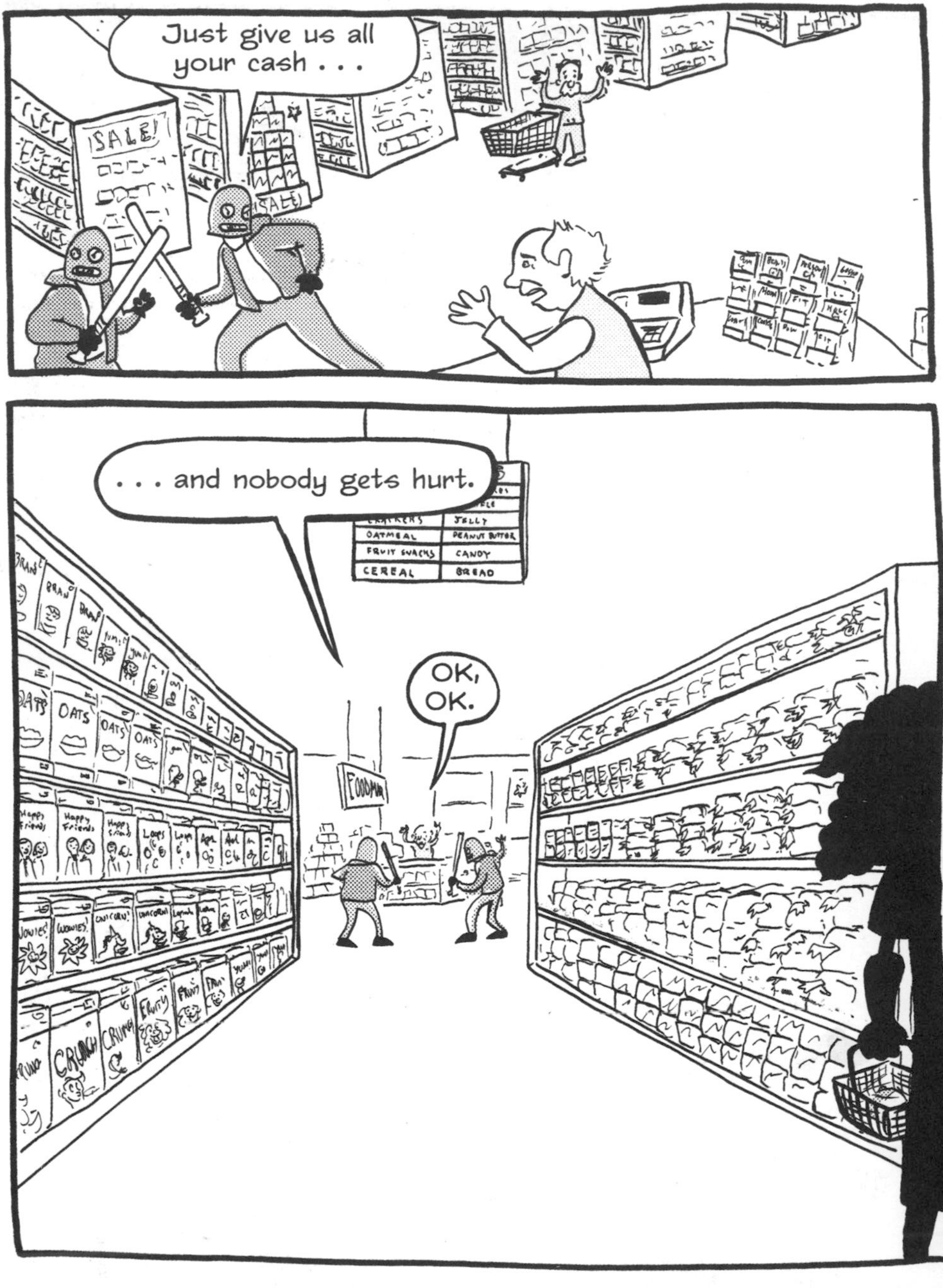
Just give us all your cash . . .
SALE!
. . . and nobody gets hurt.
OK, OK.
JELLY
OATMEAL
PEANUT BUTTER
FRUIT SNACKS
CANDY
CEREAL
BREAD

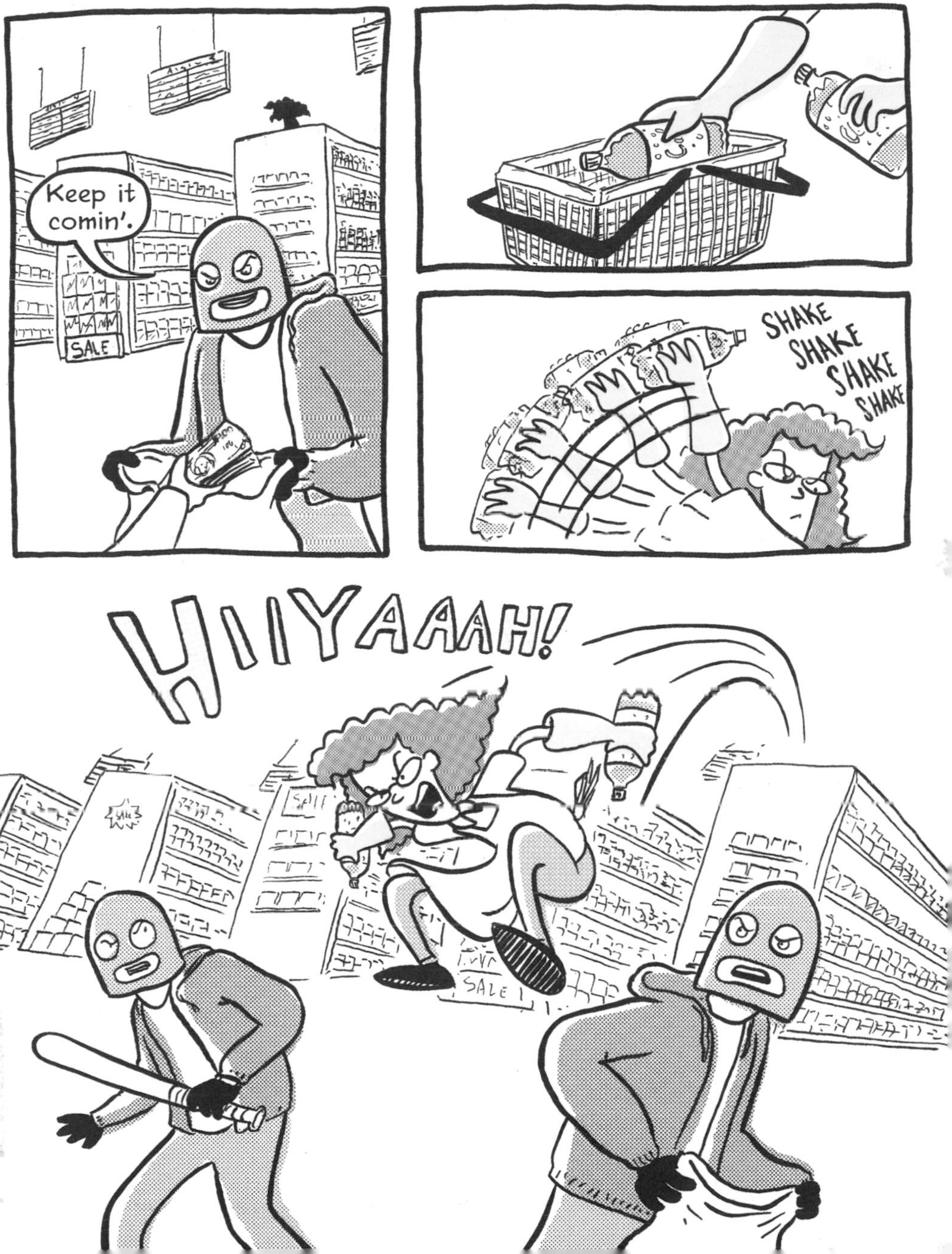
Keep it comin'.
SALE
SHAKE
SHAKE
SHAKE
SHAKE
HIIYAAAH!
SALE

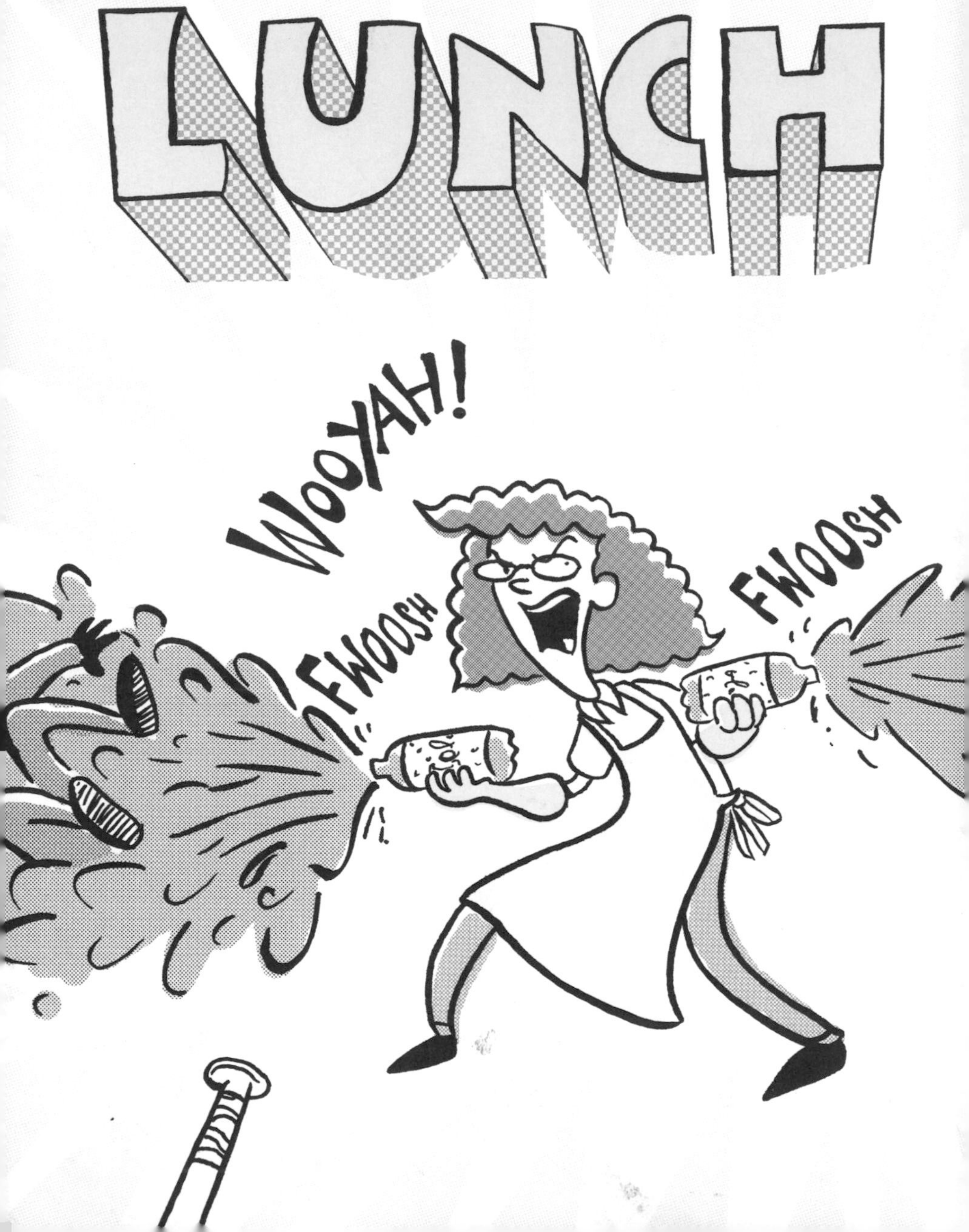
LUNCH
WOOYAH!
FWOOSH
FWOOSH

Y and the Field Trip Fiasco

Jarrett J. Krosoczka

Alfred A. Knopf ✦ New York

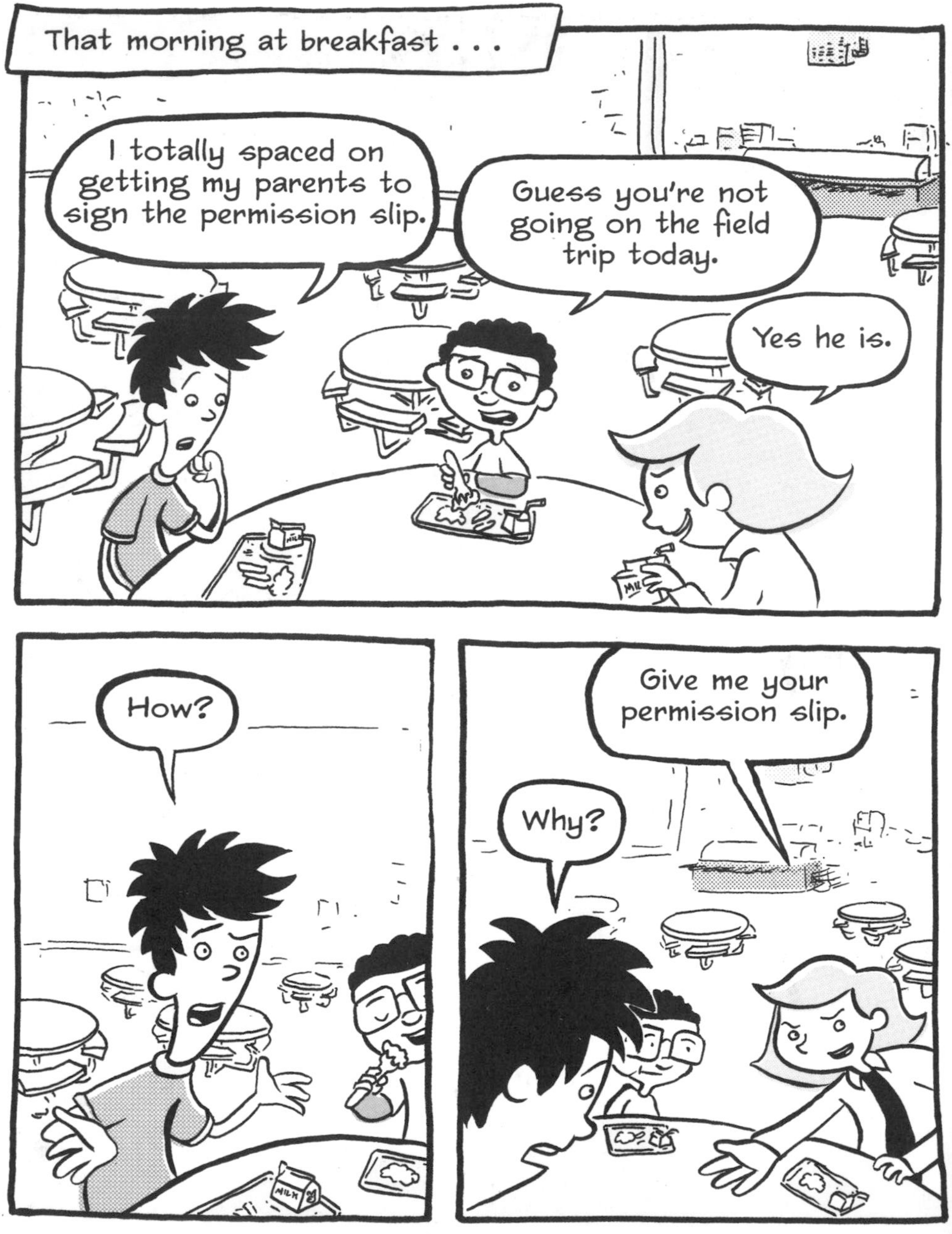
That morning at breakfast . . .
I totally spaced on getting my parents to sign the permission slip.
Guess you're not going on the field trip today.
Yes he is.
How?
Give me your permission slip.
Why?

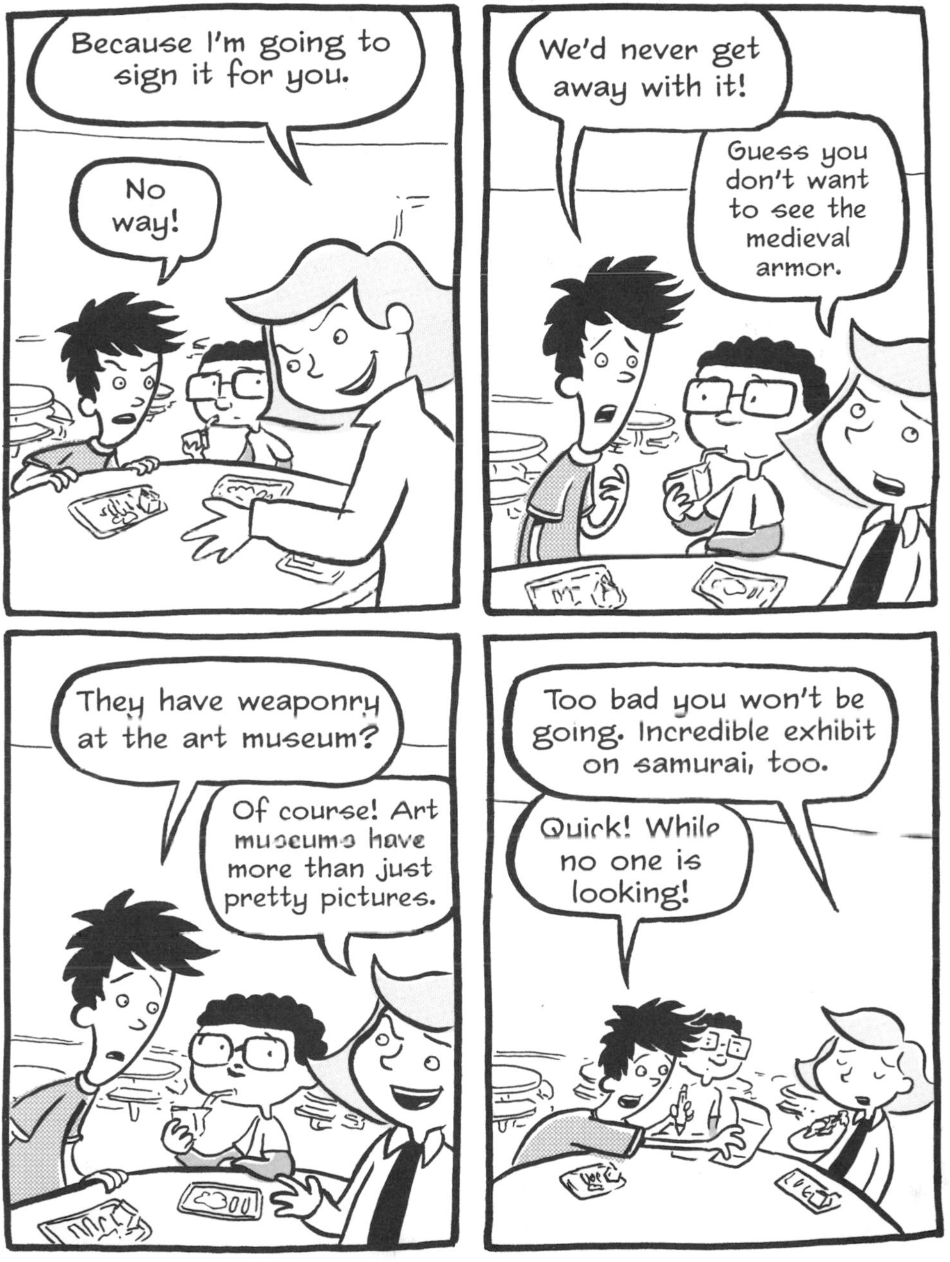
Because I'm going to sign it for you.
No way!
We'd never get away with it!
Guess you don't want to see the medieval armor.
They have weaponry at the art museum?
Of course! Art museums have more than just pretty pictures.
Too bad you won't be going. Incredible exhibit on samurai, too.
Quick! While no one is looking!

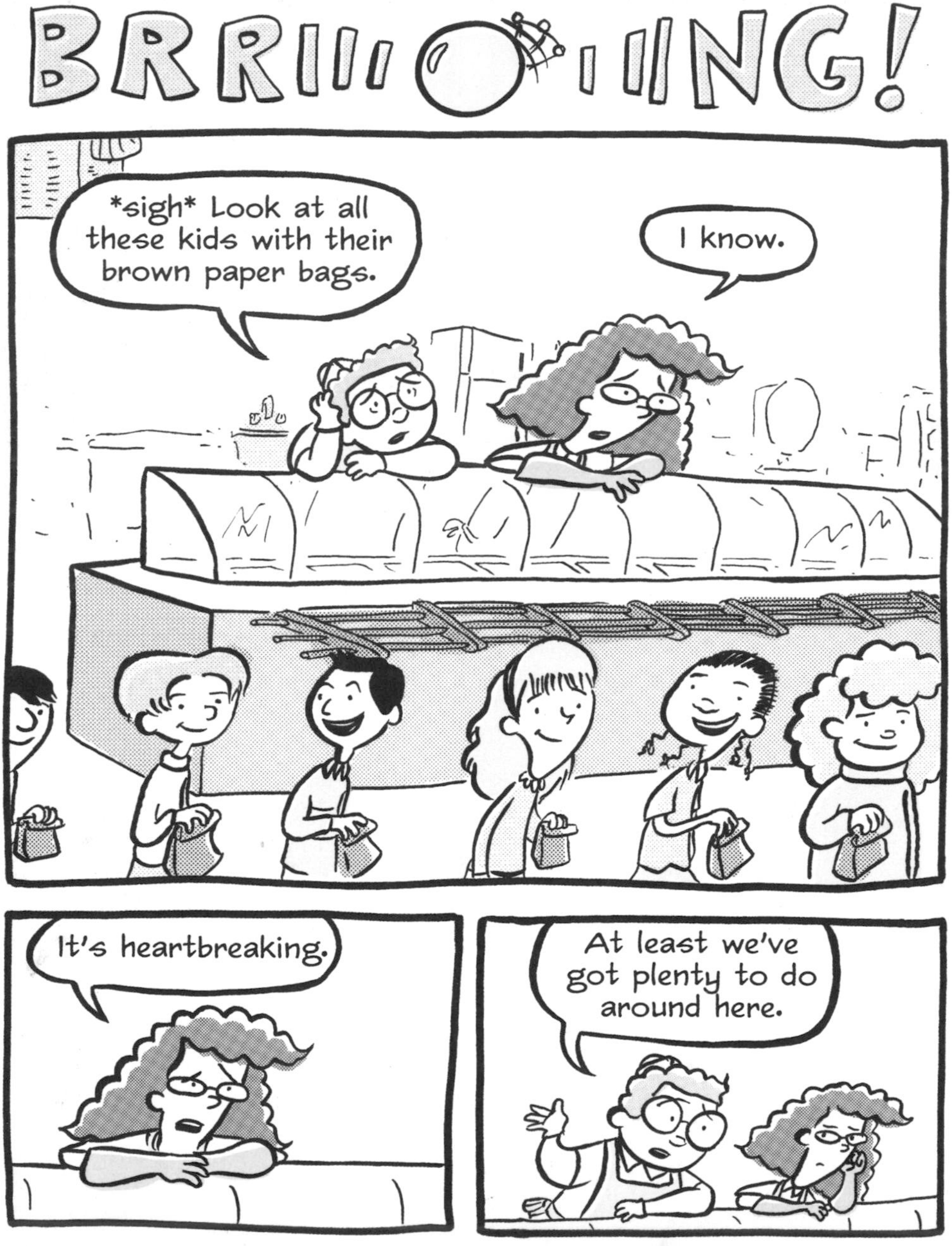
BRRIIIOIIING!
sigh Look at all these kids with their brown paper bags.
I know.
It's heartbreaking.
At least we've got plenty to do around here.

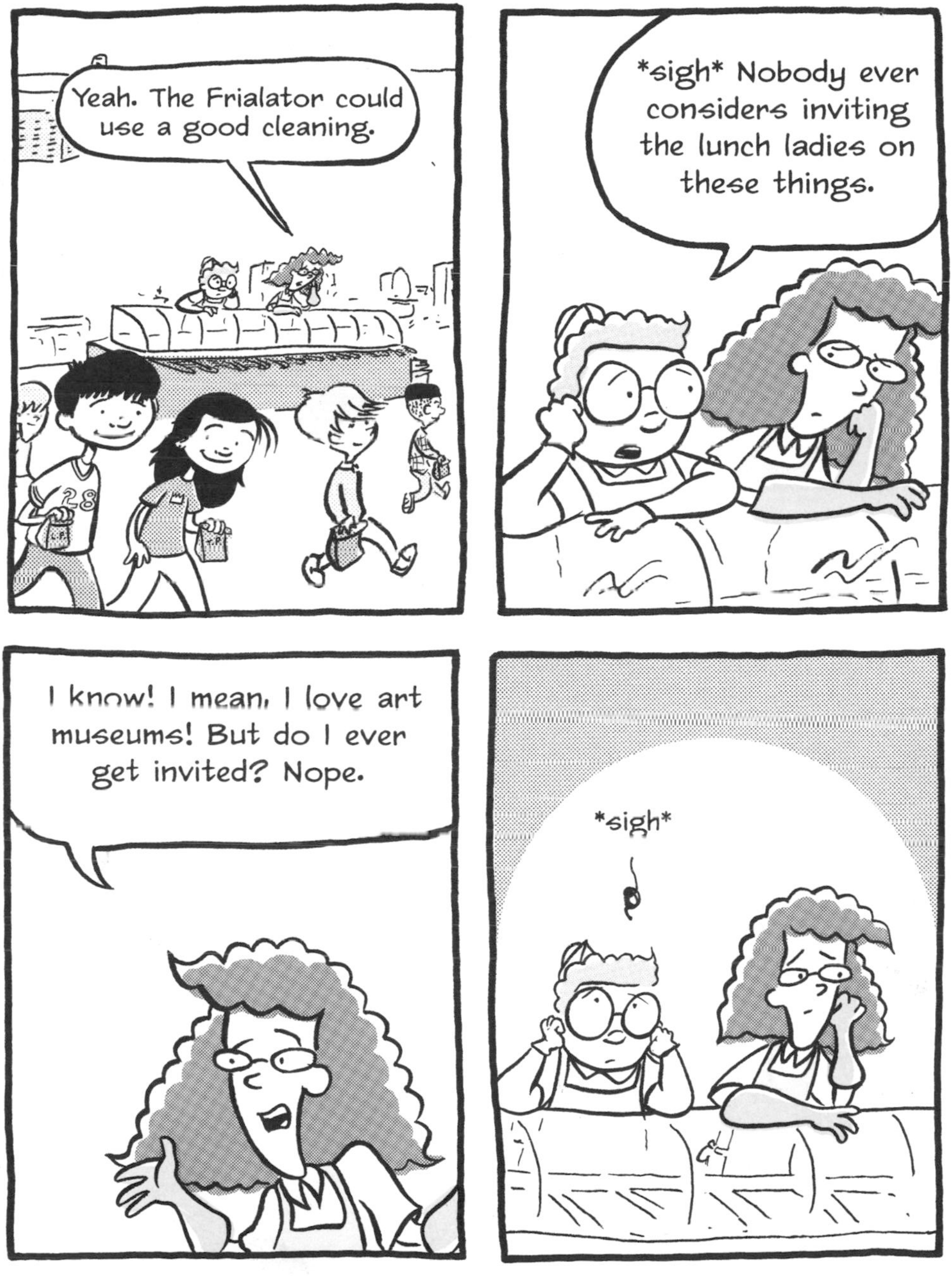
Yeah. The Frialator could use a good cleaning.
sigh Nobody ever considers inviting the lunch ladies on these things.
I know! I mean, I love art museums! But do I ever get invited? Nope.
sigh

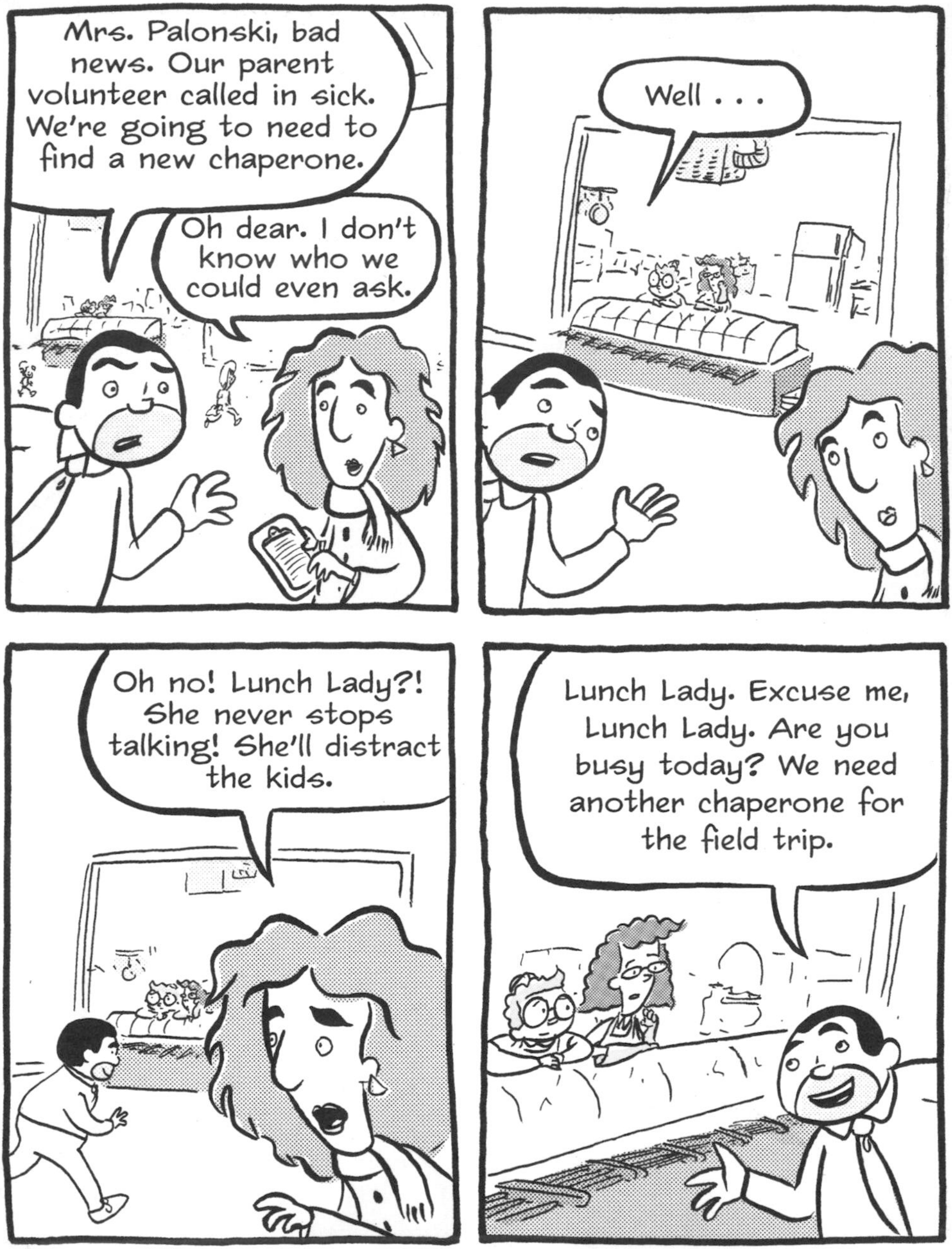
Mrs. Palonski, bad news. Our parent volunteer called in sick. We're going to need to find a new chaperone.
Oh dear. I don't know who we could even ask.
Well . . .
Oh no! Lunch Lady?! She never stops talking! She'll distract the kids.
Lunch Lady. Excuse me, Lunch Lady. Are you busy today? We need another chaperone for the field trip.

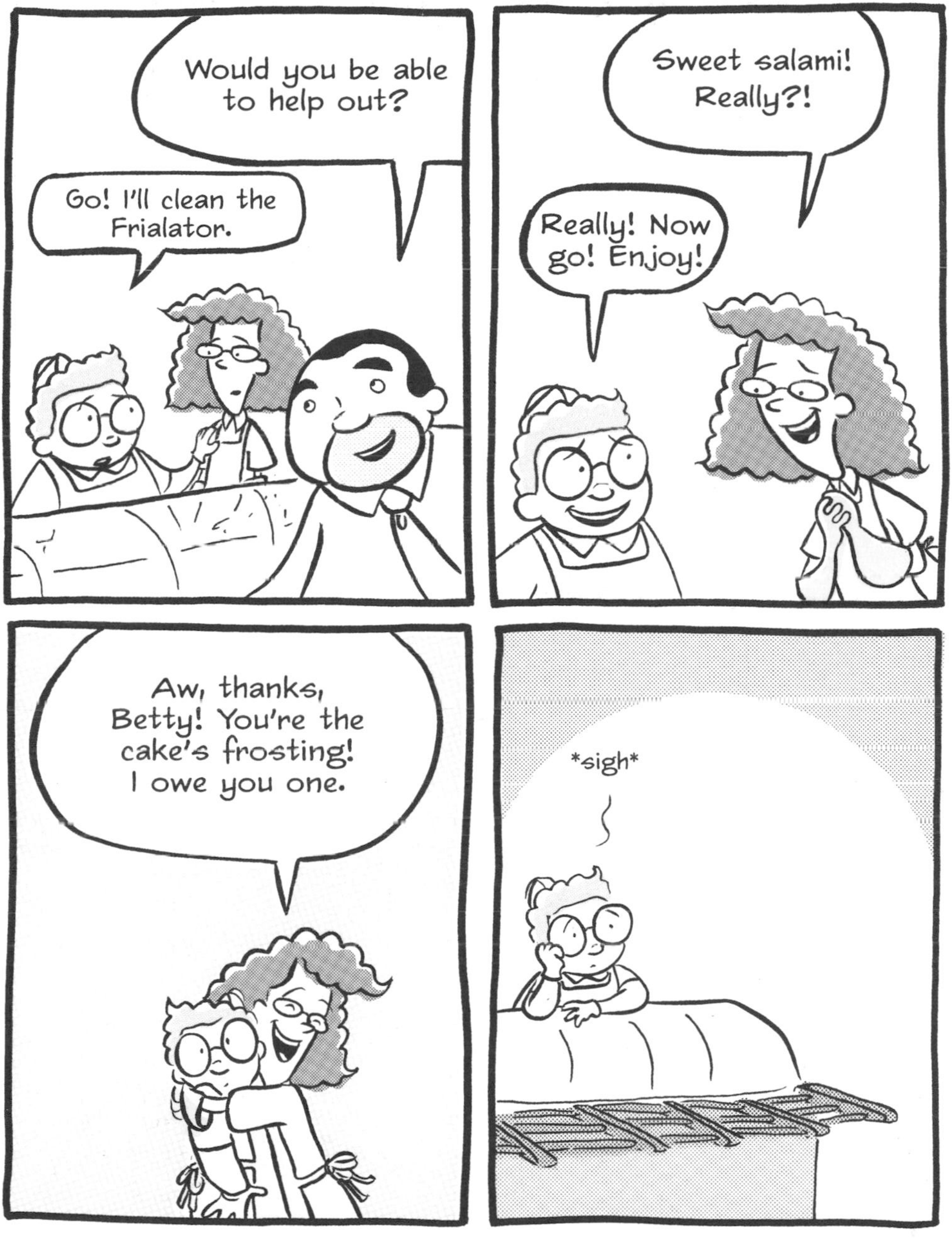
Would you be able to help out?
Go! I'll clean the Frialator.
Sweet salami! Really?!
Really! Now go! Enjoy!
Aw, thanks, Betty! You're the cake's frosting! I owe you one.
sigh

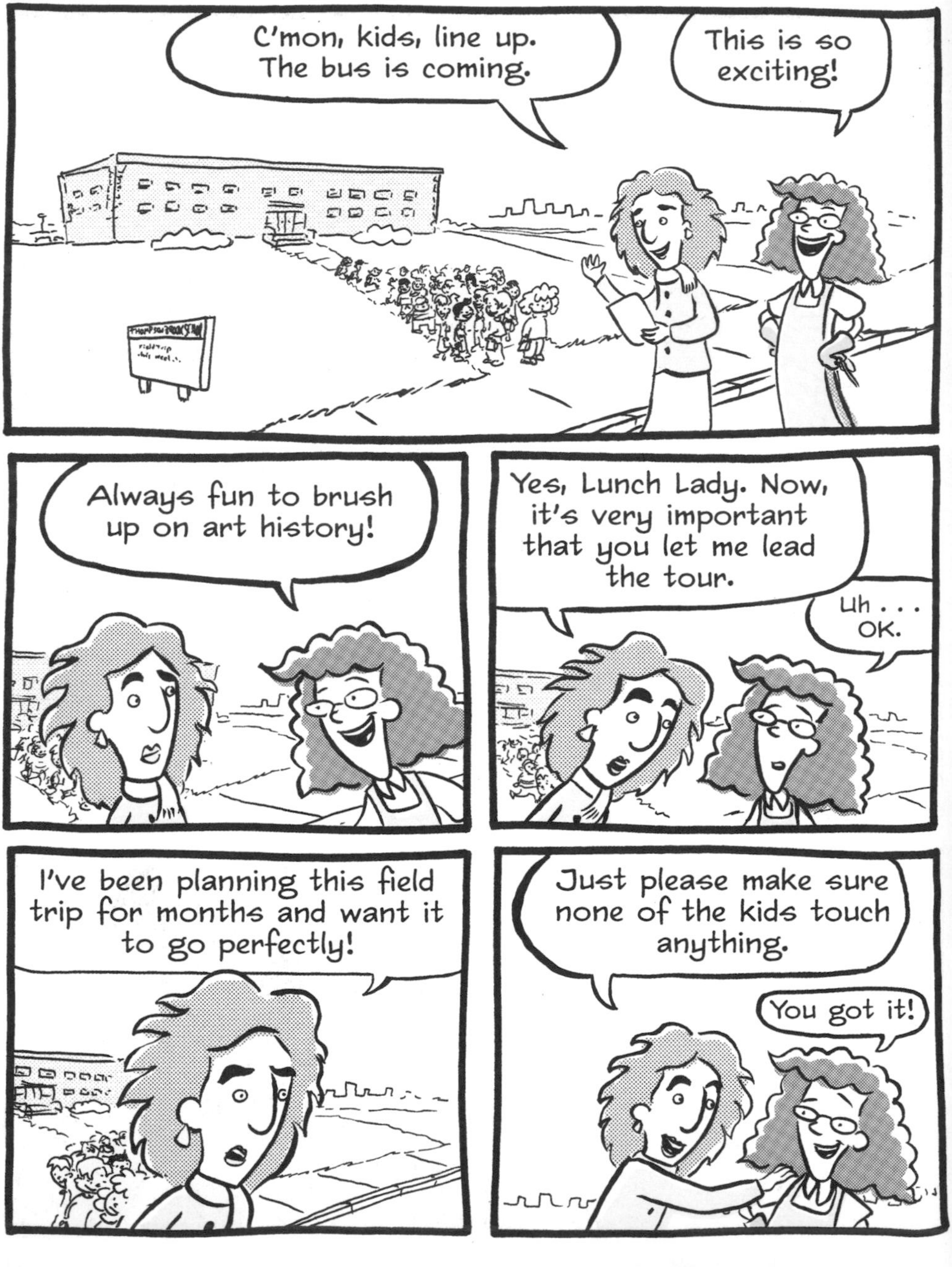
C'mon, kids, line up. The bus is coming.
This is so exciting!
Always fun to brush up on art history!
Yes, Lunch Lady. Now, it's very important that you let me lead the tour.
Uh . . . OK.
I've been planning this field trip for months and want it to go perfectly!
Just please make sure none of the kids touch anything.
You got it!

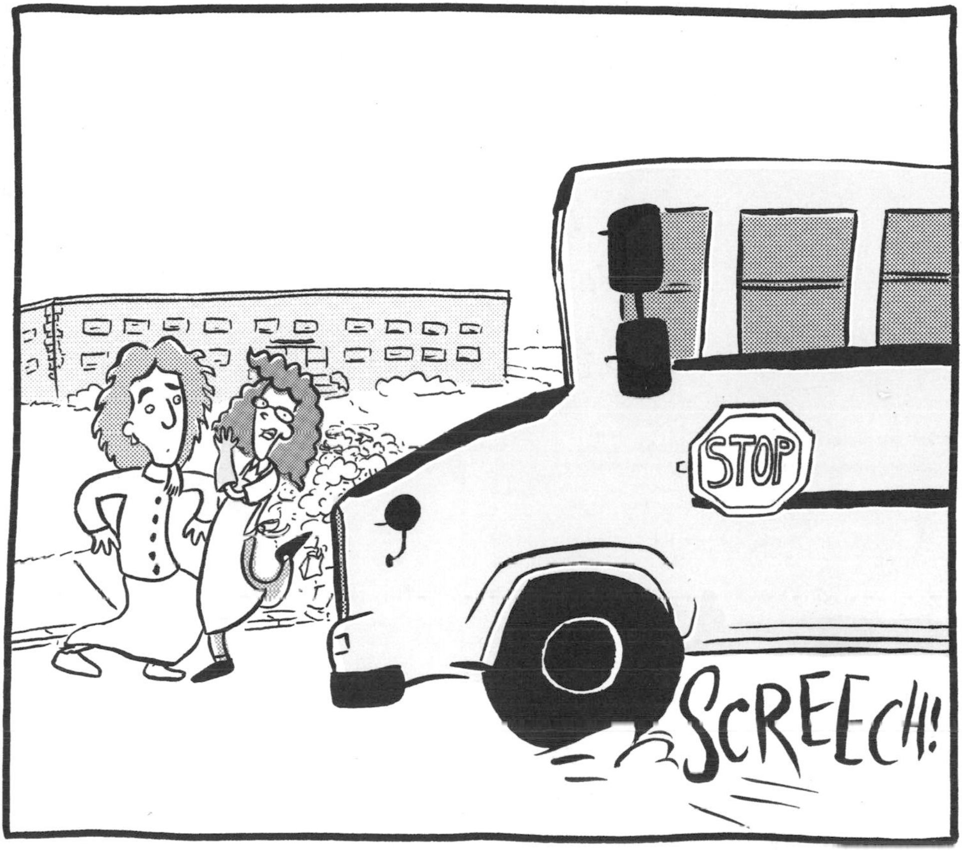
STOP
SCREECH!

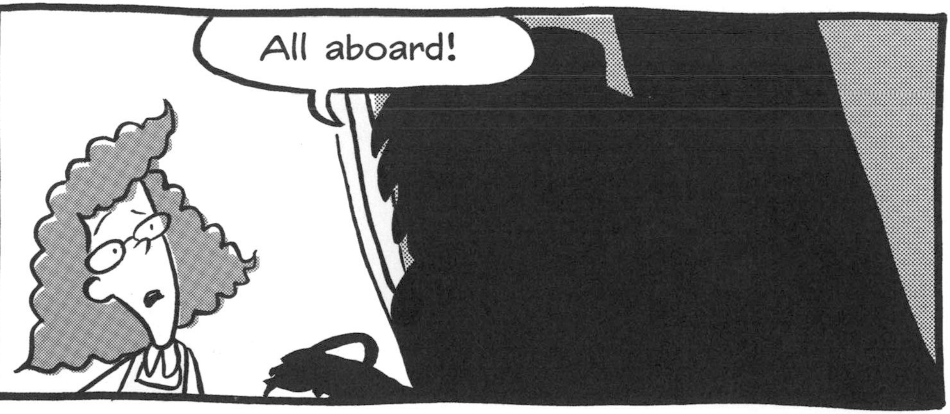
All aboard!

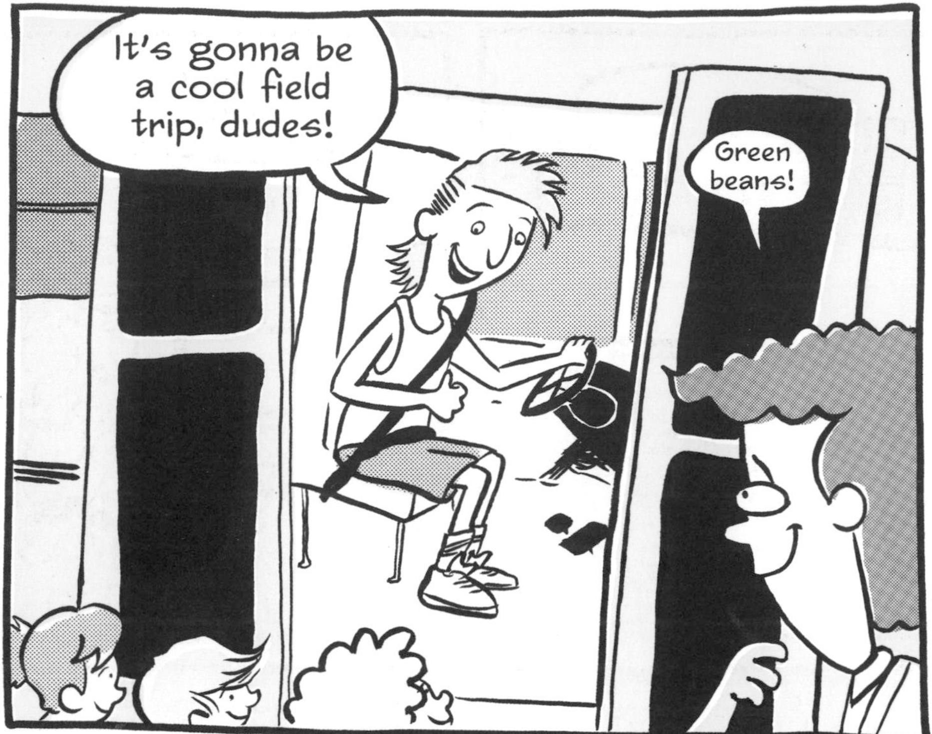
It's gonna be a cool field trip, dudes!
Green beans!

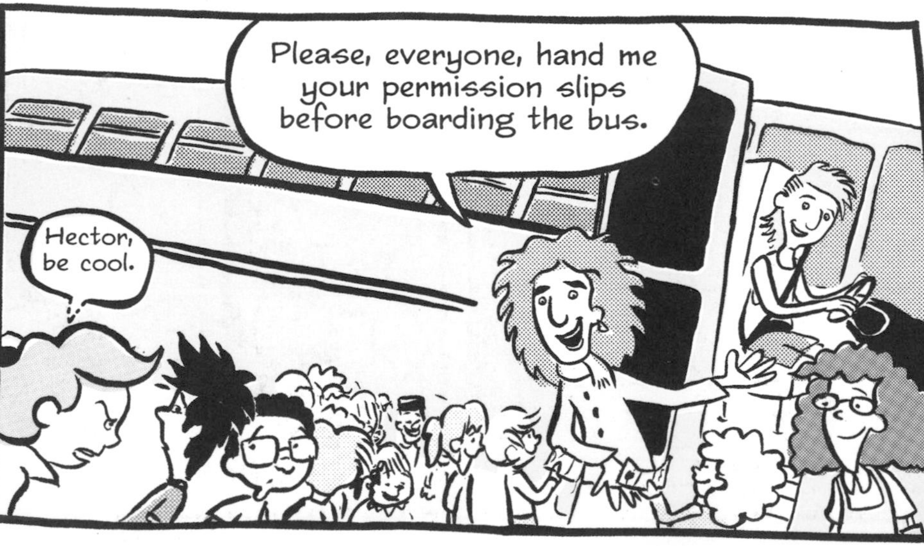
Please, everyone, hand me your permission slips before boarding the bus.
Hector, be cool.

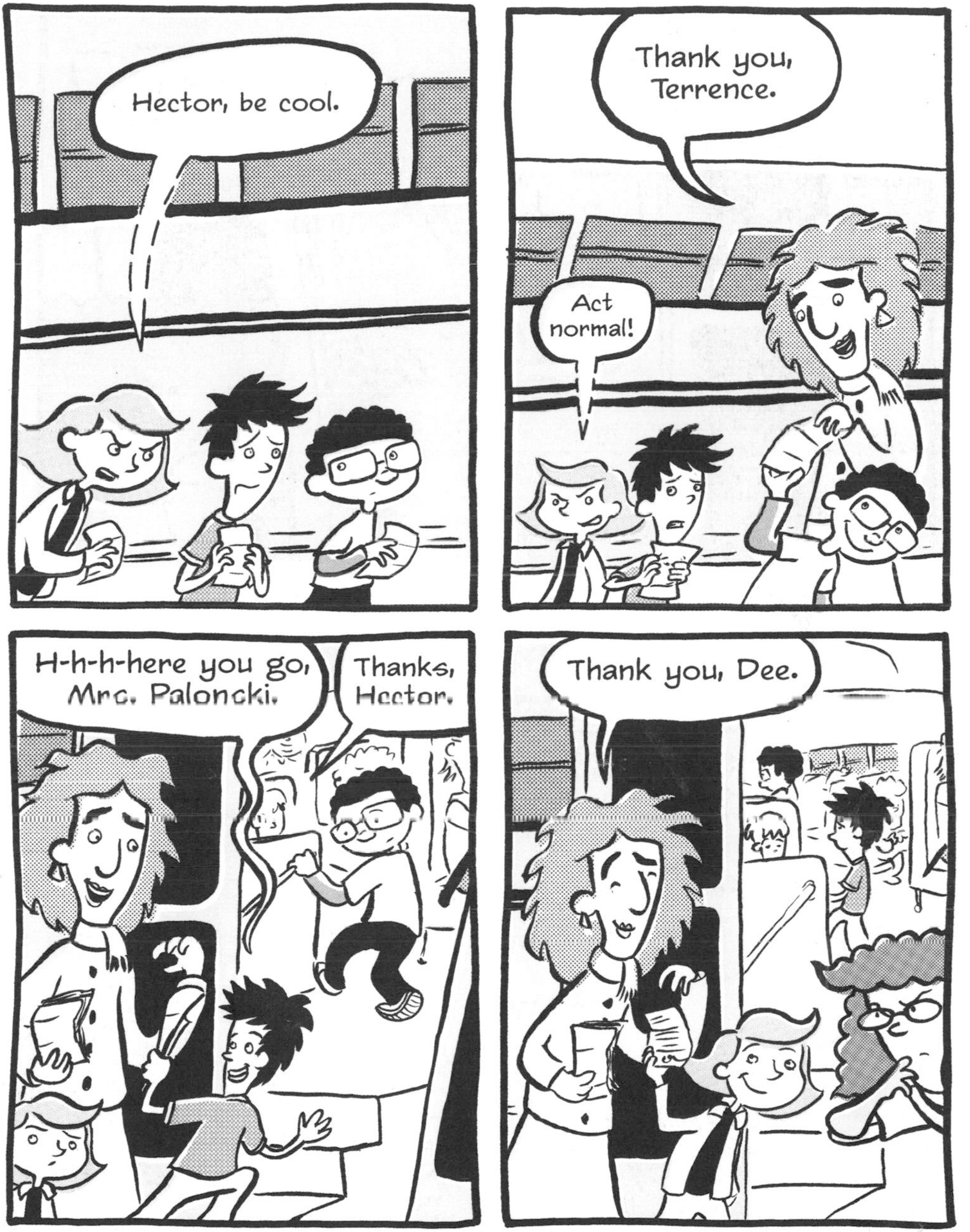
Hector, be cool.
Thank you, Terrence.
Act normal!
H-h-h-here you go, Mrs. Palonski.
Thanks, Hector.
Thank you, Dee.

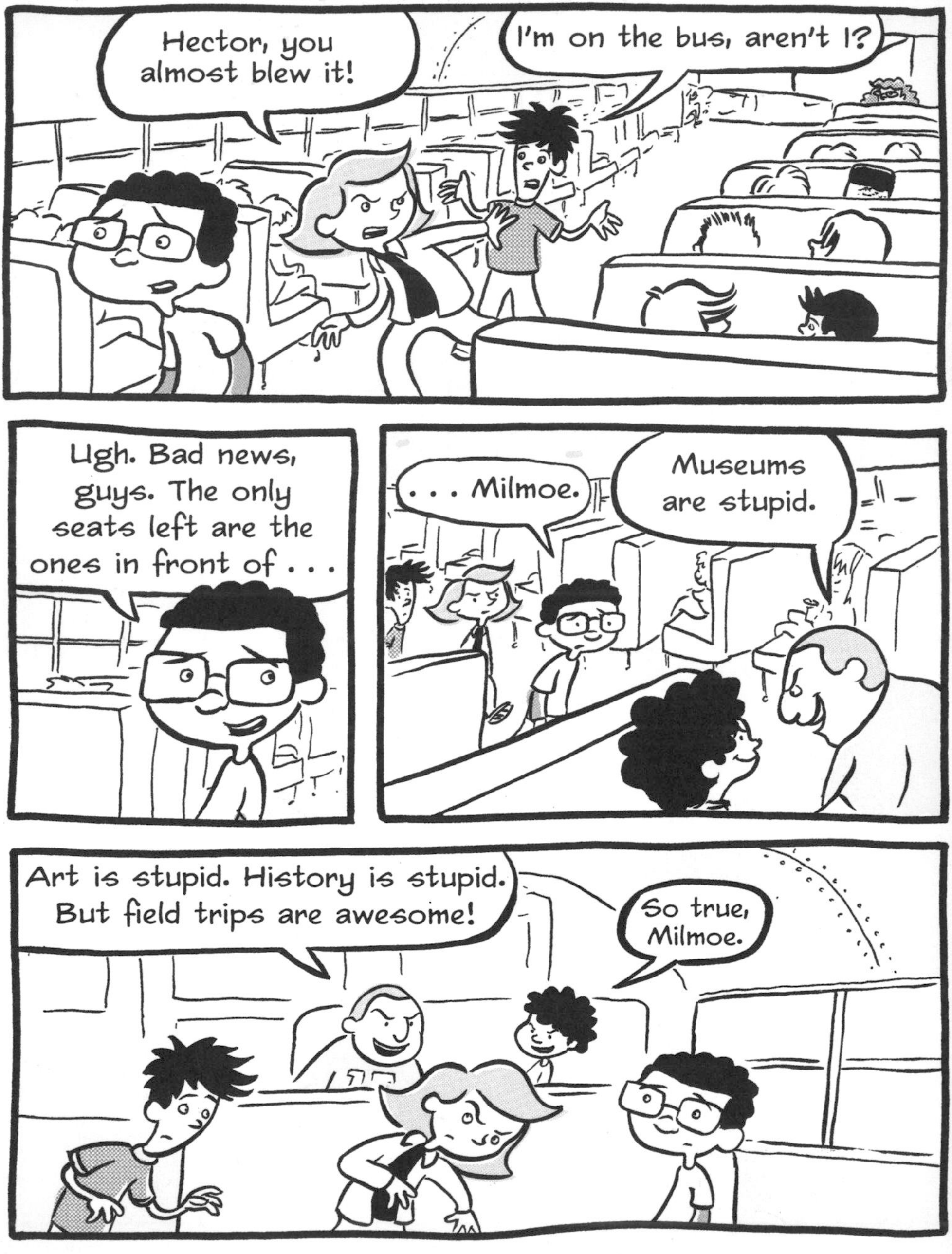
Hector, you almost blew it!
I'm on the bus, aren't I?
Ugh. Bad news, guys. The only seats left are the ones in front of . . .
. . . Milmoe.
Museums are stupid.
Art is stupid. History is stupid. But field trips are awesome!
So true, Milmoe.

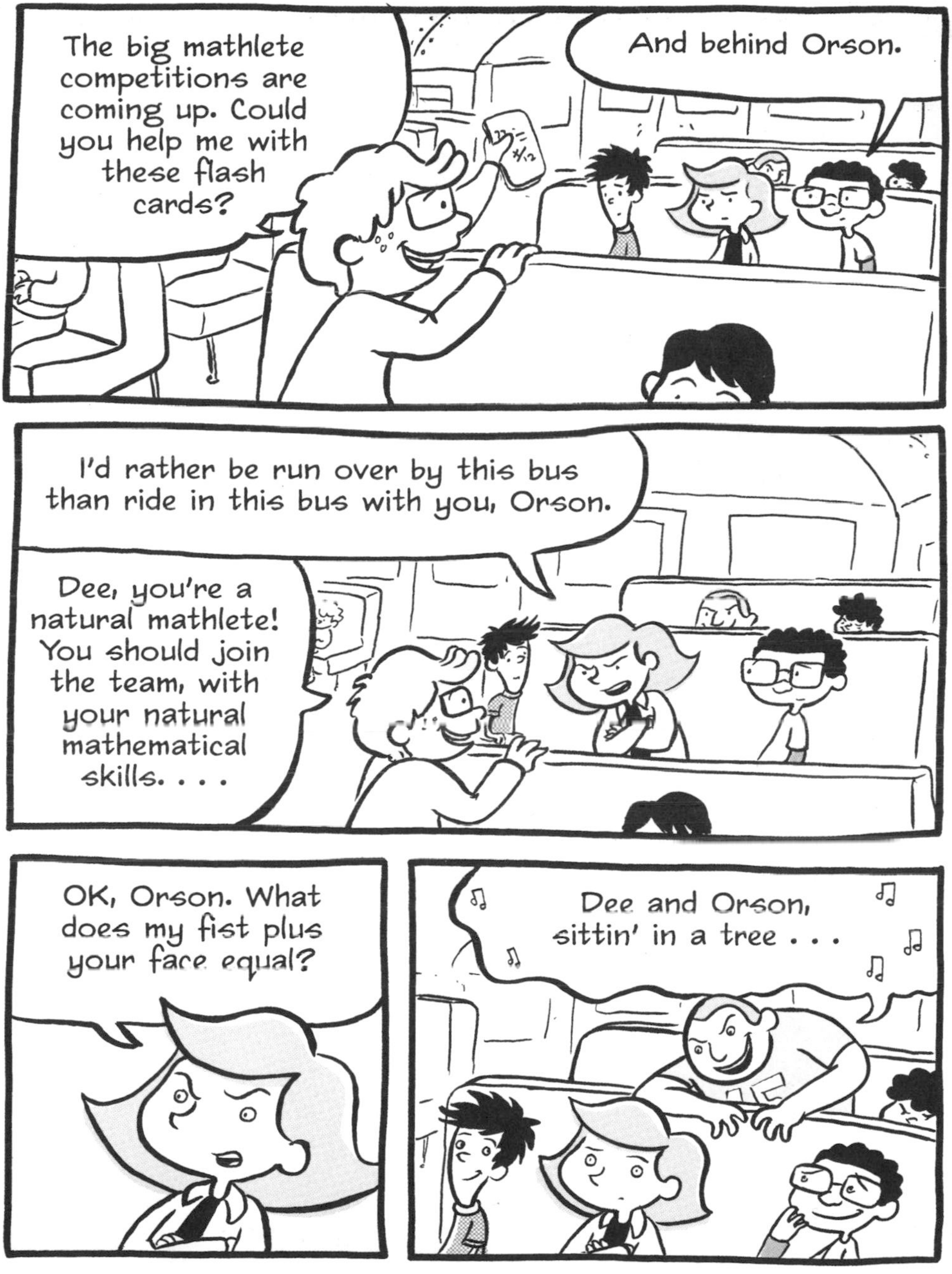

The big mathlete competitions are coming up. Could you help me with these flash cards?
And behind Orson.
I'd rather be run over by this bus than ride in this bus with you, Orson.
Dee, you're a natural mathlete! You should join the team, with your natural mathematical skills. . . .
OK, Orson. What does my fist plus your face equal?
Dee and Orson, sittin' in a tree . . .

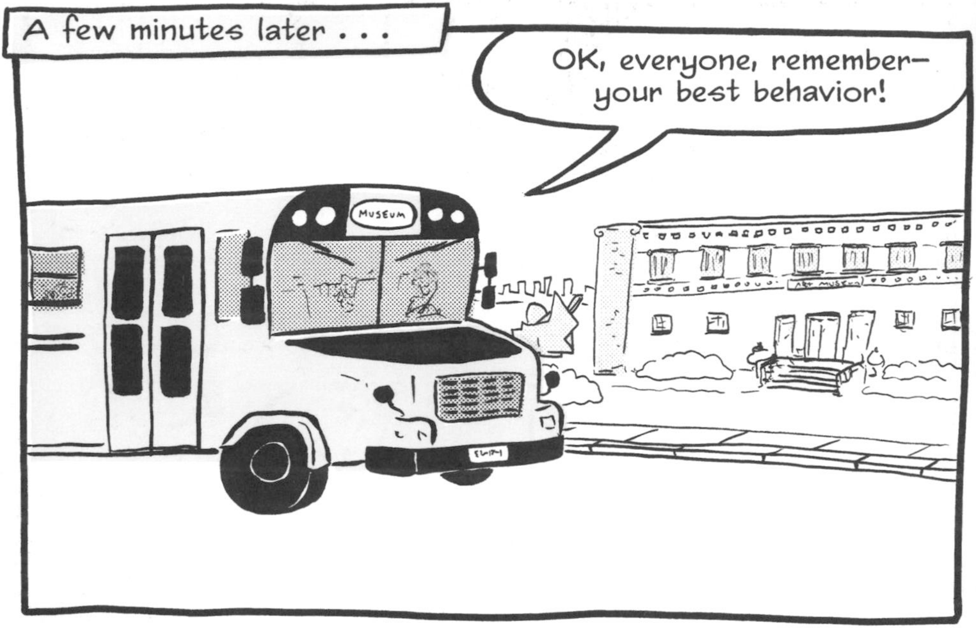
A few minutes later . . .
OK, everyone, remember—your best behavior!
MUSEUM
ART MUSEUM

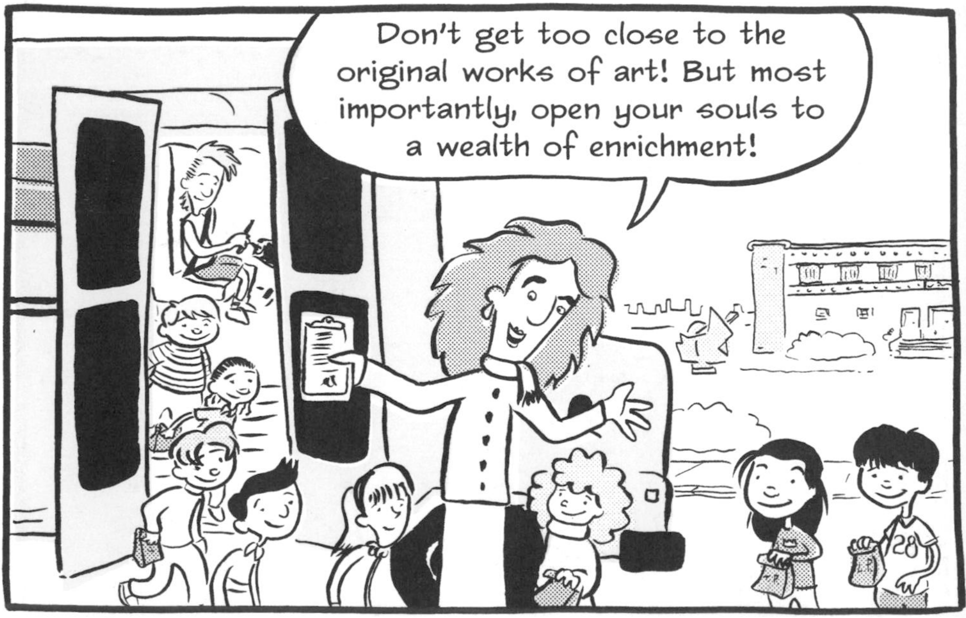
Don't get too close to the original works of art! But most importantly, open your souls to a wealth of enrichment!
28

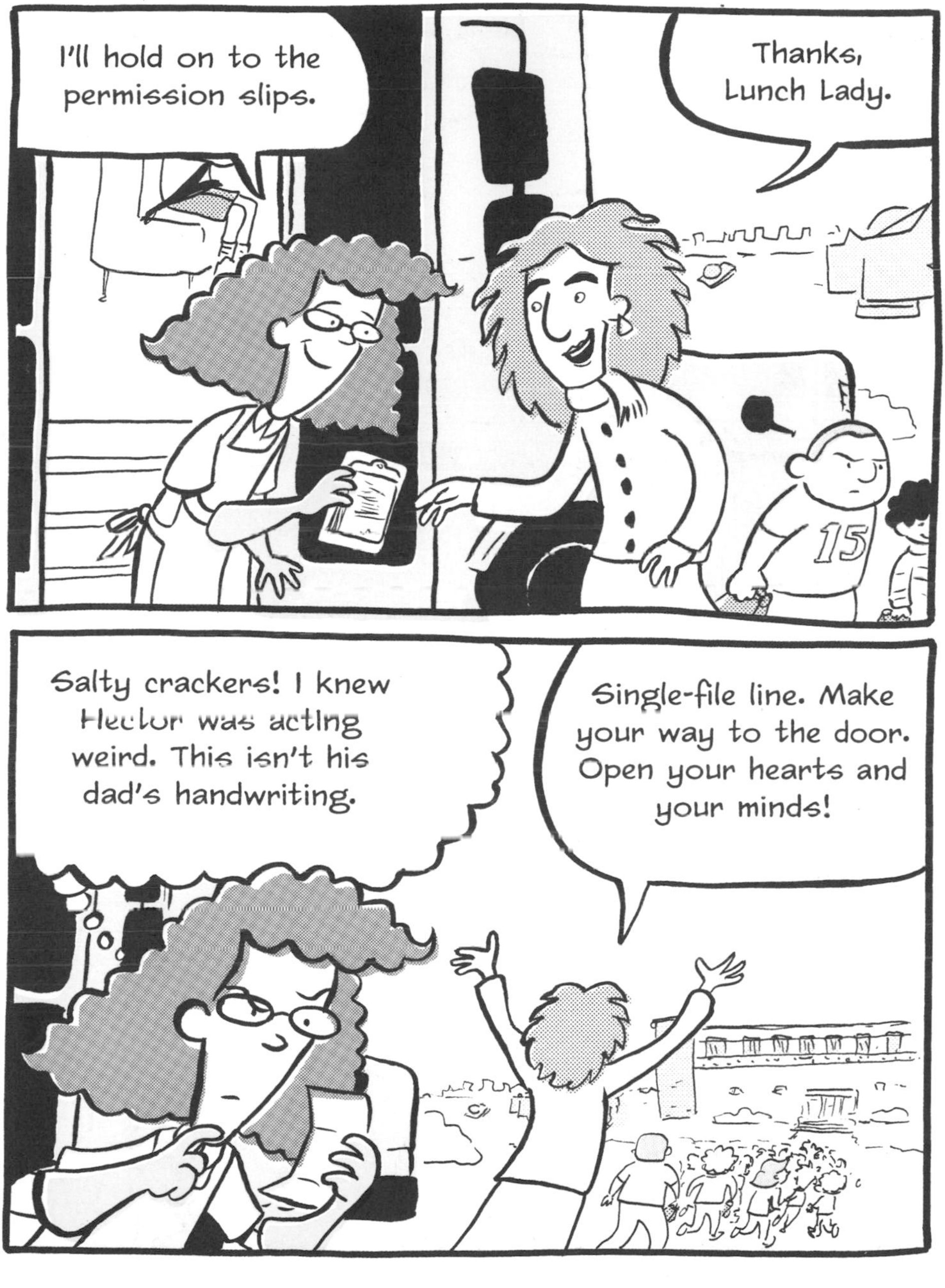
I'll hold on to the permission slips.
Thanks, Lunch Lady.
15
Salty crackers! I knew Hector was acting weird. This isn't his dad's handwriting.
Single-file line. Make your way to the door. Open your hearts and your minds!

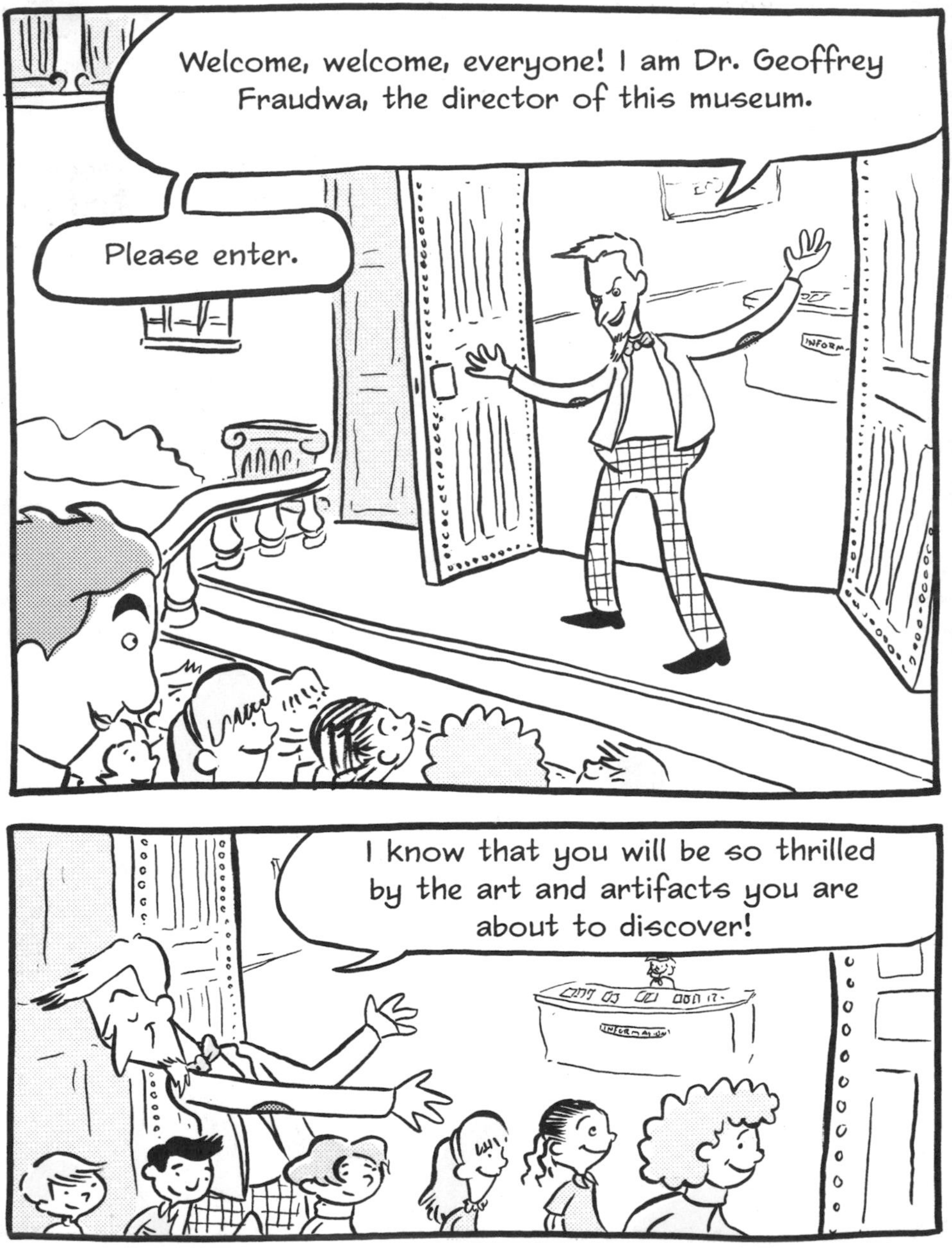
Welcome, welcome, everyone! I am Dr. Geoffrey Fraudwa, the director of this museum.
Please enter.
I know that you will be so thrilled by the art and artifacts you are about to discover!

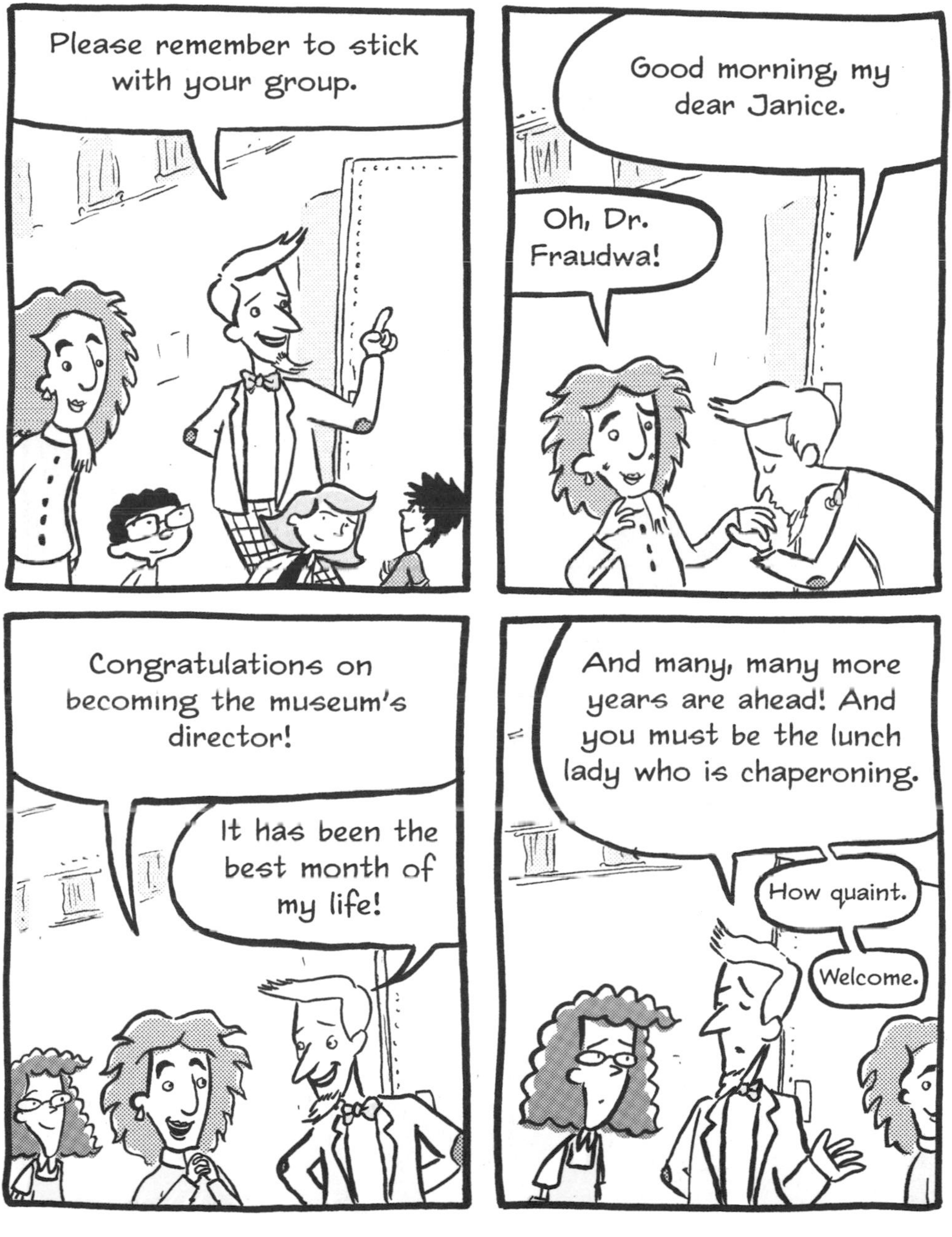

Please remember to stick with your group.
Good morning, my dear Janice.
Oh, Dr. Fraudwa!
Congratulations on becoming the museum's director!
It has been the best month of my life!
And many, many more years are ahead! And you must be the lunch lady who is chaperoning.
How quaint.
Welcome.

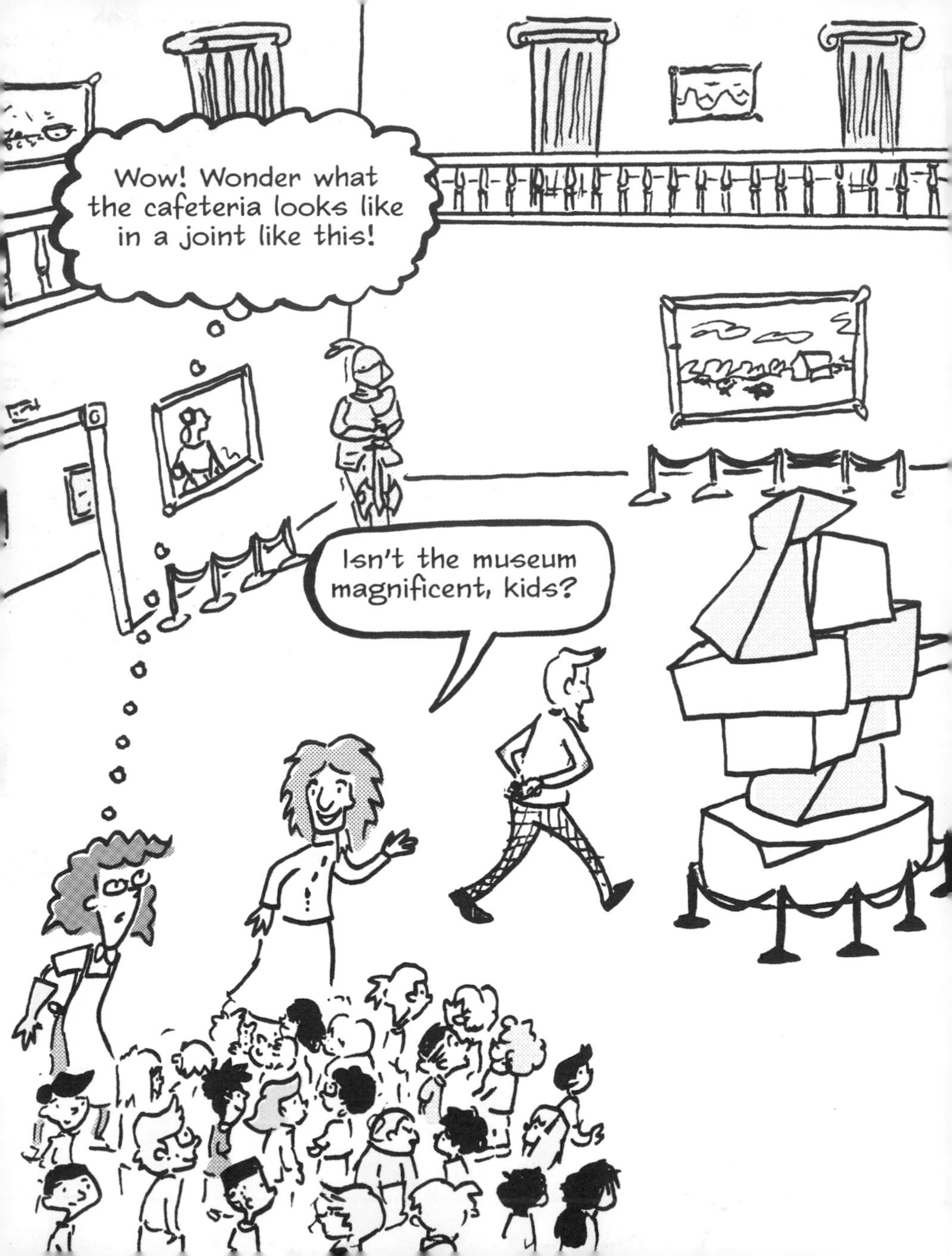
Wow! Wonder what the cafeteria looks like in a joint like this!
Isn't the museum magnificent, kids?

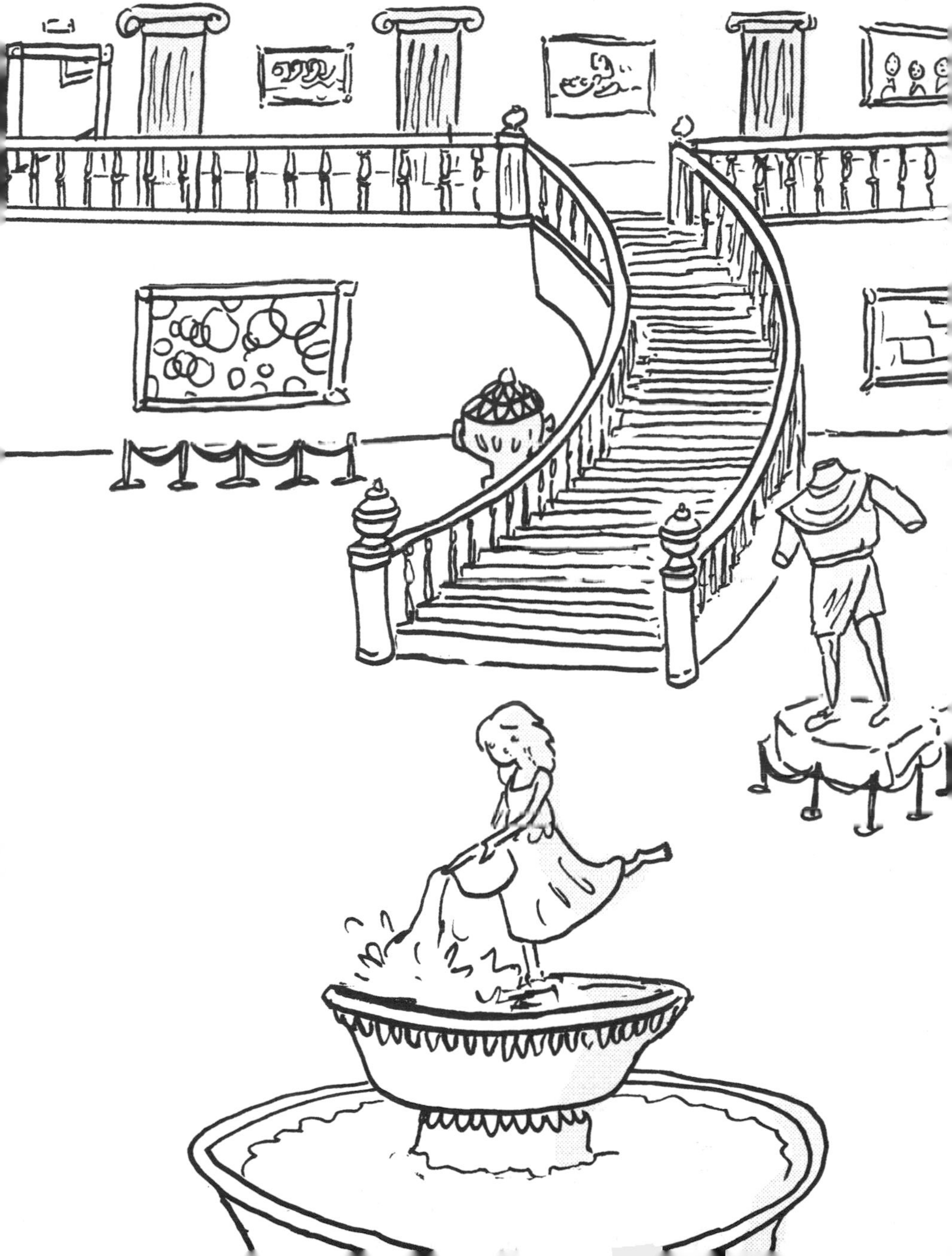

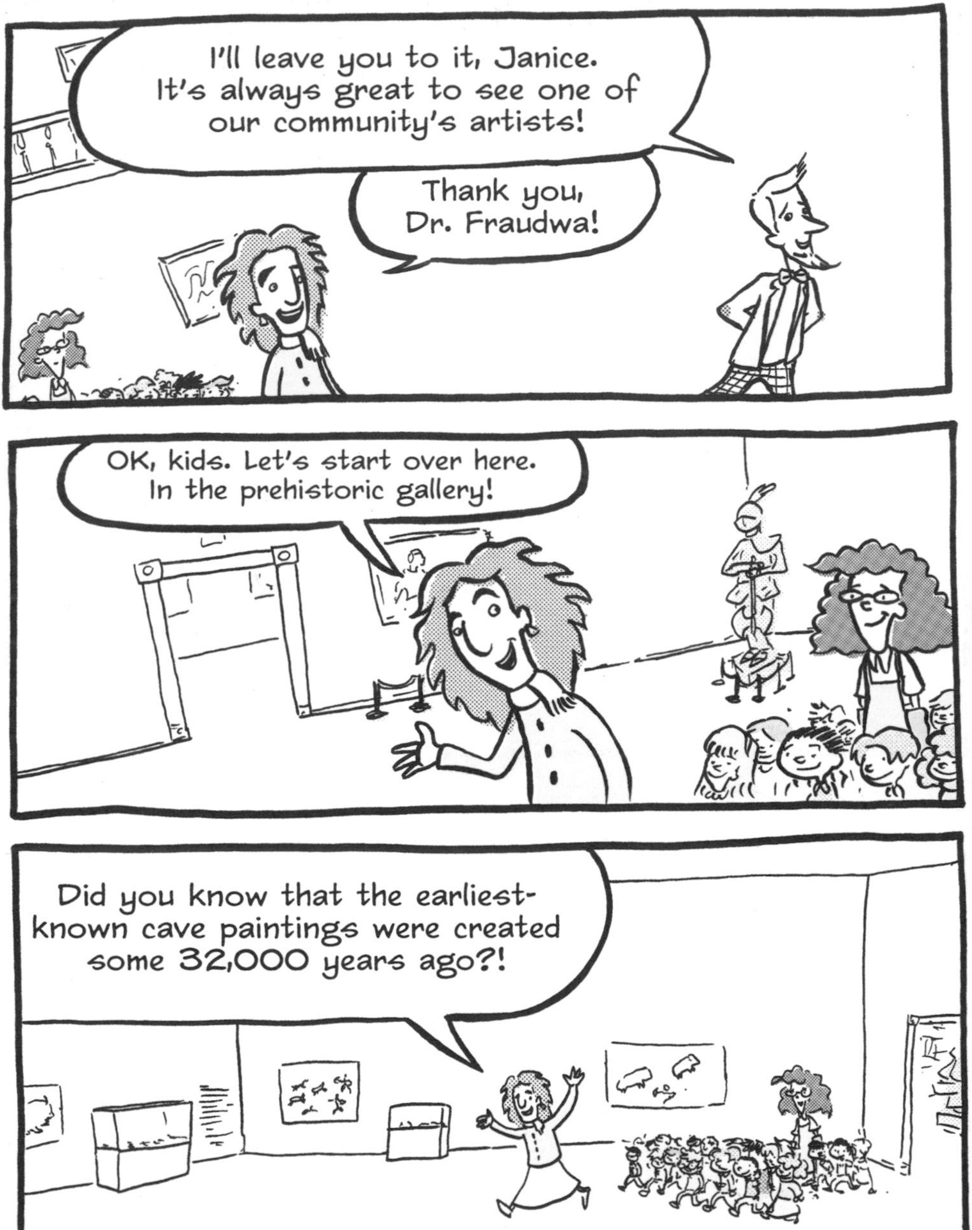
I'll leave you to it, Janice. It's always great to see one of our community's artists!
Thank you, Dr. Fraudwa!
OK, kids. Let's start over here. In the prehistoric gallery!
Did you know that the earliest-known cave paintings were created some 32,000 years ago?!

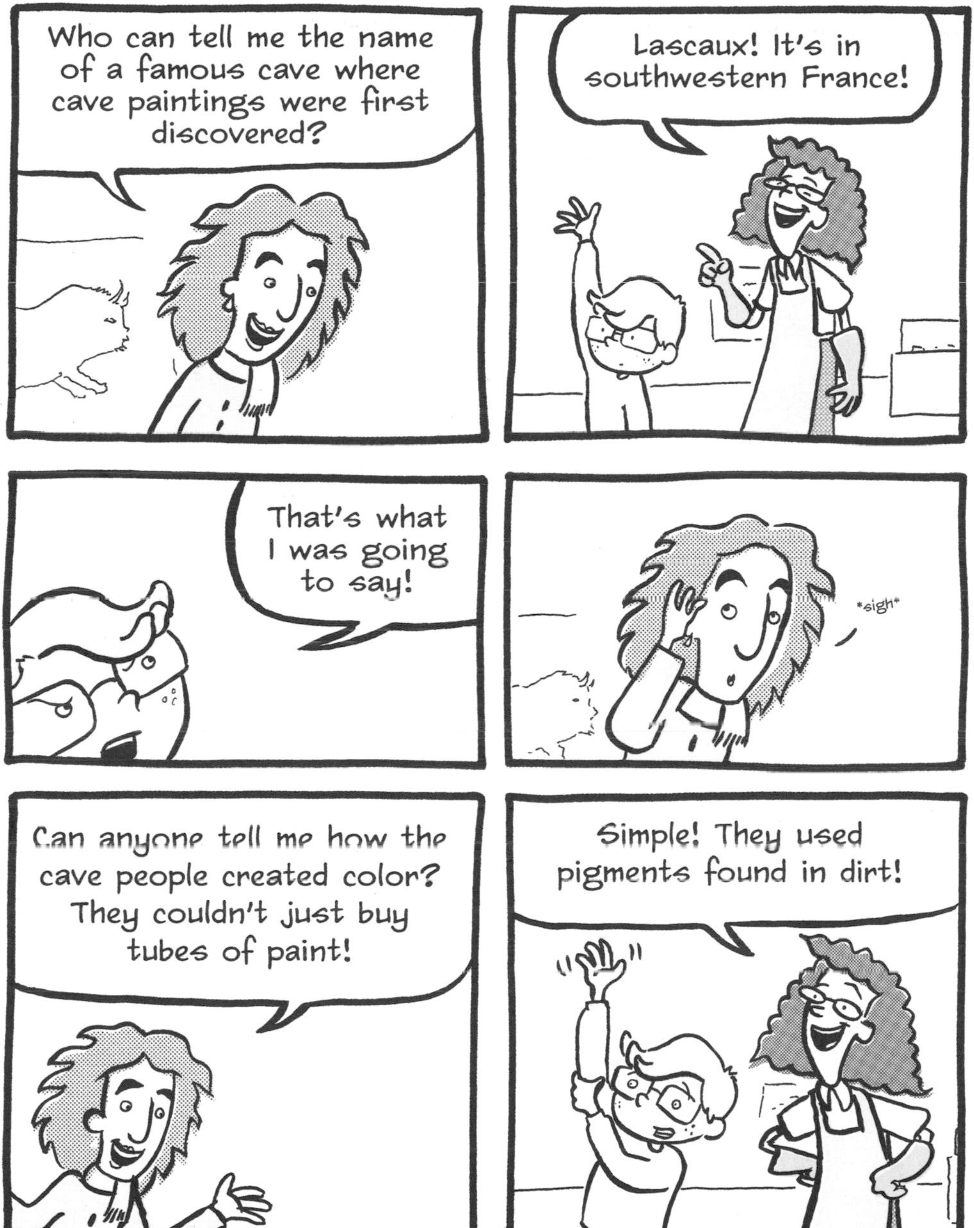
Who can tell me the name of a famous cave where cave paintings were first discovered?
Lascaux! It's in southwestern France!
That's what I was going to say!
sigh
Can anyone tell me how the cave people created color? They couldn't just buy tubes of paint!
Simple! They used pigments found in dirt!

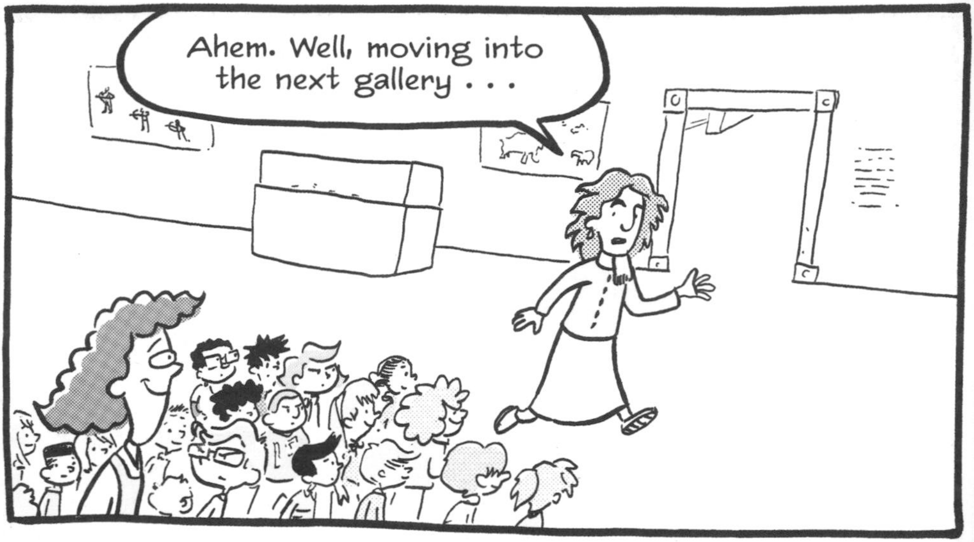
Ahem. Well, moving into the next gallery . . .

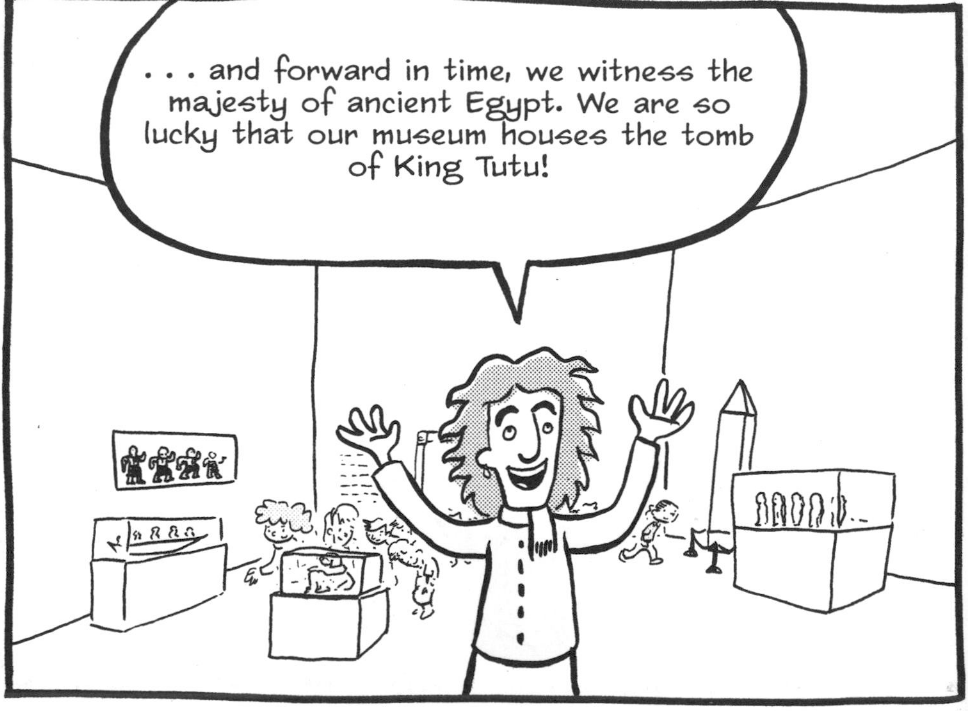
. . . and forward in time, we witness the majesty of ancient Egypt. We are so lucky that our museum houses the tomb of King Tutu!

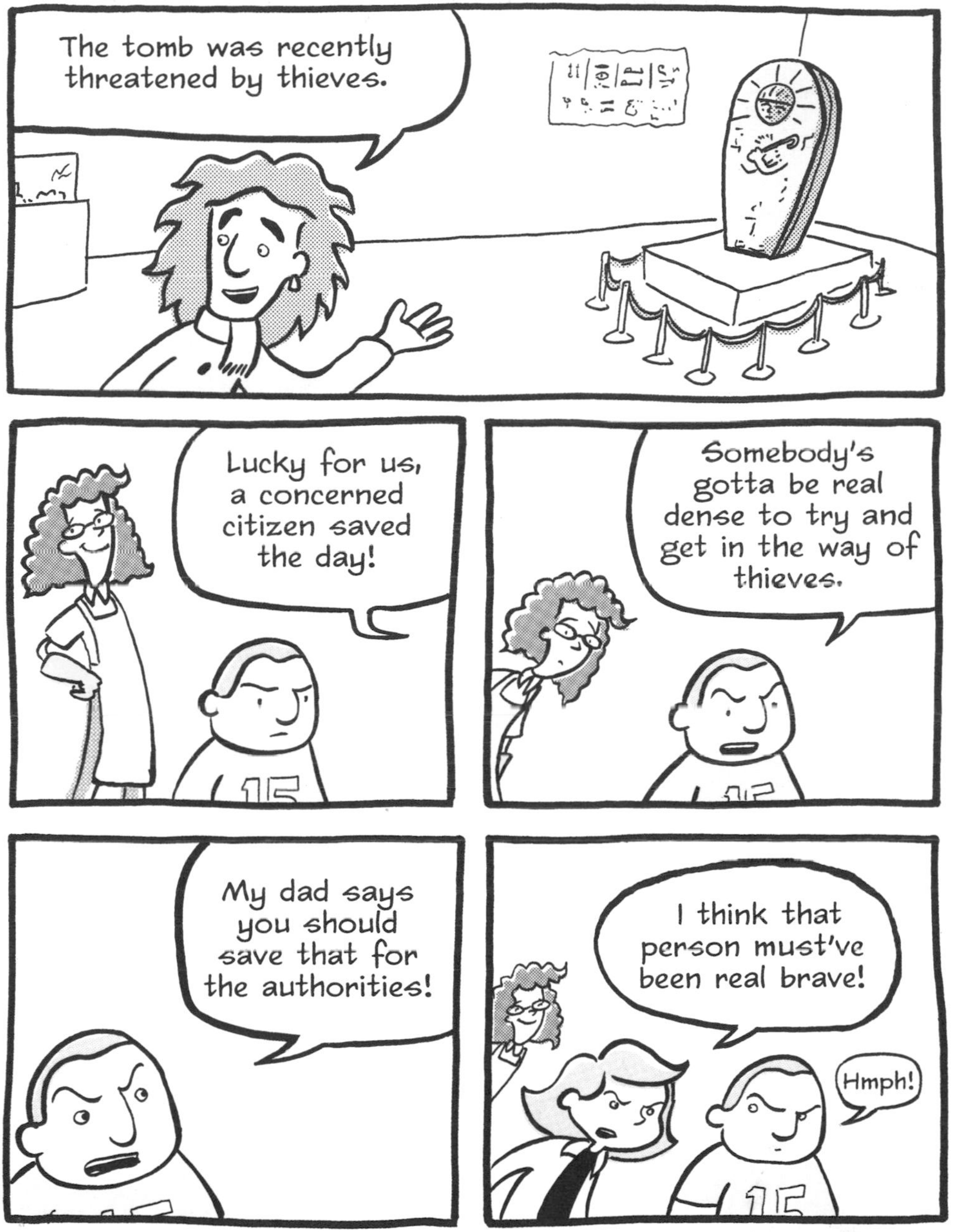
The tomb was recently threatened by thieves.
Lucky for us, a concerned citizen saved the day!
Somebody's gotta be real dense to try and get in the way of thieves.
My dad says you should save that for the authorities!
I think that person must've been real brave!
Hmph!

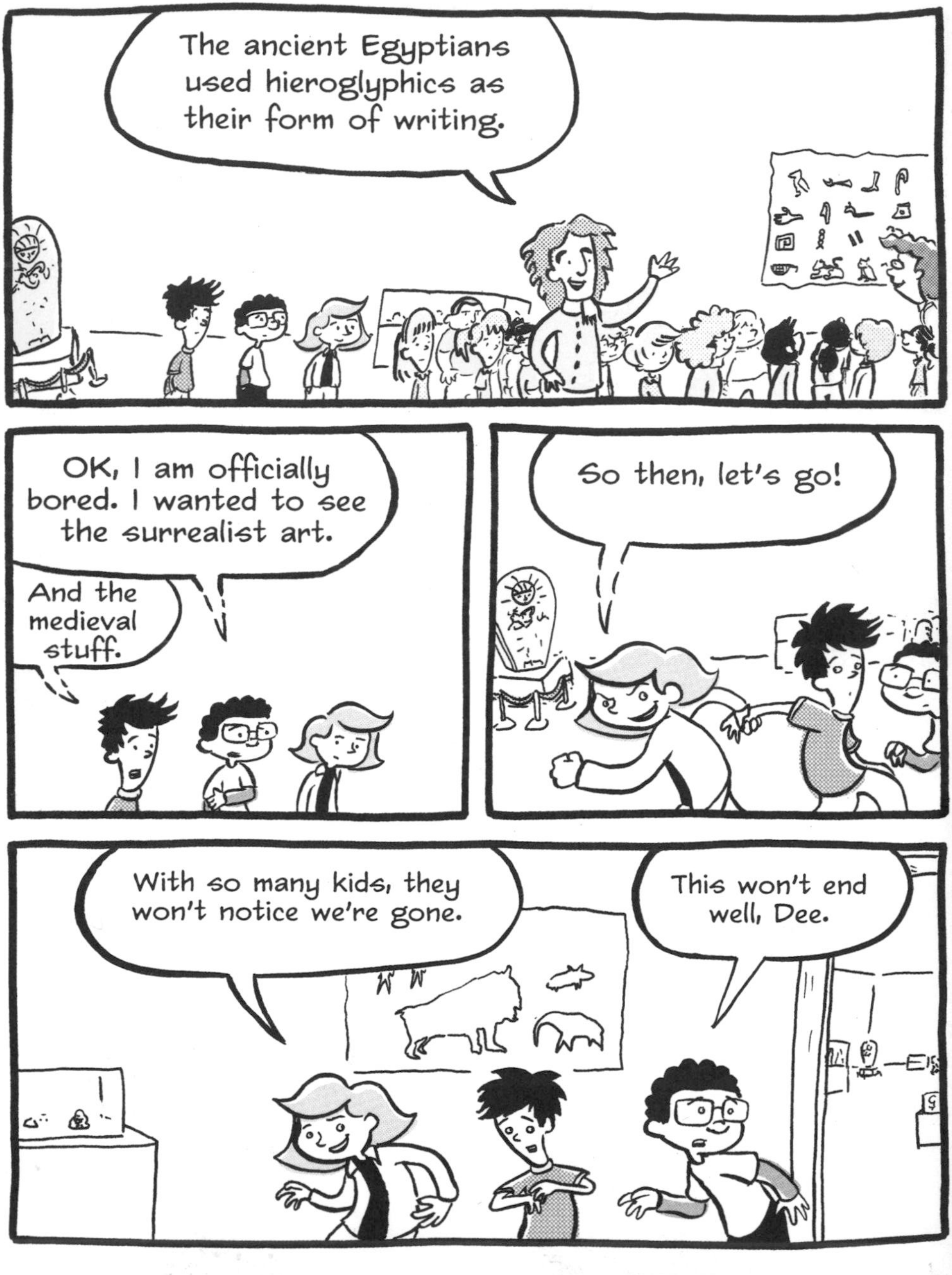
The ancient Egyptians used hieroglyphics as their form of writing.
OK, I am officially bored. I wanted to see the surrealist art.
And the medieval stuff.
So then, let's go!
With so many kids, they won't notice we're gone.
This won't end well, Dee.

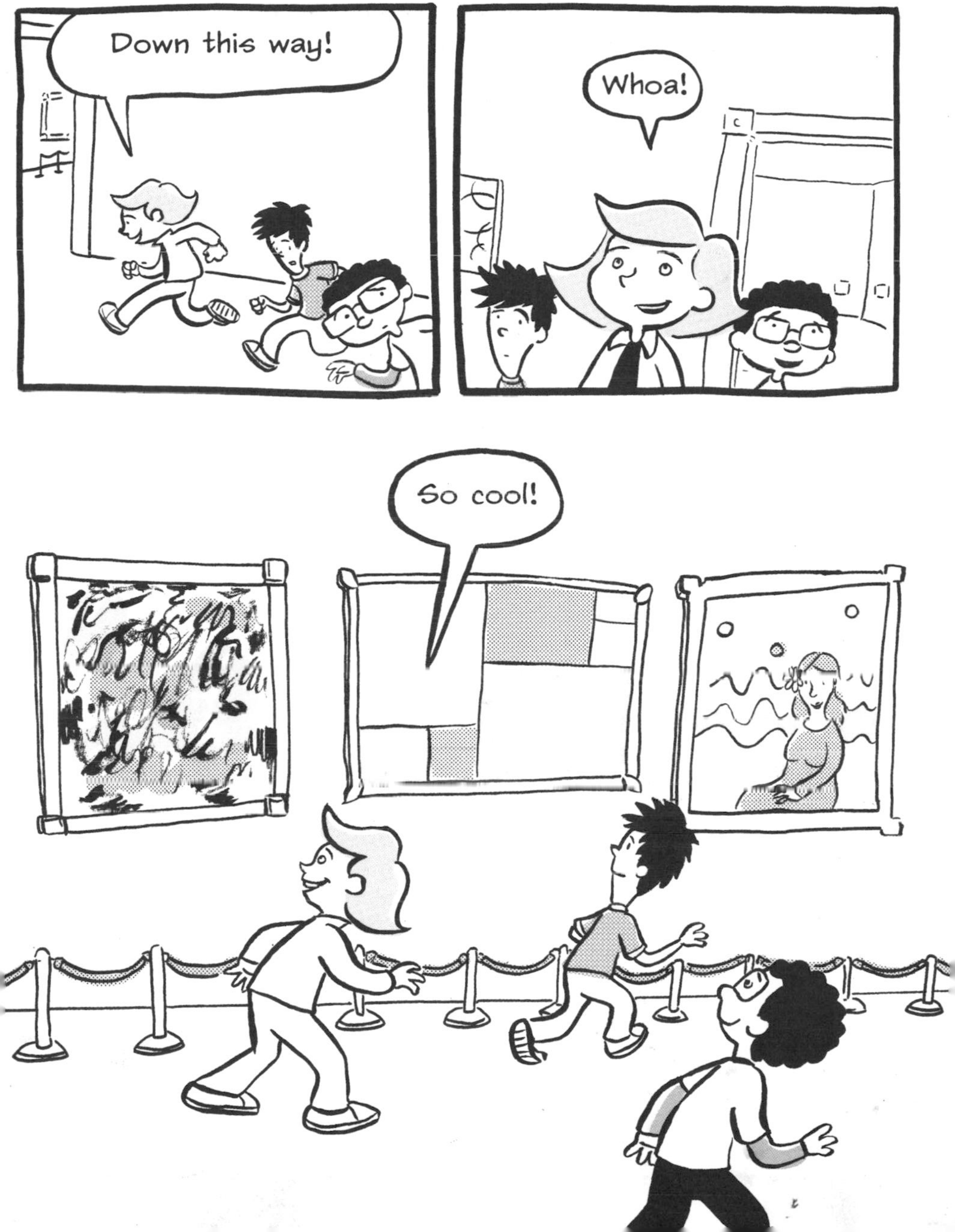
Down this way!
Whoa!
So cool!

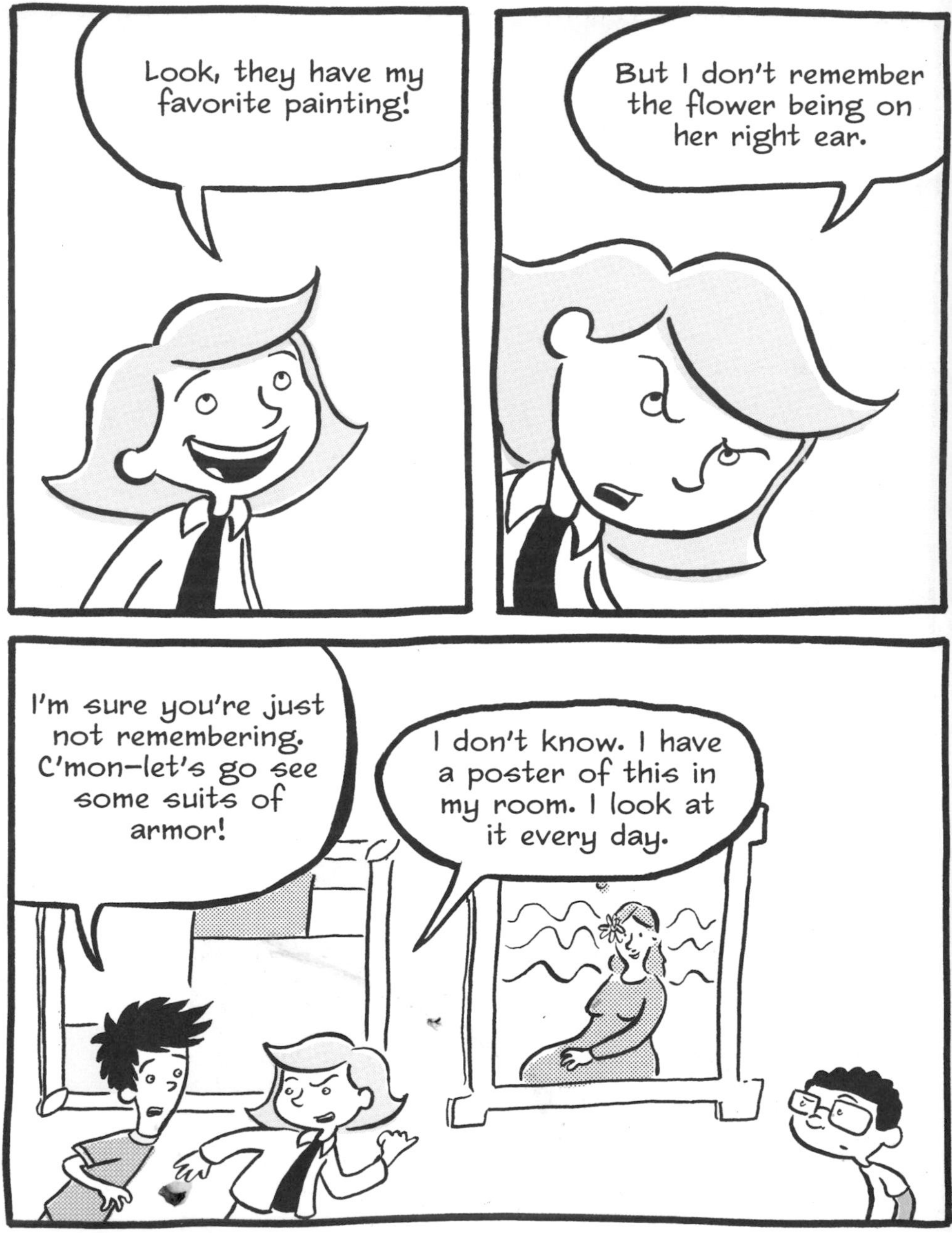
Look, they have my favorite painting!
But I don't remember the flower being on her right ear.
I'm sure you're just not remembering. C'mon—let's go see some suits of armor!
I don't know. I have a poster of this in my room. I look at it every day.

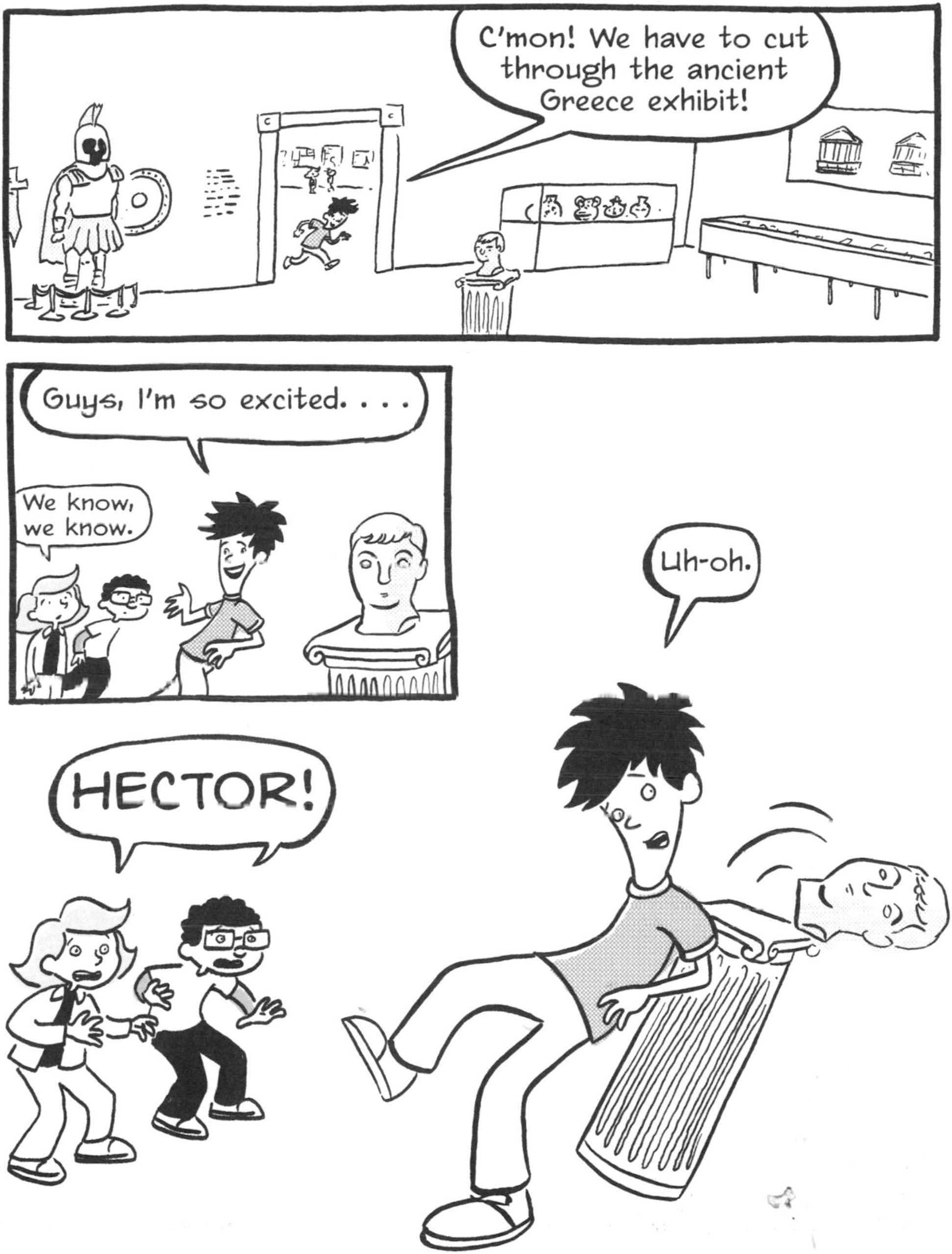
C'mon! We have to cut through the ancient Greece exhibit!
Guys, I'm so excited. . . .
We know, we know.
Uh-oh.
HECTOR!

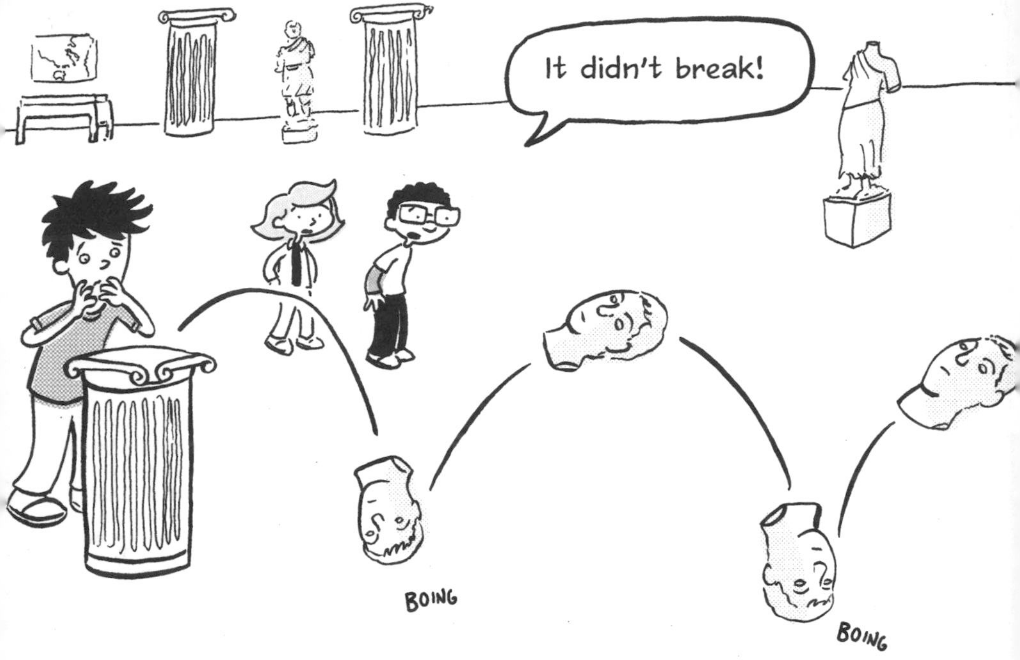
It didn't break!
BOING
BOING

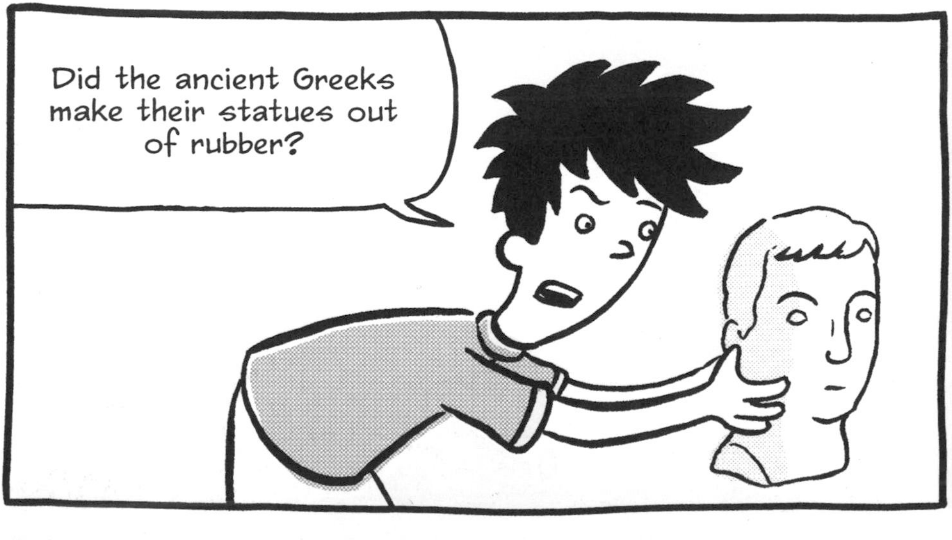
Did the ancient Greeks make their statues out of rubber?

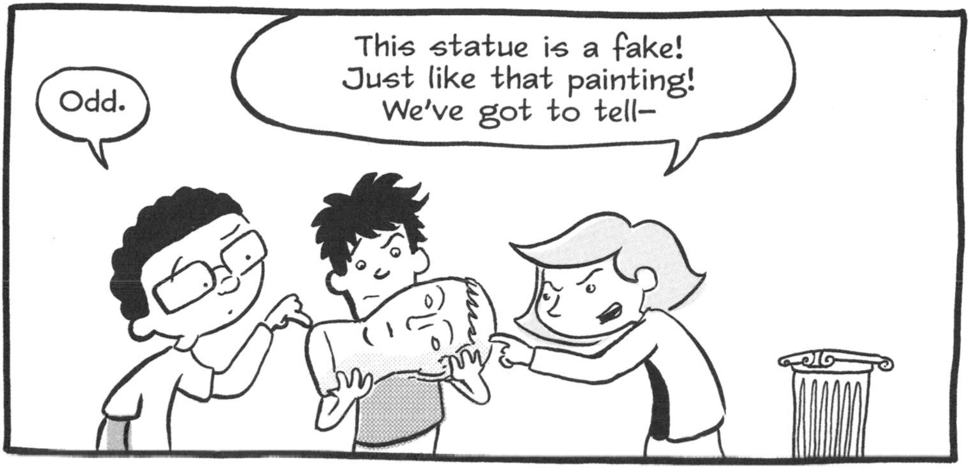
Odd.
This statue is a fake! Just like that painting! We've got to tell–

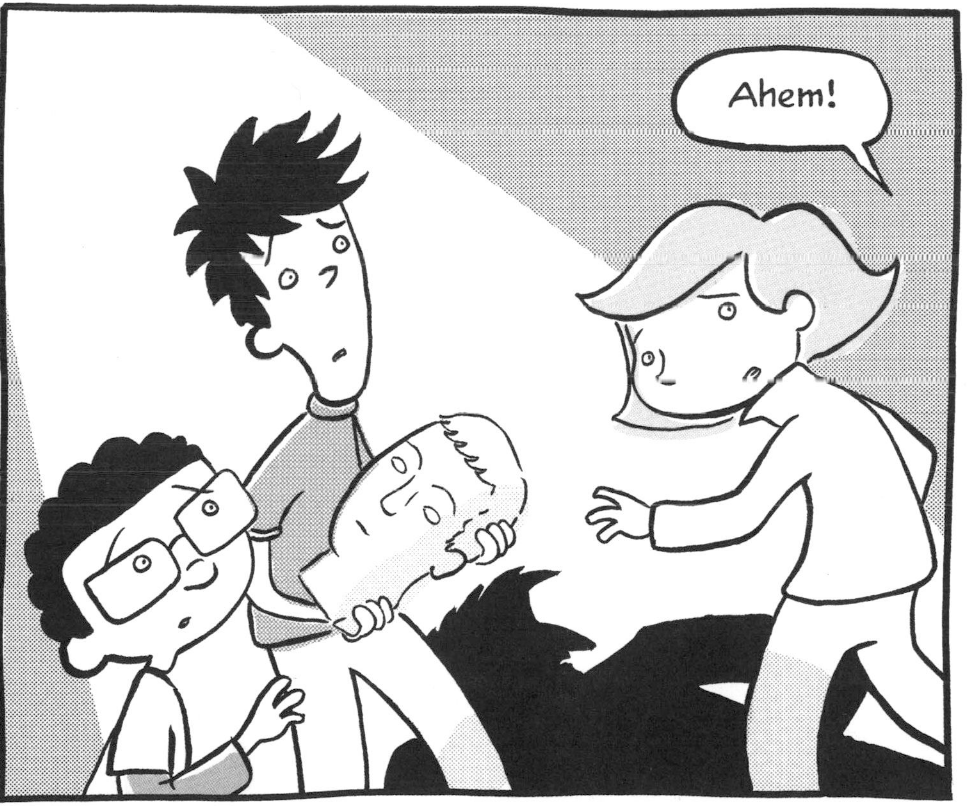
Ahem!

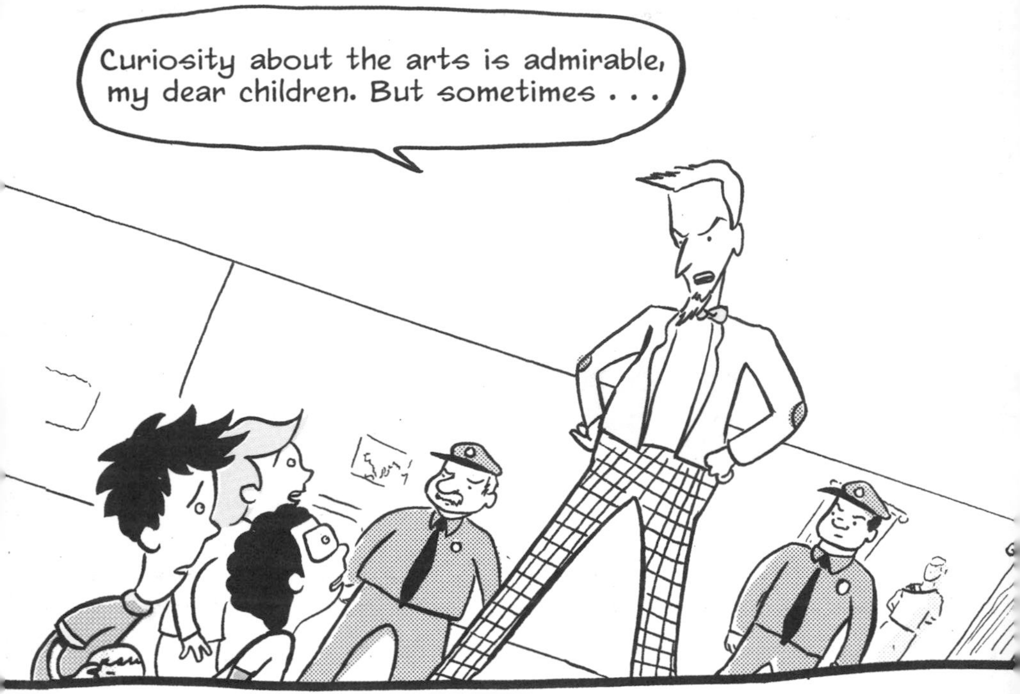
Curiosity about the arts is admirable, my dear children. But sometimes . . .

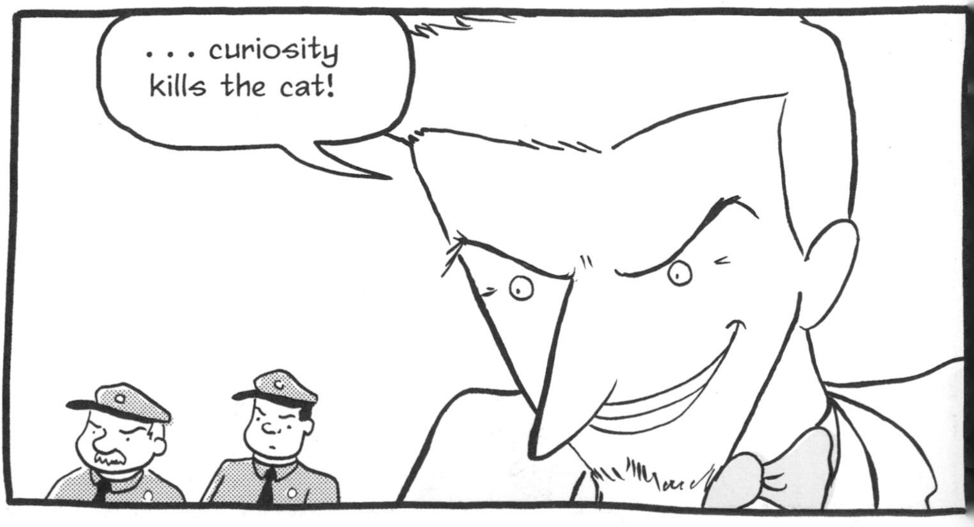
. . . curiosity kills the cat!

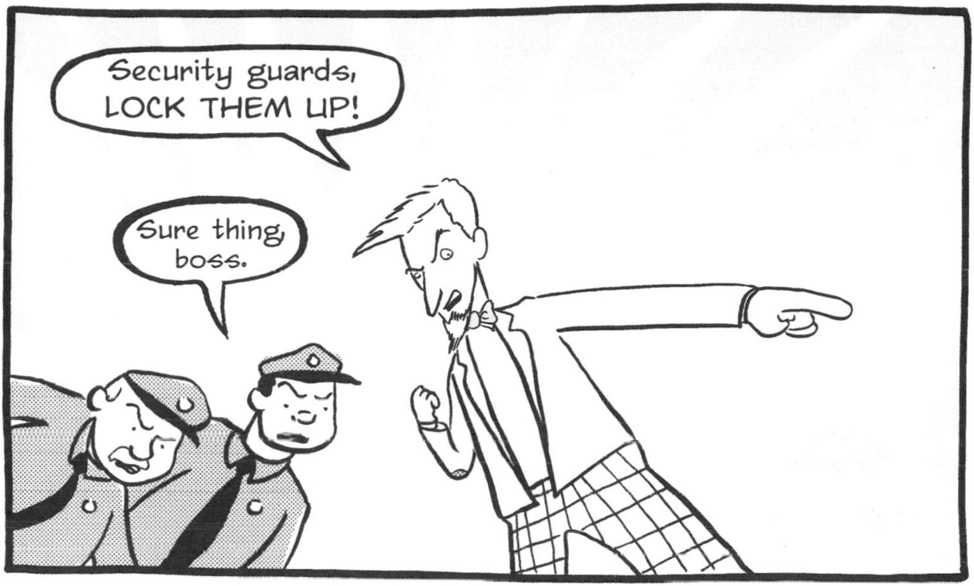
Security guards, LOCK THEM UP!
Sure thing, boss.

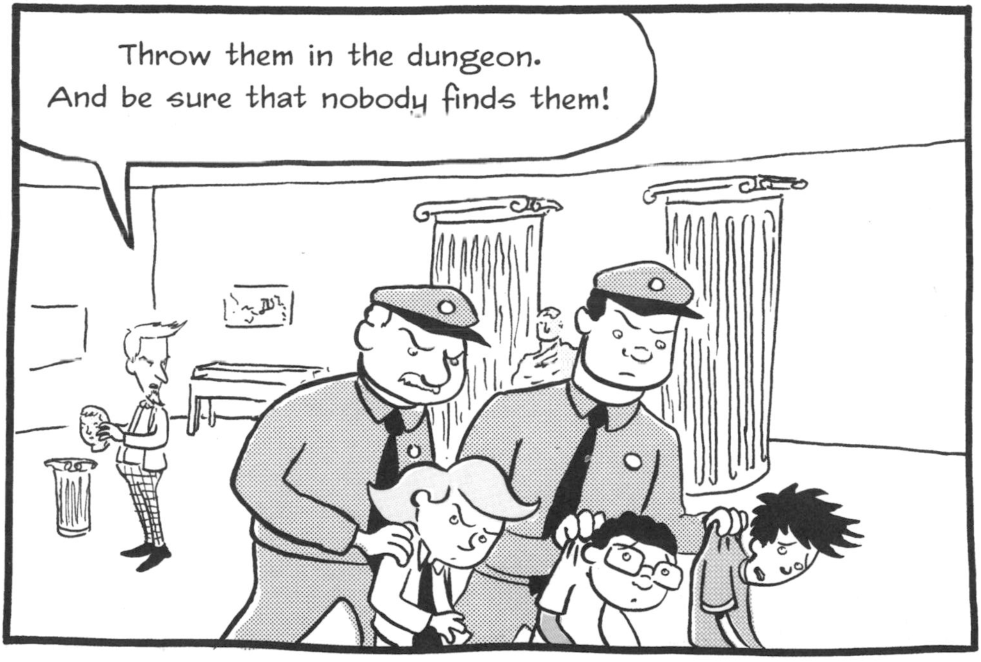
Throw them in the dungeon. And be sure that nobody finds them!

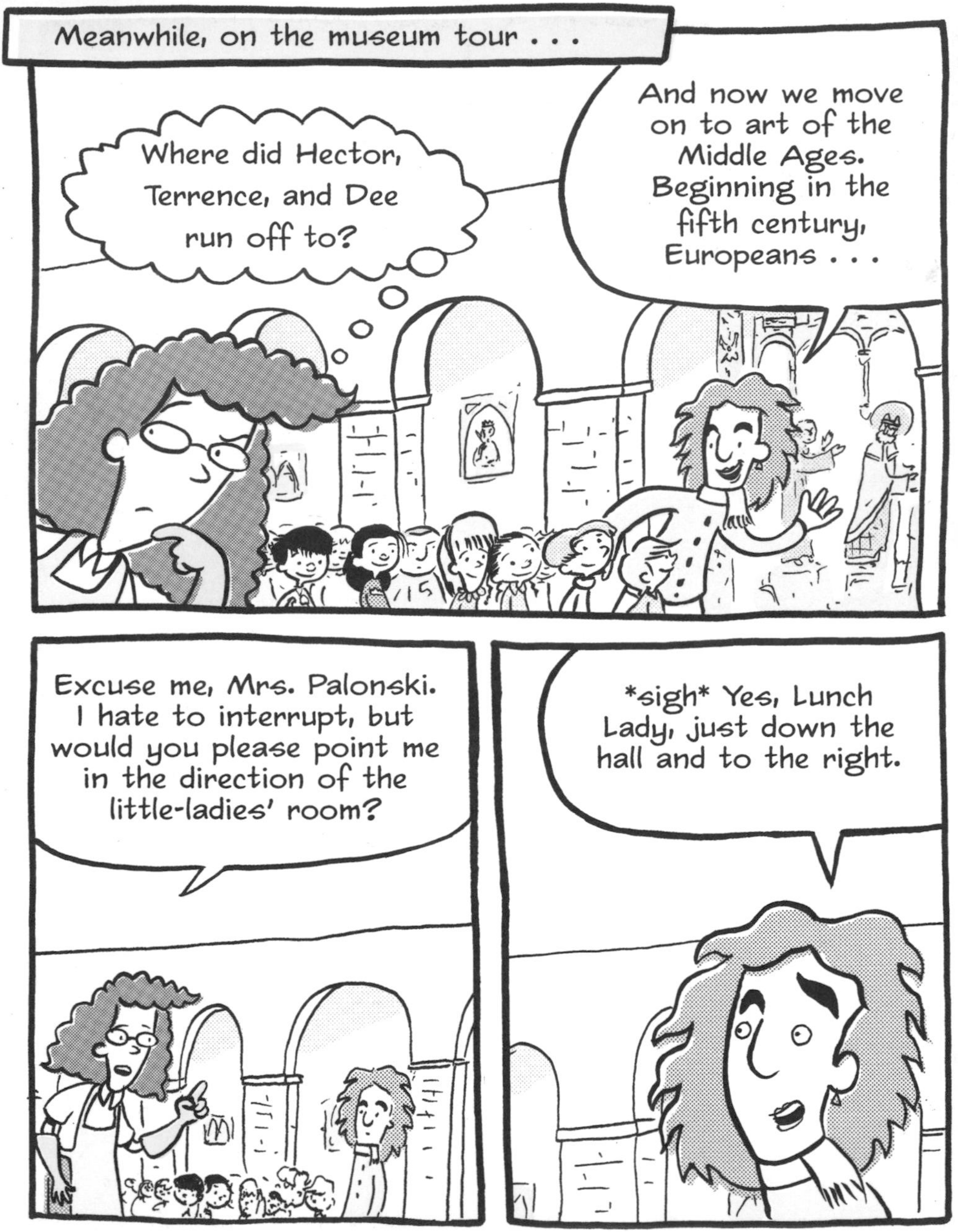
Meanwhile, on the museum tour . . .
Where did Hector, Terrence, and Dee run off to?
And now we move on to art of the Middle Ages. Beginning in the fifth century, Europeans . . .
Excuse me, Mrs. Palonski. I hate to interrupt, but would you please point me in the direction of the little-ladies' room?
sigh Yes, Lunch Lady, just down the hall and to the right.

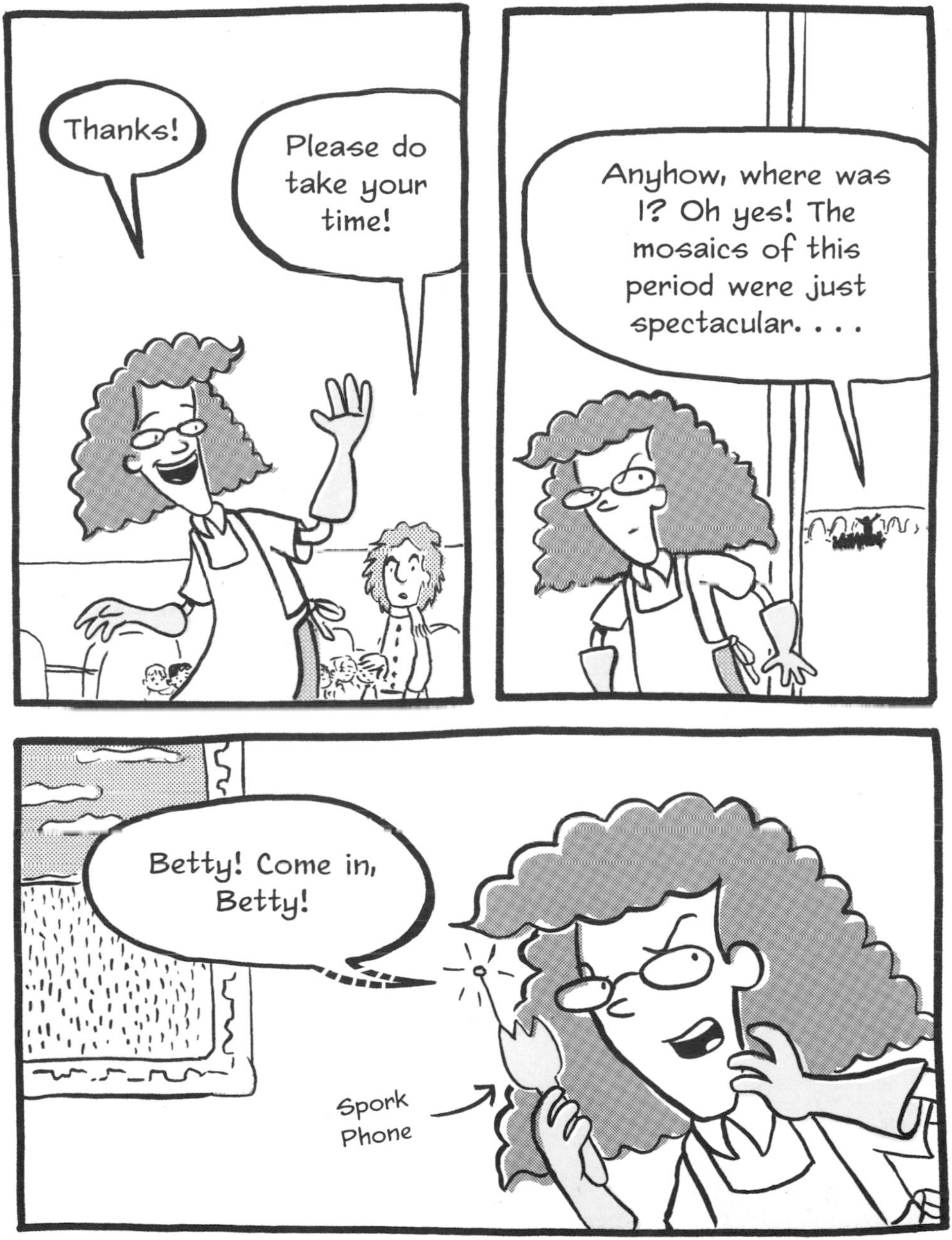
Thanks!
Please do take your time!
Anyhow, where was I? Oh yes! The mosaics of this period were just spectacular. . . .
Betty! Come in, Betty!
Spork Phone

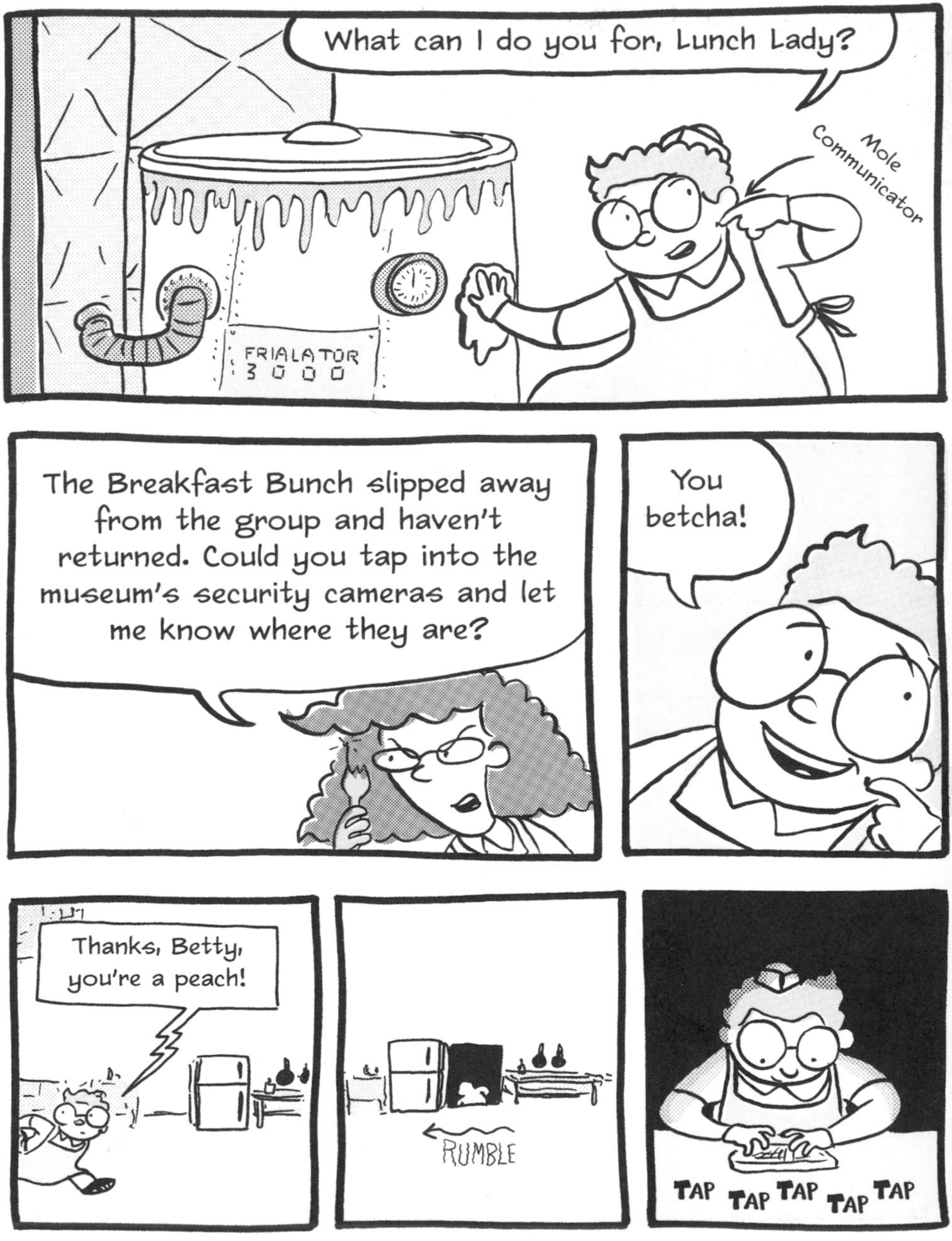
What can I do you for, Lunch Lady?
Mole Communicator
FRIALATOR 3000
The Breakfast Bunch slipped away from the group and haven't returned. Could you tap into the museum's security cameras and let me know where they are?
You betcha!
Thanks, Betty, you're a peach!
RUMBLE
TAP TAP TAP TAP TAP

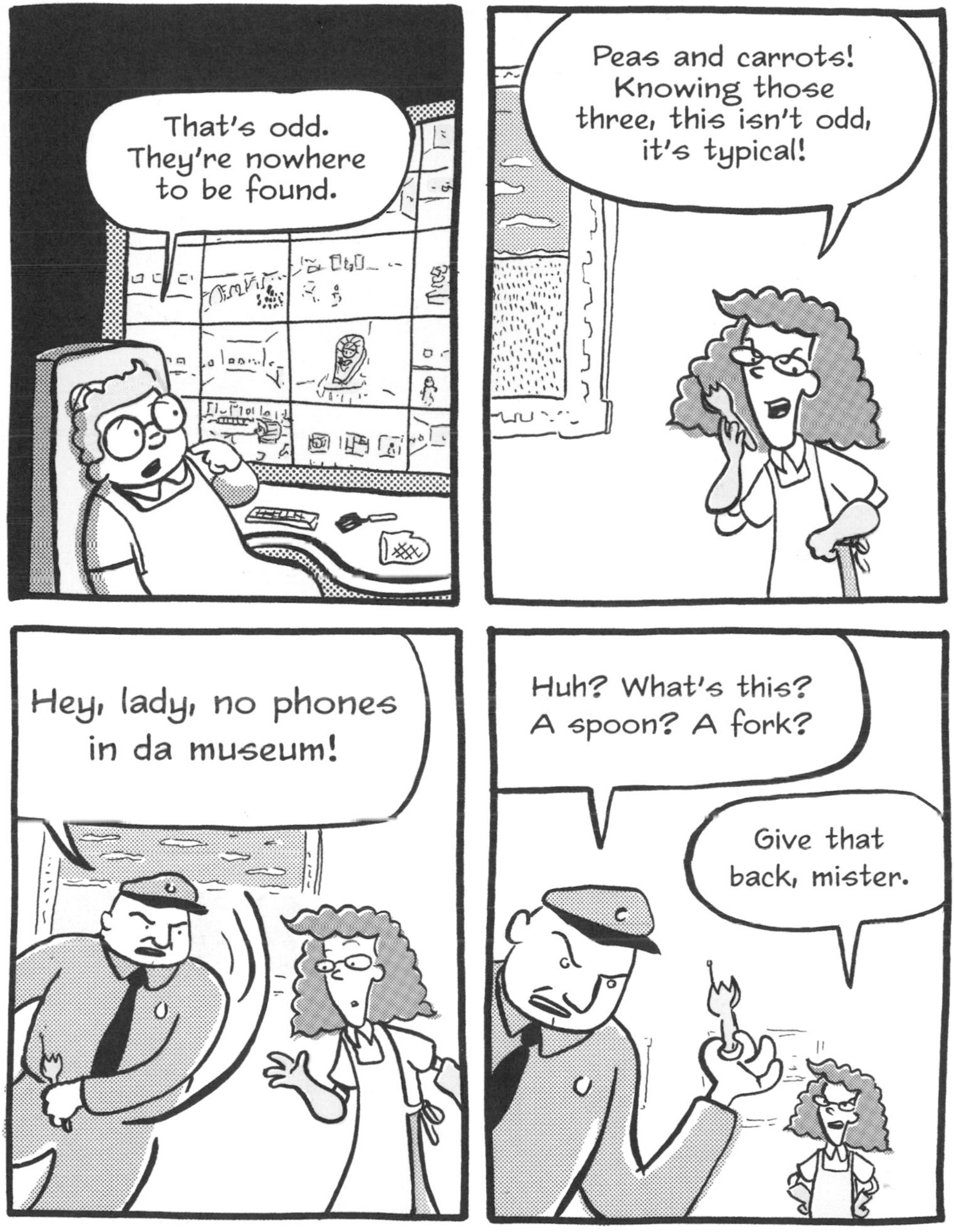
That's odd. They're nowhere to be found.
Peas and carrots! Knowing those three, this isn't odd, it's typical!
Hey, lady, no phones in da museum!
Huh? What's this? A spoon? A fork?
Give that back, mister.

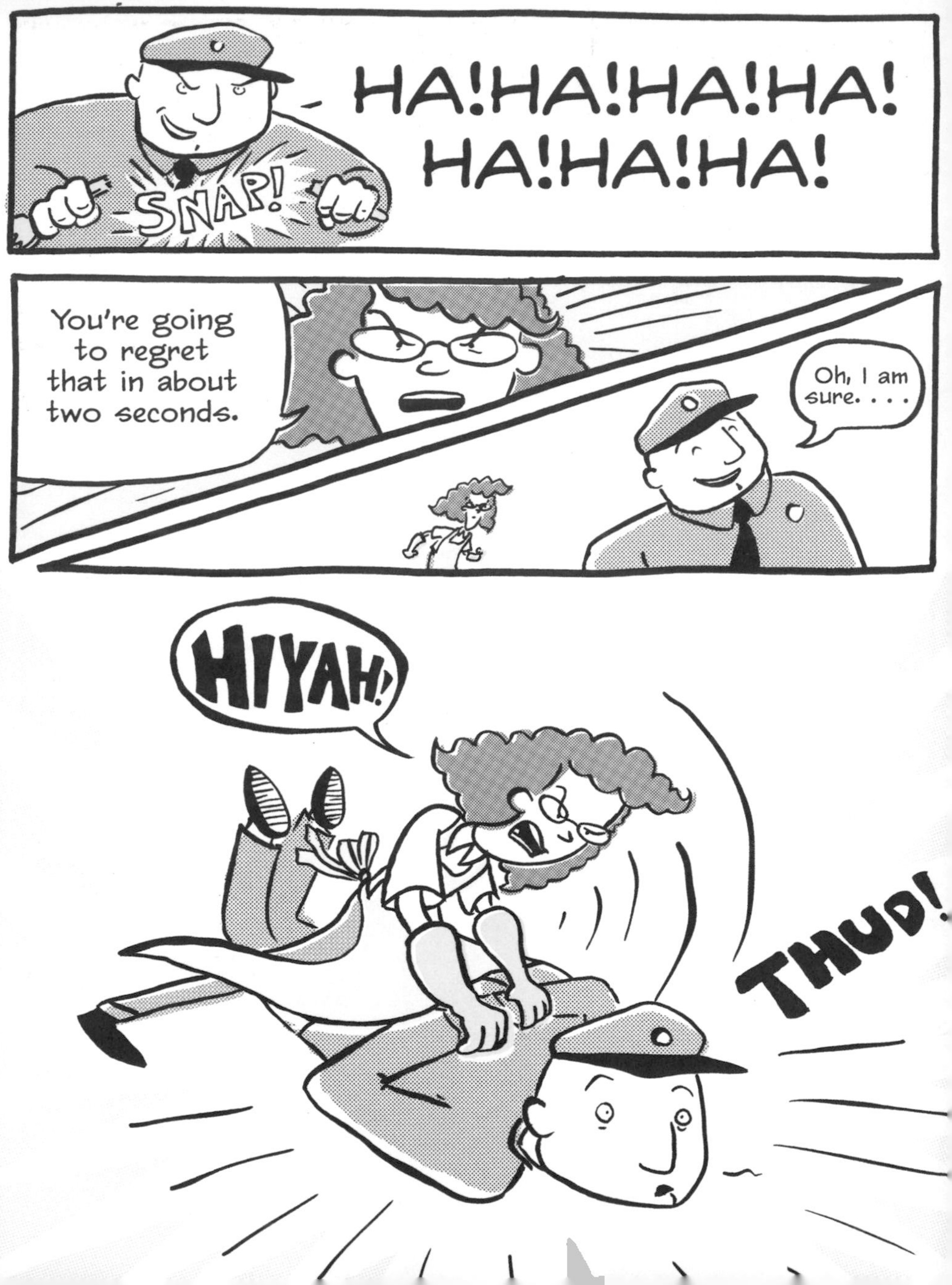
SNAP!
HA!HA!HA!HA!
HA!HA!HA!
You're going to regret that in about two seconds.
Oh, I am sure. . . .
HIYAH!
THUD!

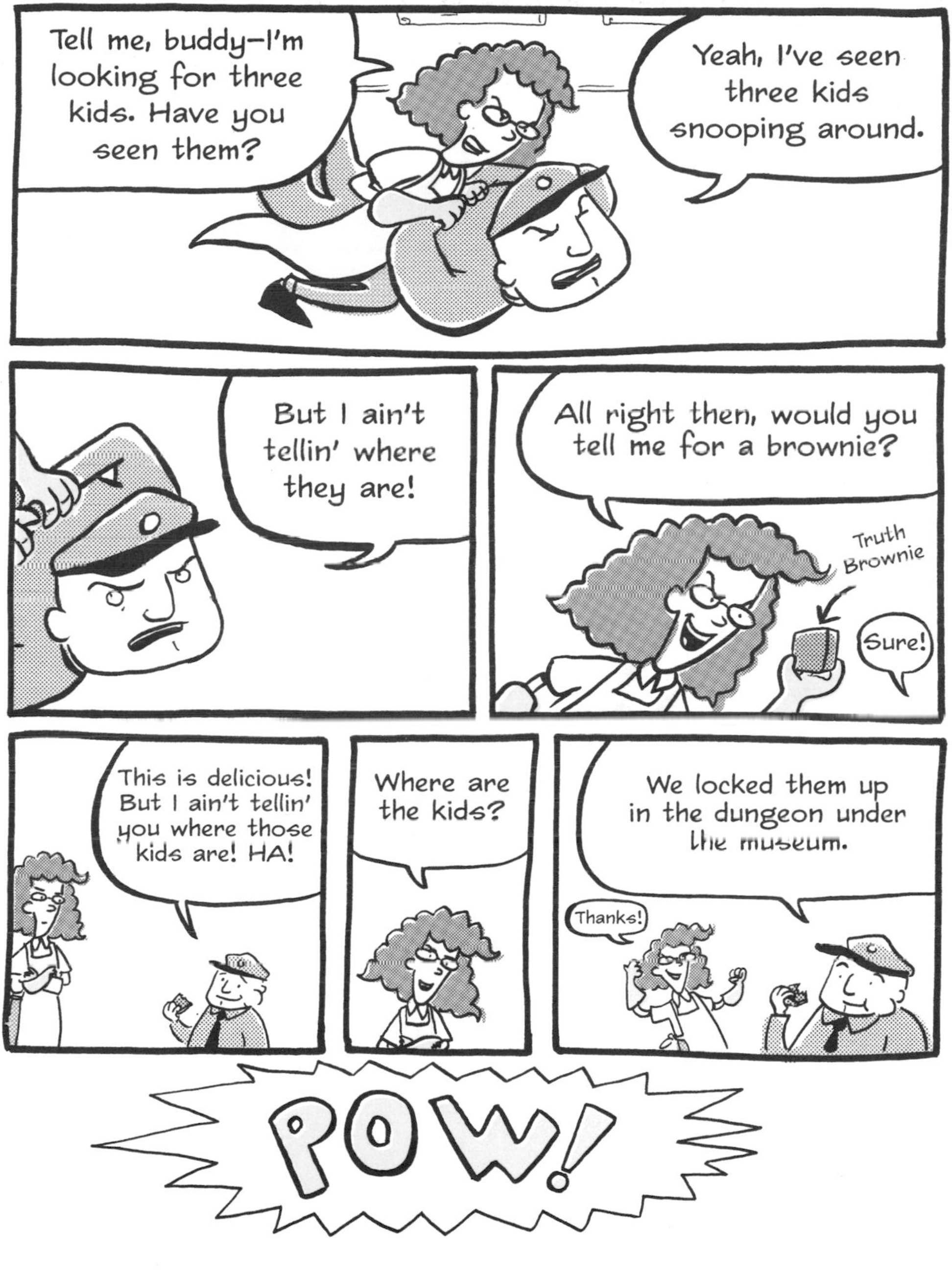
Tell me, buddy—I'm looking for three kids. Have you seen them?
Yeah, I've seen three kids snooping around.
But I ain't tellin' where they are!
All right then, would you tell me for a brownie?
Truth Brownie
Sure!
This is delicious! But I ain't tellin' you where those kids are! HA!
Where are the kids?
We locked them up in the dungeon under the museum.
Thanks!
POW!

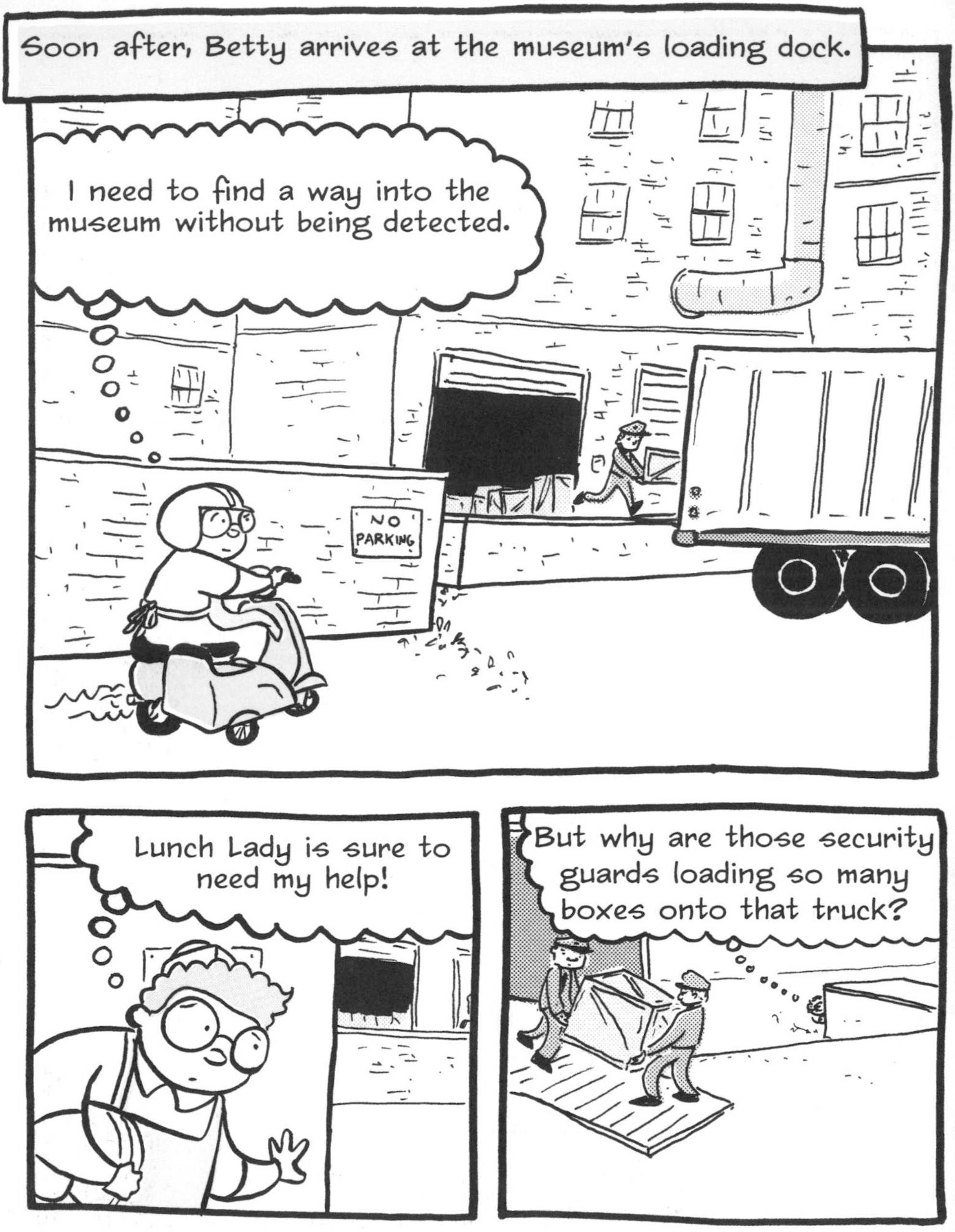
Soon after, Betty arrives at the museum's loading dock.
I need to find a way into the museum without being detected.
NO PARKING
Lunch Lady is sure to need my help!
But why are those security guards loading so many boxes onto that truck?

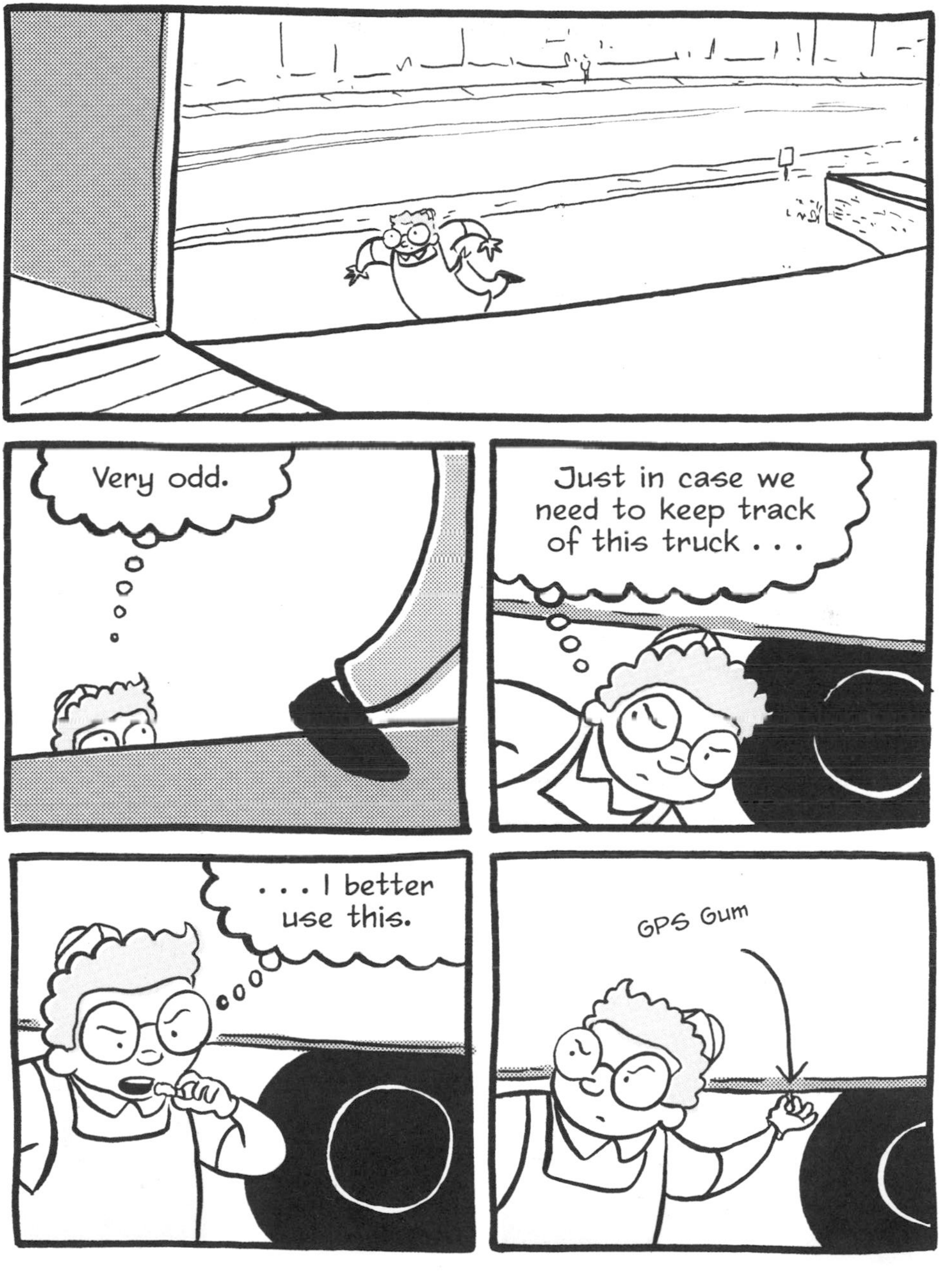
Very odd.
Just in case we need to keep track of this truck . . .
. . . I better use this.
GPS Gum

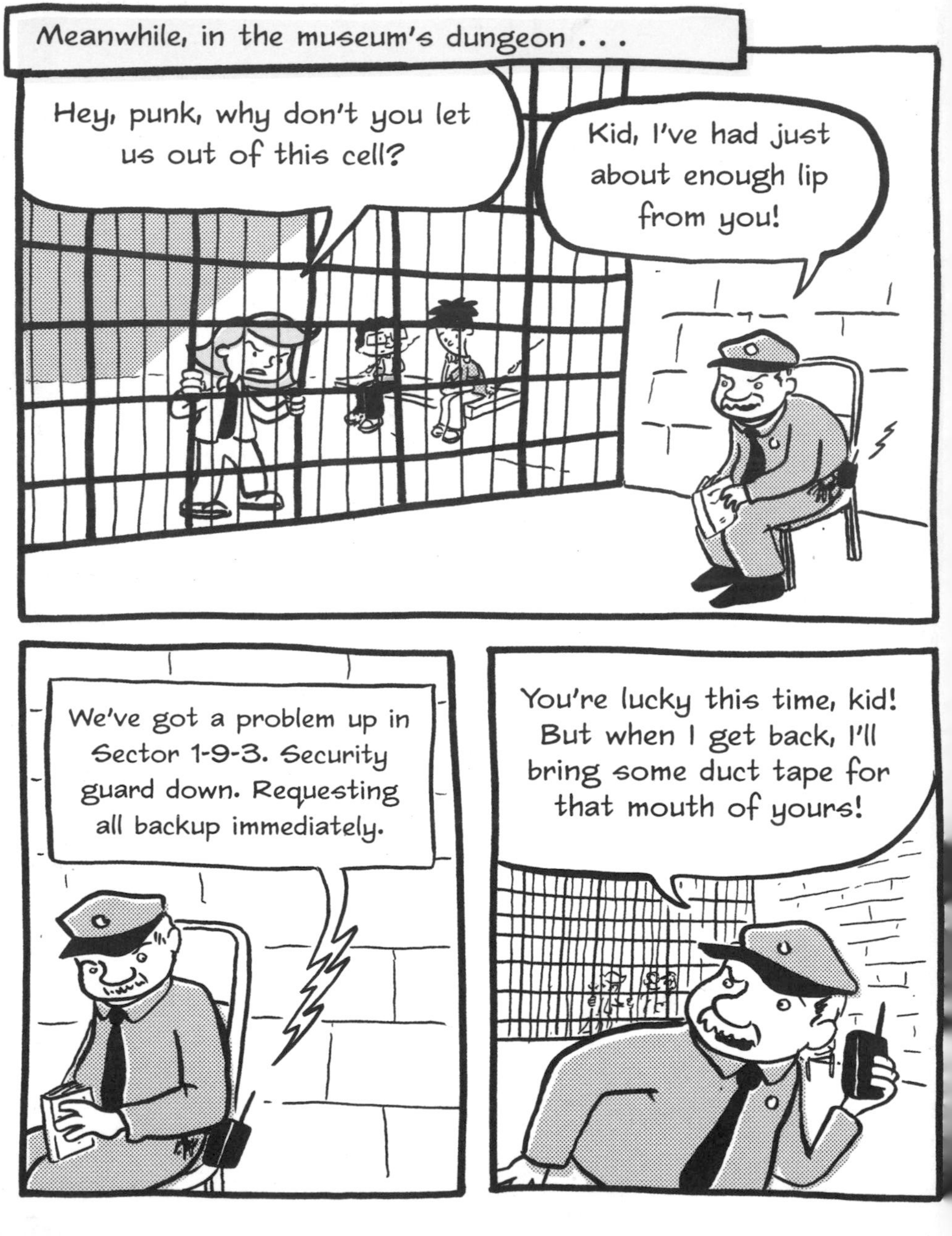
Meanwhile, in the museum's dungeon . . .
Hey, punk, why don't you let us out of this cell?
Kid, I've had just about enough lip from you!
We've got a problem up in Sector 1-9-3. Security guard down. Requesting all backup immediately.
You're lucky this time, kid! But when I get back, I'll bring some duct tape for that mouth of yours!

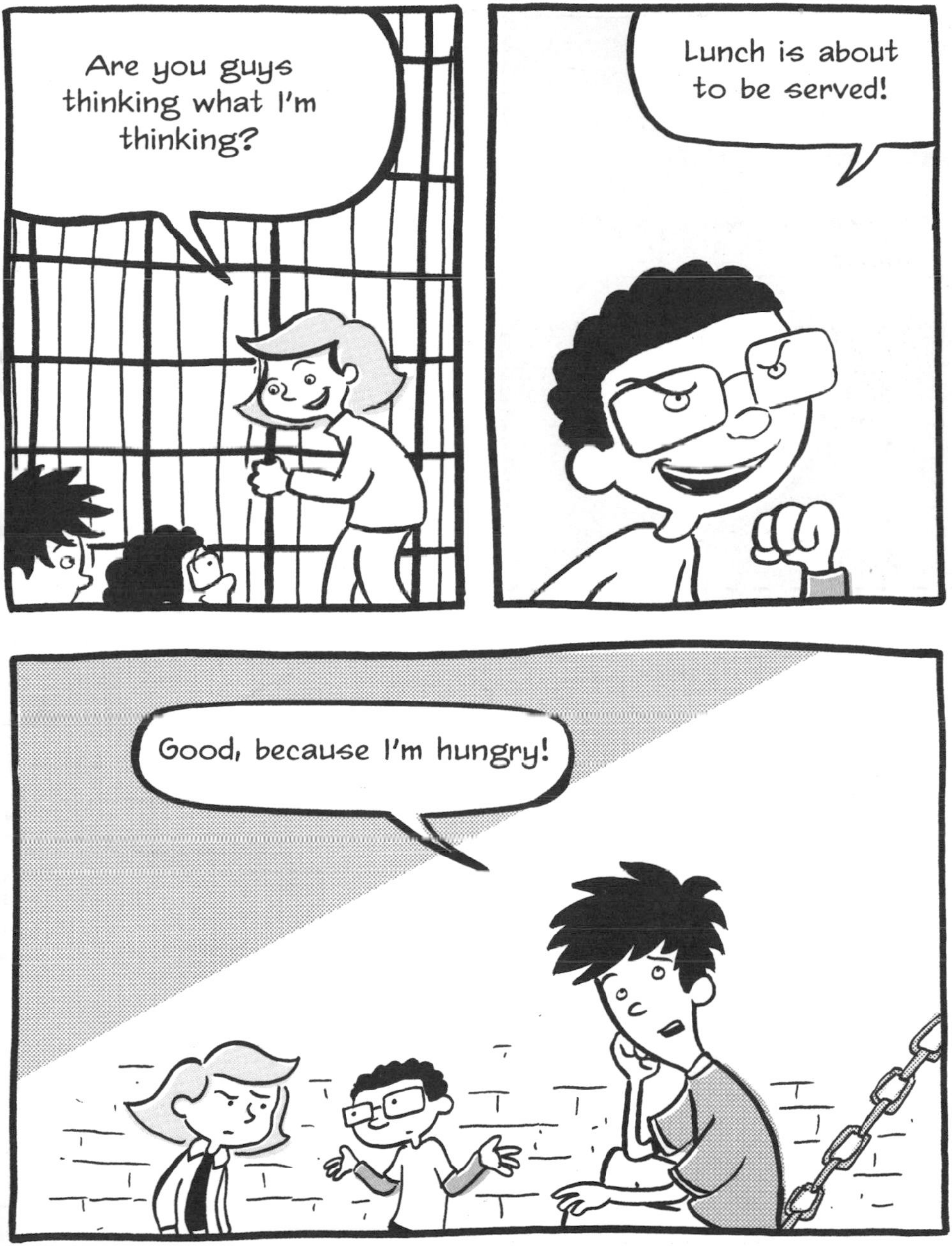
Are you guys thinking what I'm thinking?
Lunch is about to be served!
Good, because I'm hungry!

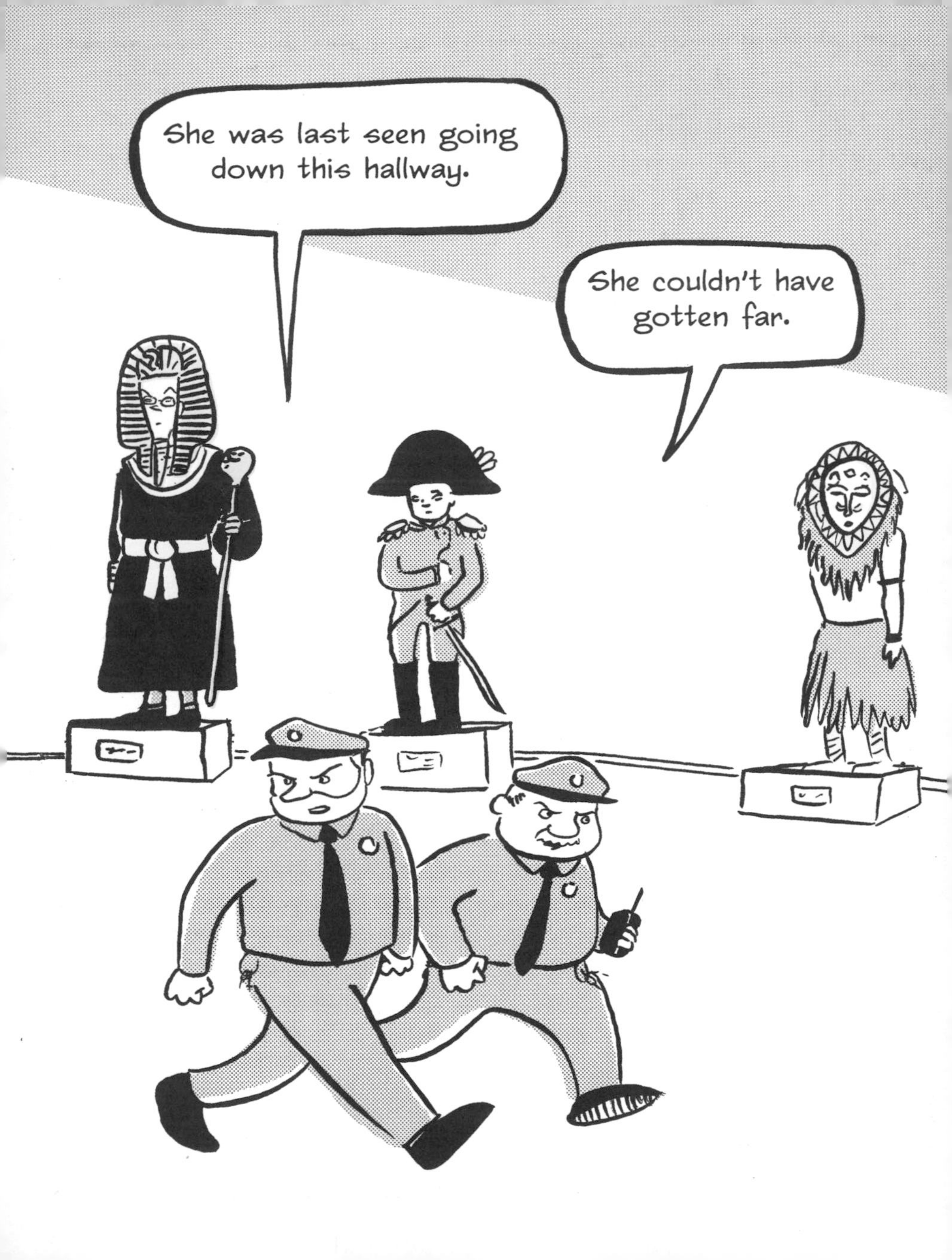
She was last seen going down this hallway.
She couldn't have gotten far.

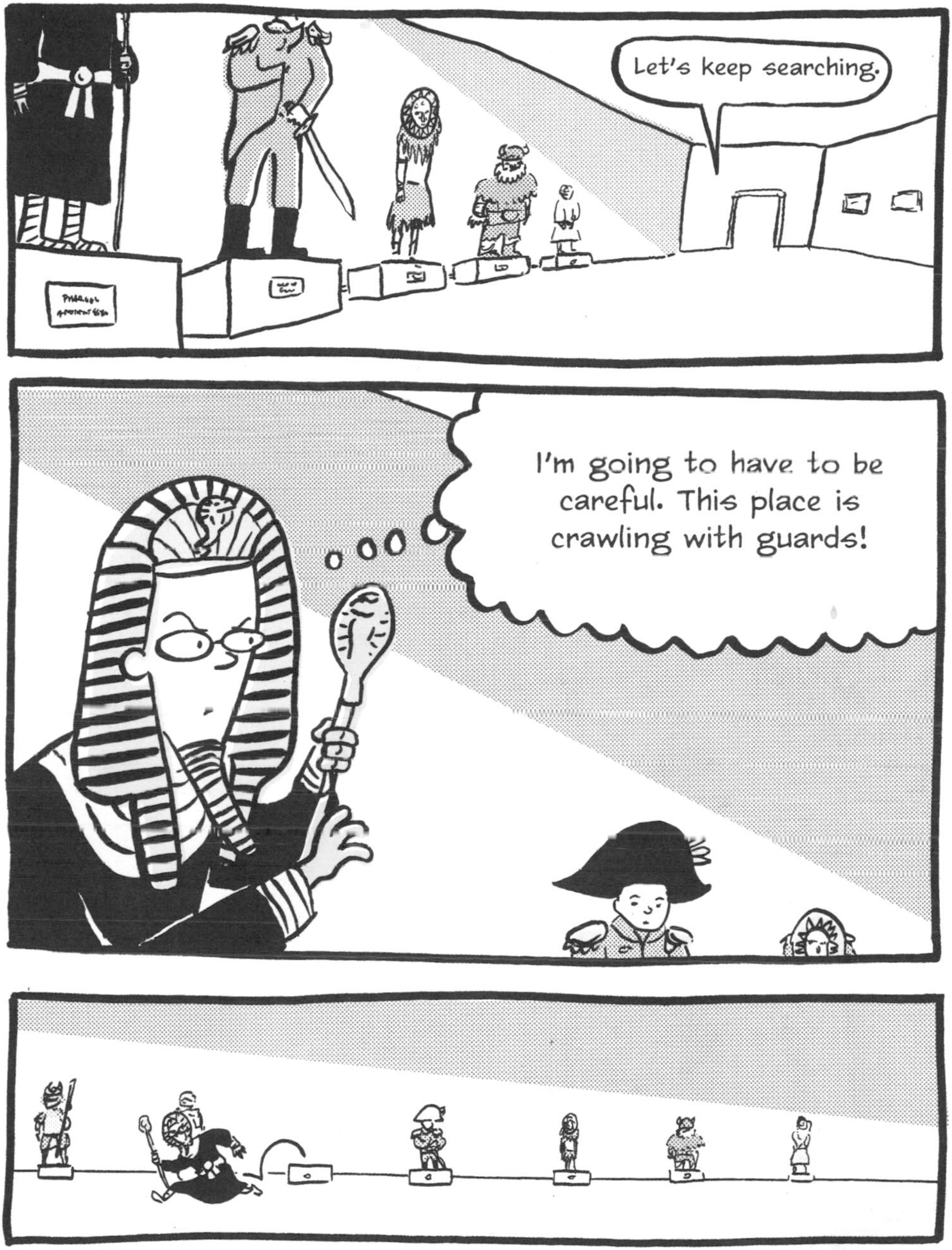
Let's keep searching.
I'm going to have to be careful. This place is crawling with guards!

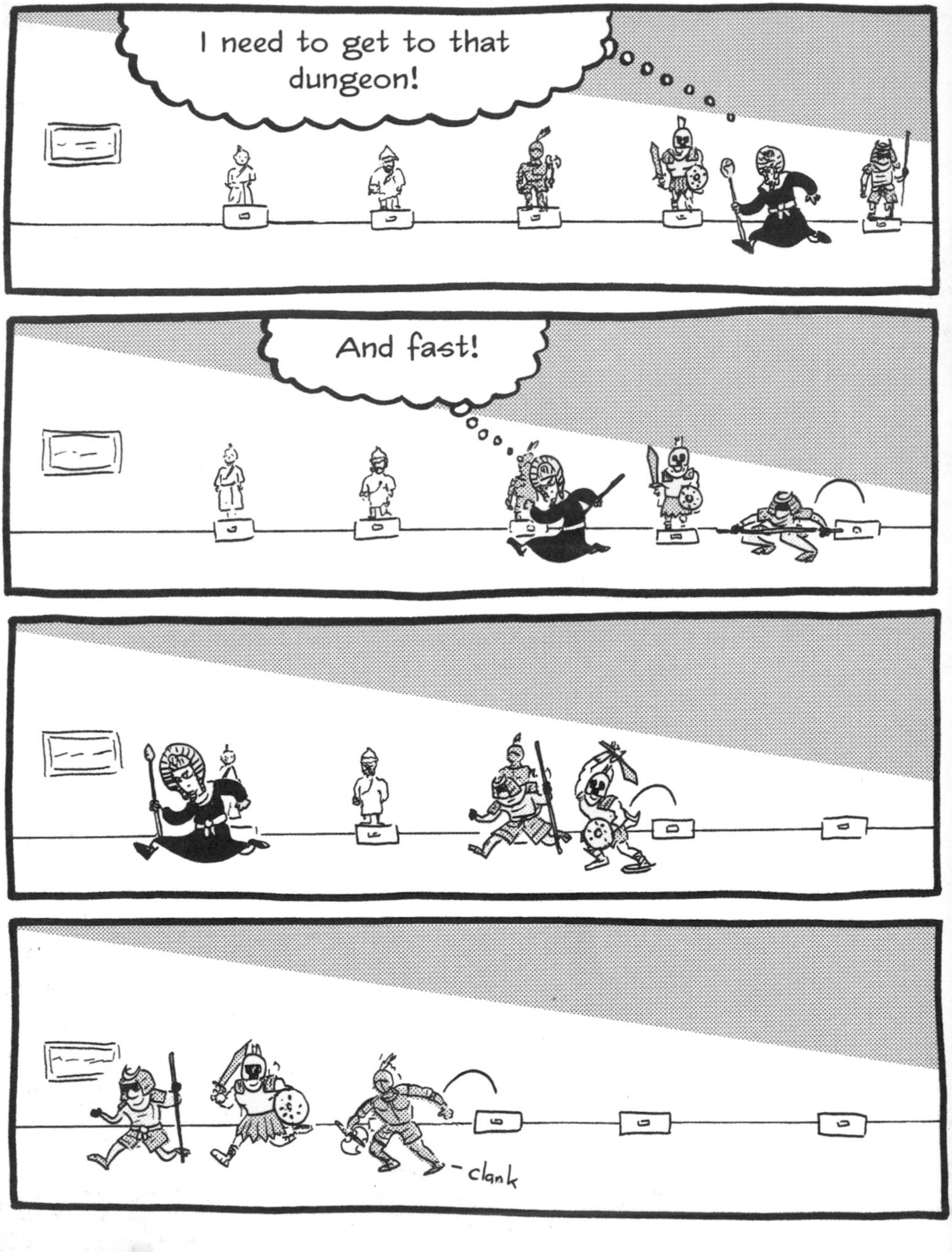
I need to get to that dungeon!
And fast!
clank

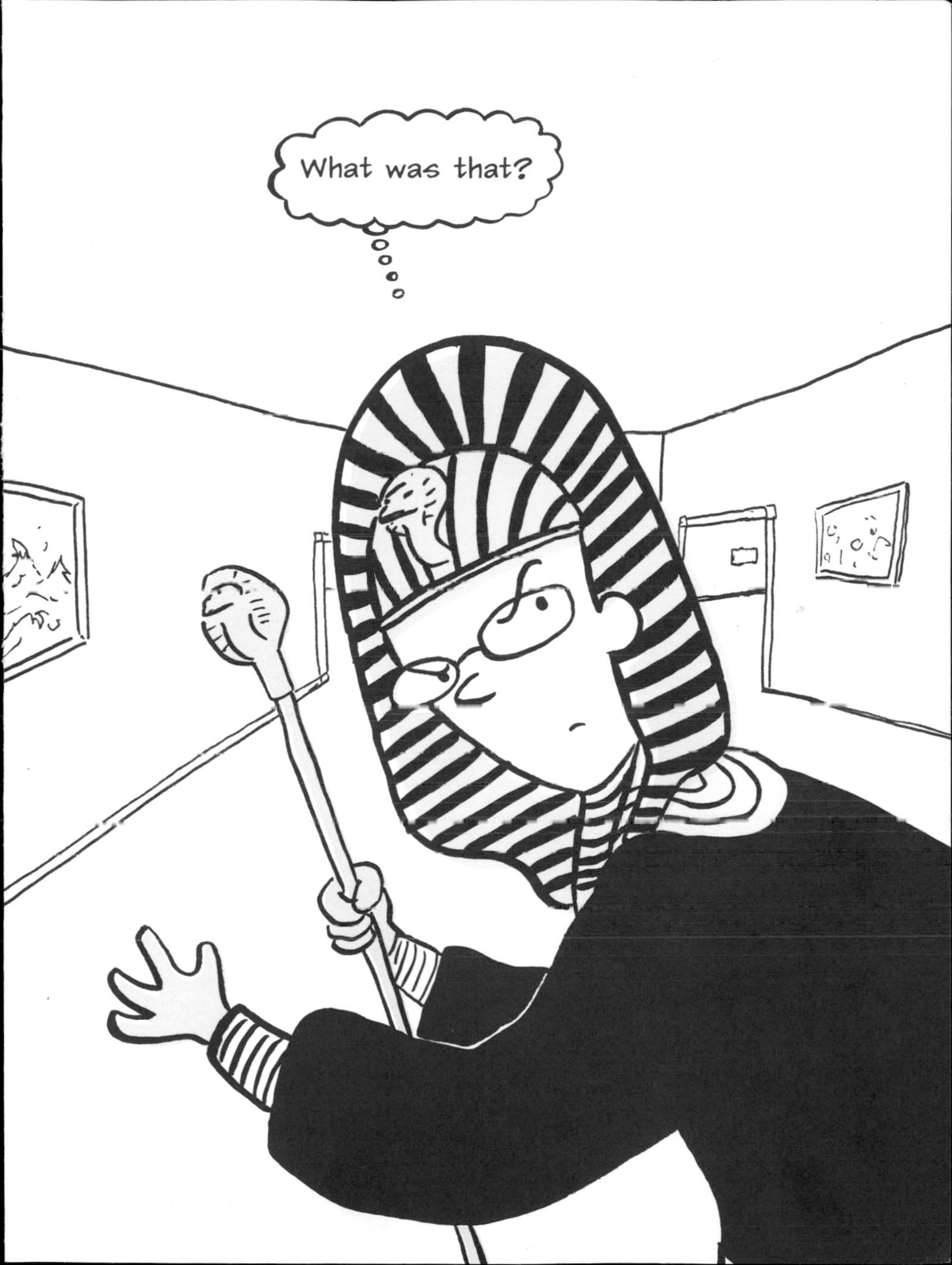
What was that?

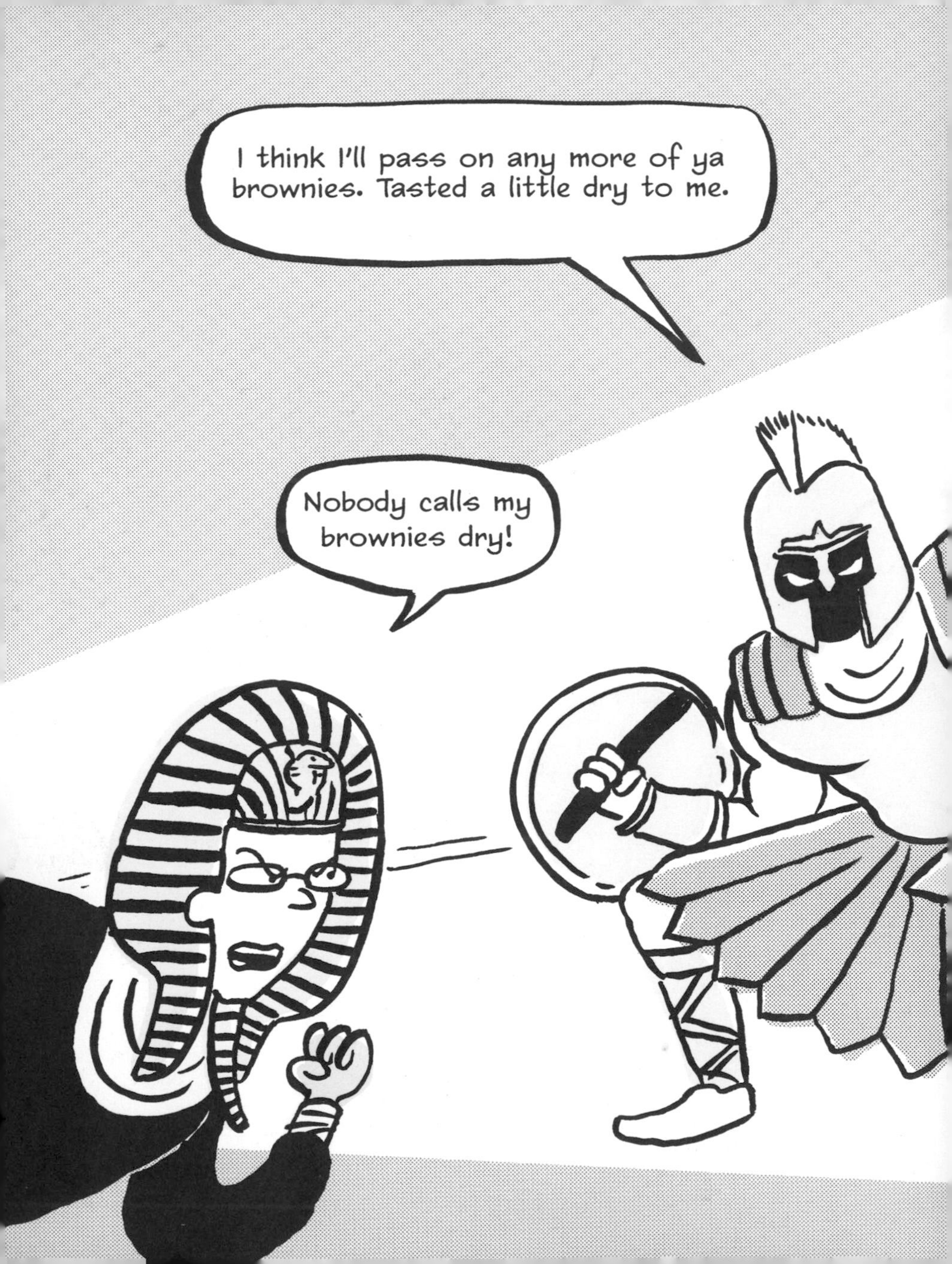
I think I'll pass on any more of ya brownies. Tasted a little dry to me.
Nobody calls my brownies dry!

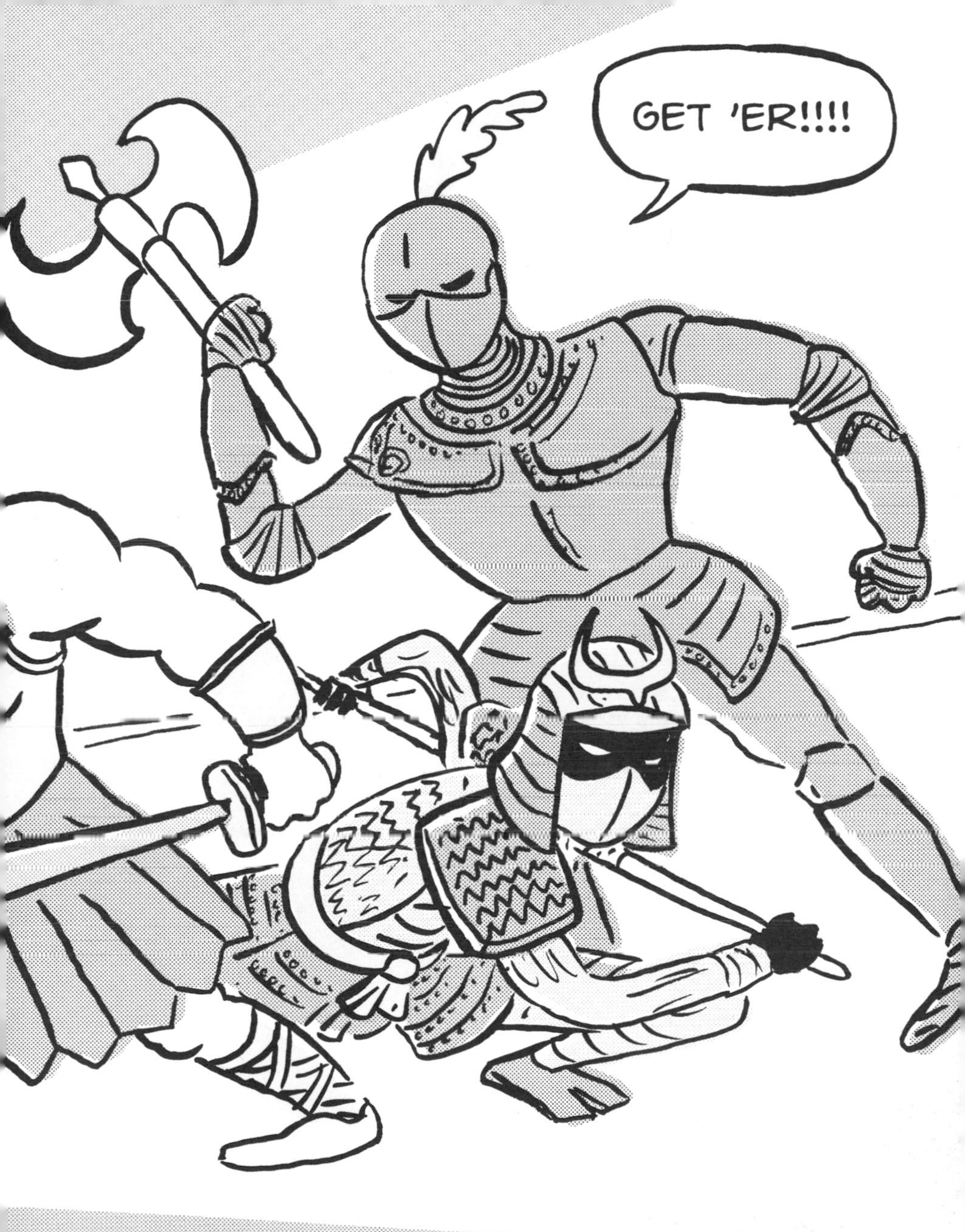
GET 'ER!!!!

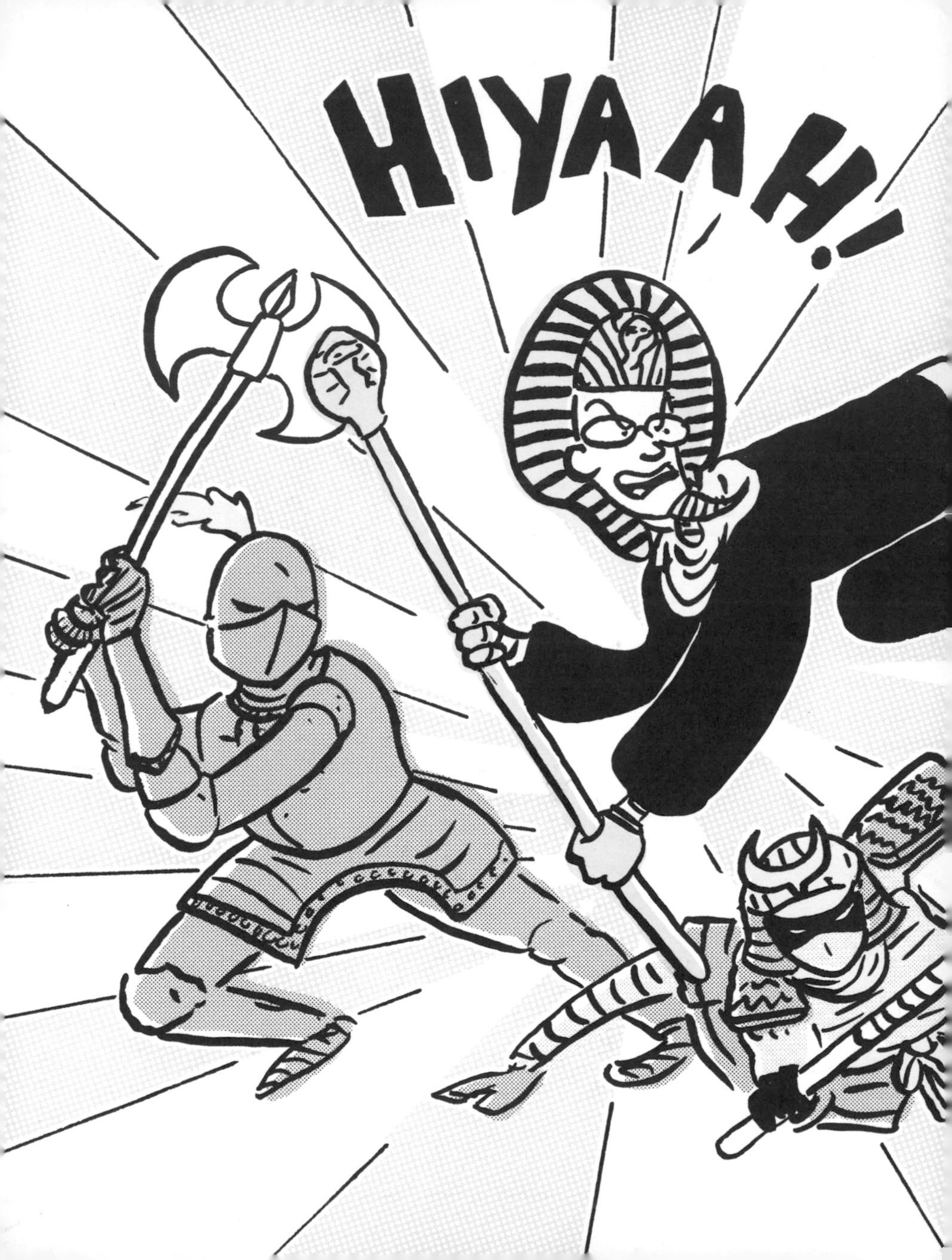
HIYAAH!

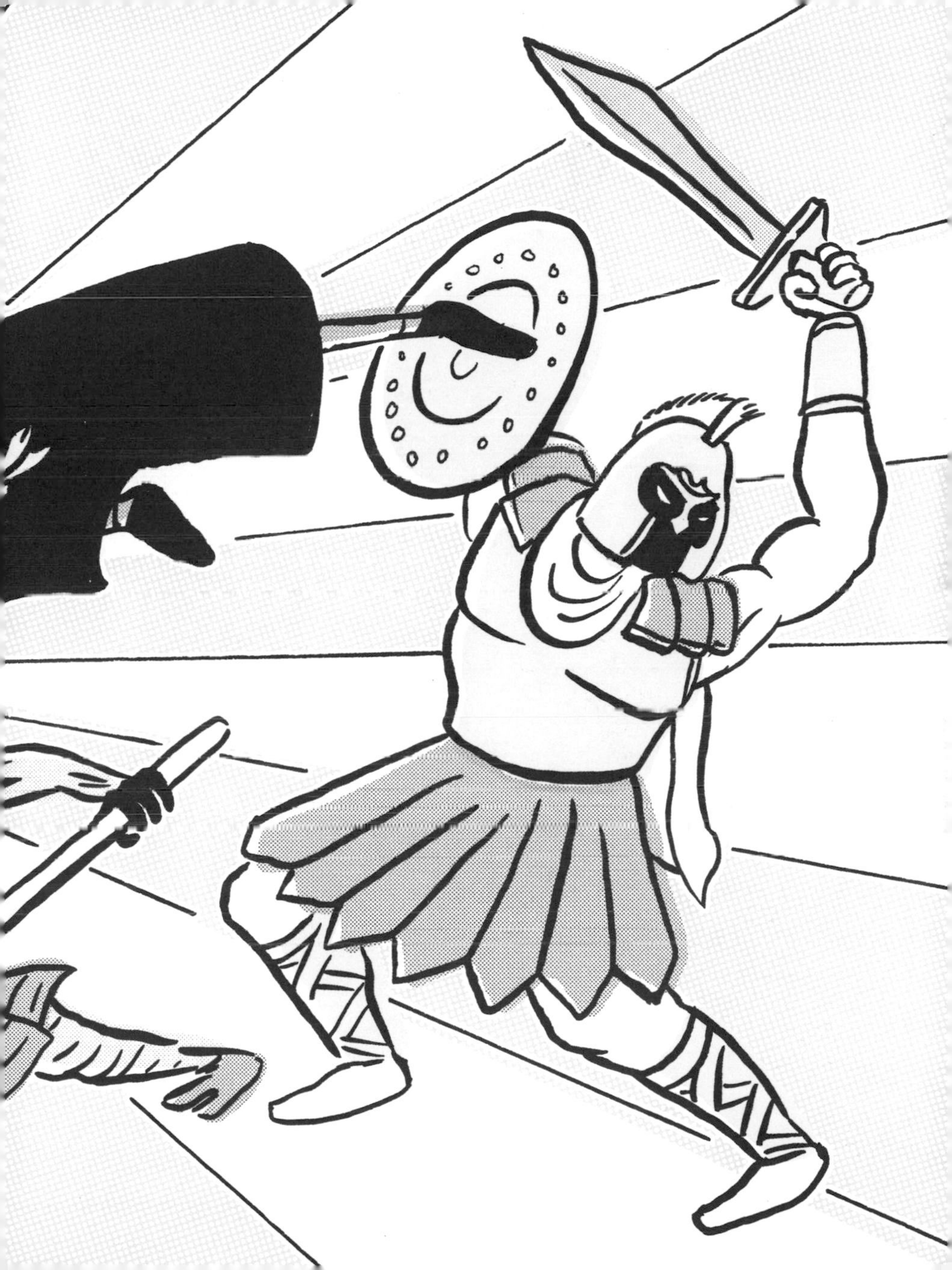

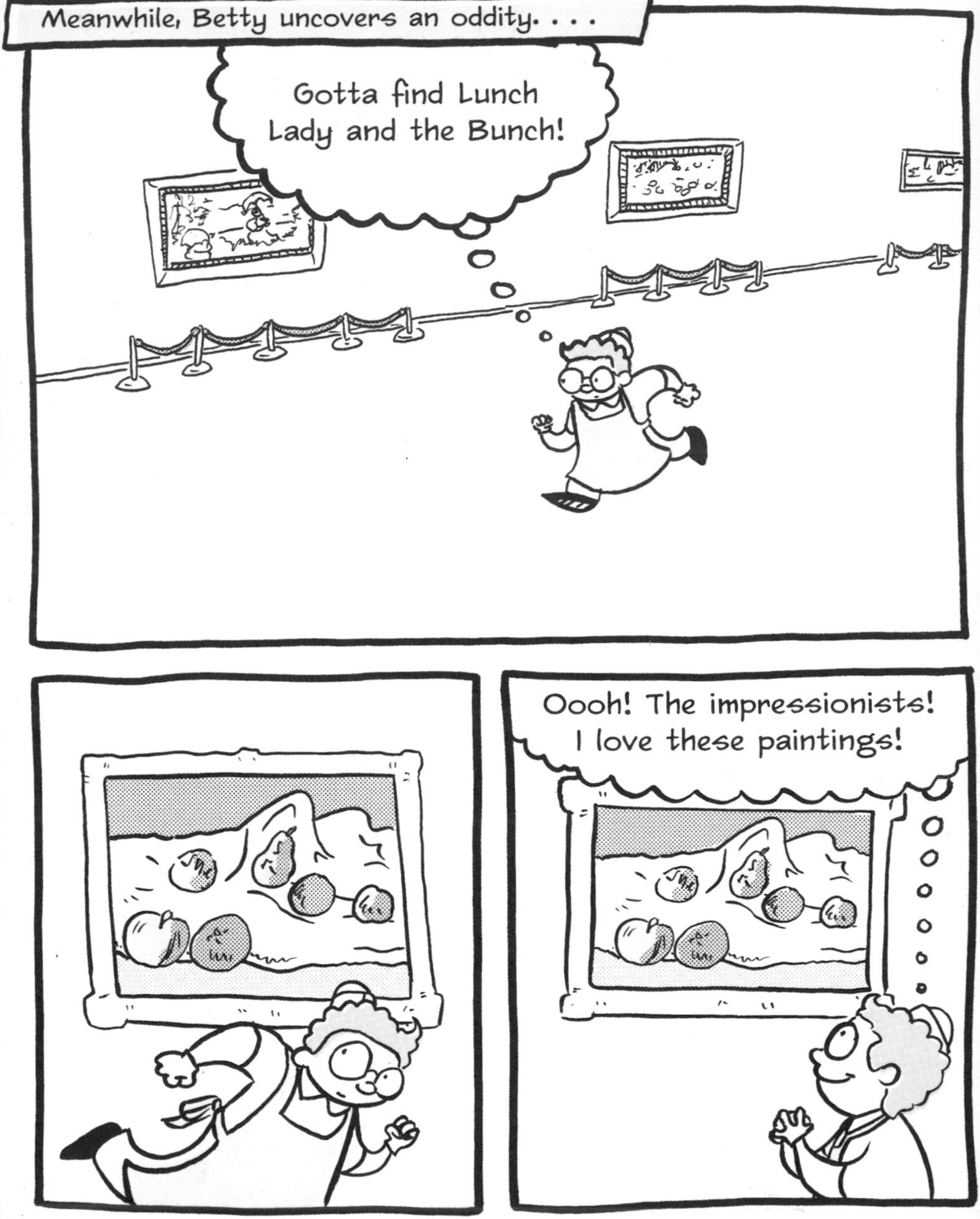

Meanwhile, Betty uncovers an oddity. . . .
Gotta find Lunch Lady and the Bunch!
Oooh! The impressionists! I love these paintings!

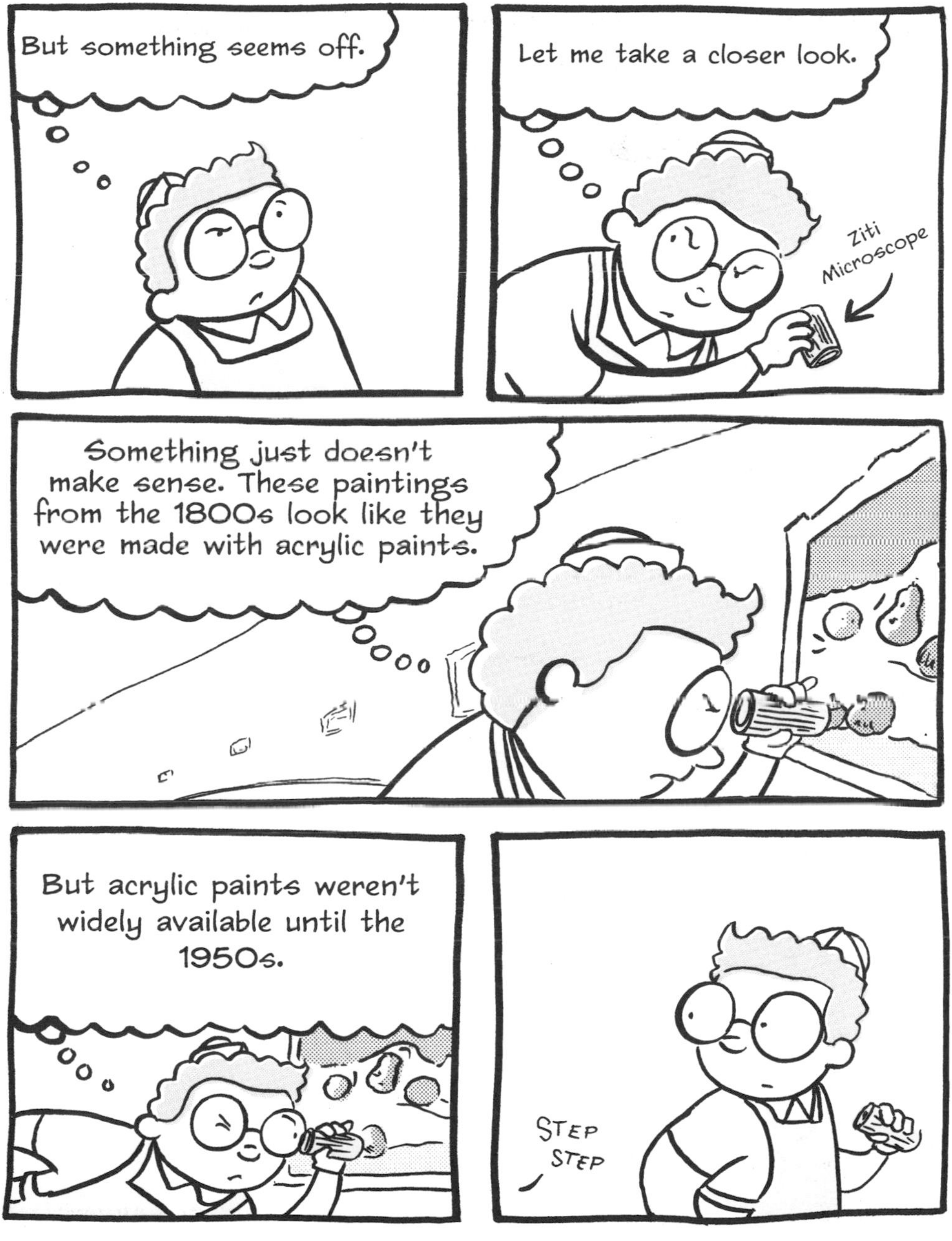
But something seems off.
Let me take a closer look.
Ziti Microscope
Something just doesn't make sense. These paintings from the 1800s look like they were made with acrylic paints.
But acrylic paints weren't widely available until the 1950s.
STEP
STEP

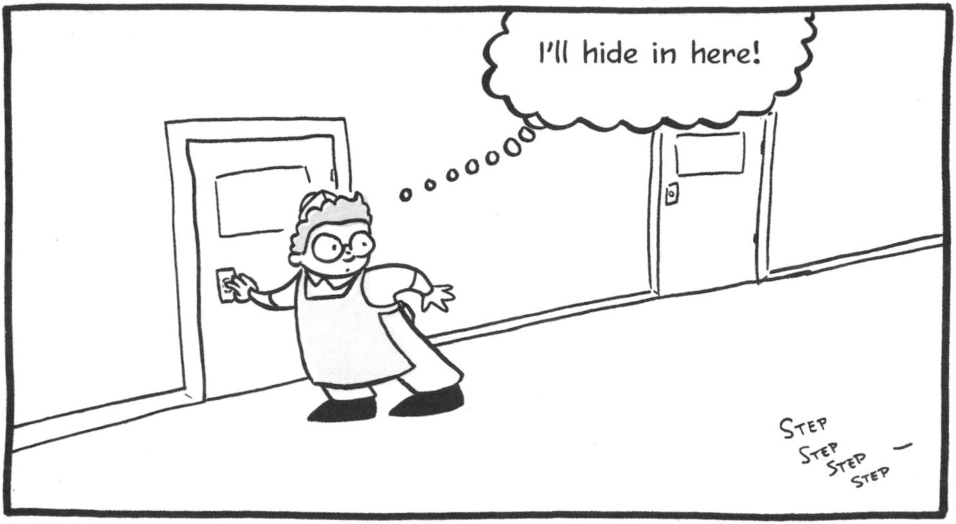
I'll hide in here!
STEP
STEP
STEP
STEP

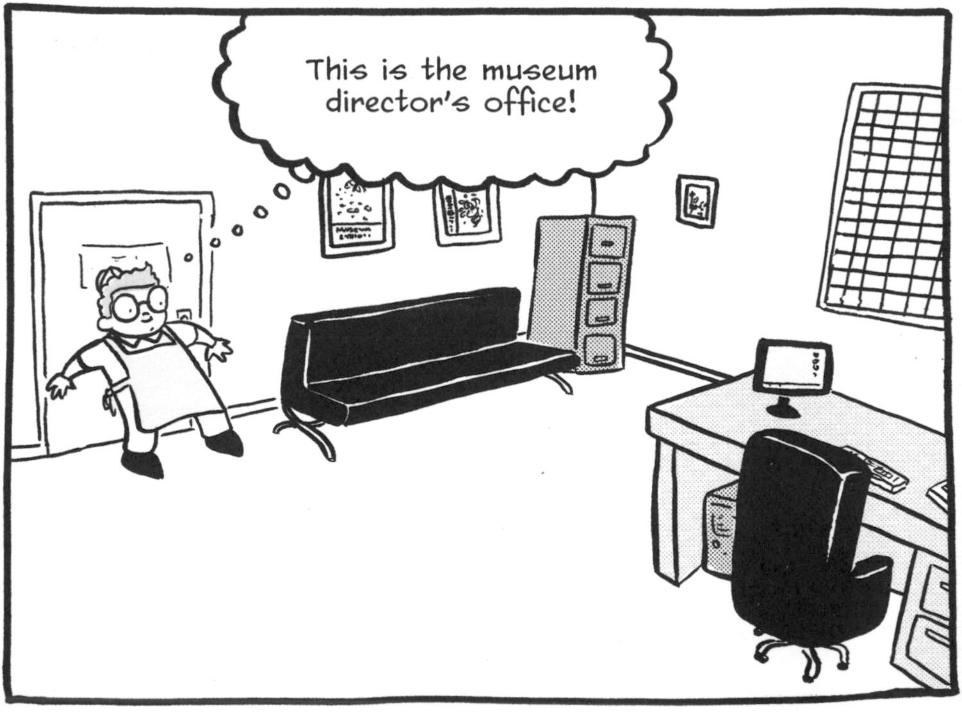
This is the museum director's office!

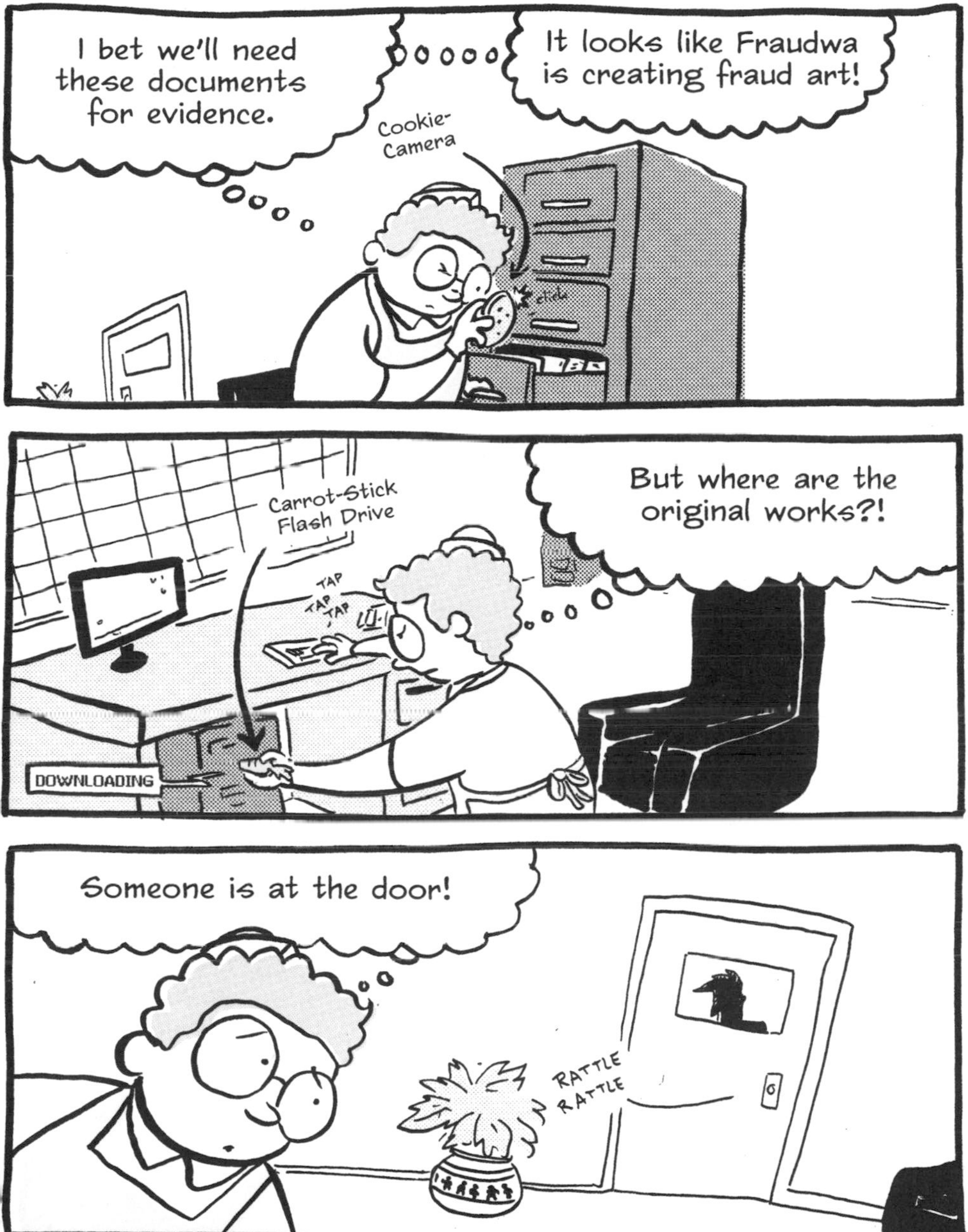
I bet we'll need these documents for evidence.
It looks like Fraudwa is creating fraud art!
Cookie-Camera
click
Carrot-Stick Flash Drive
But where are the original works?!
TAP
TAP
TAP
DOWNLOADING
Someone is at the door!
RATTLE
RATTLE

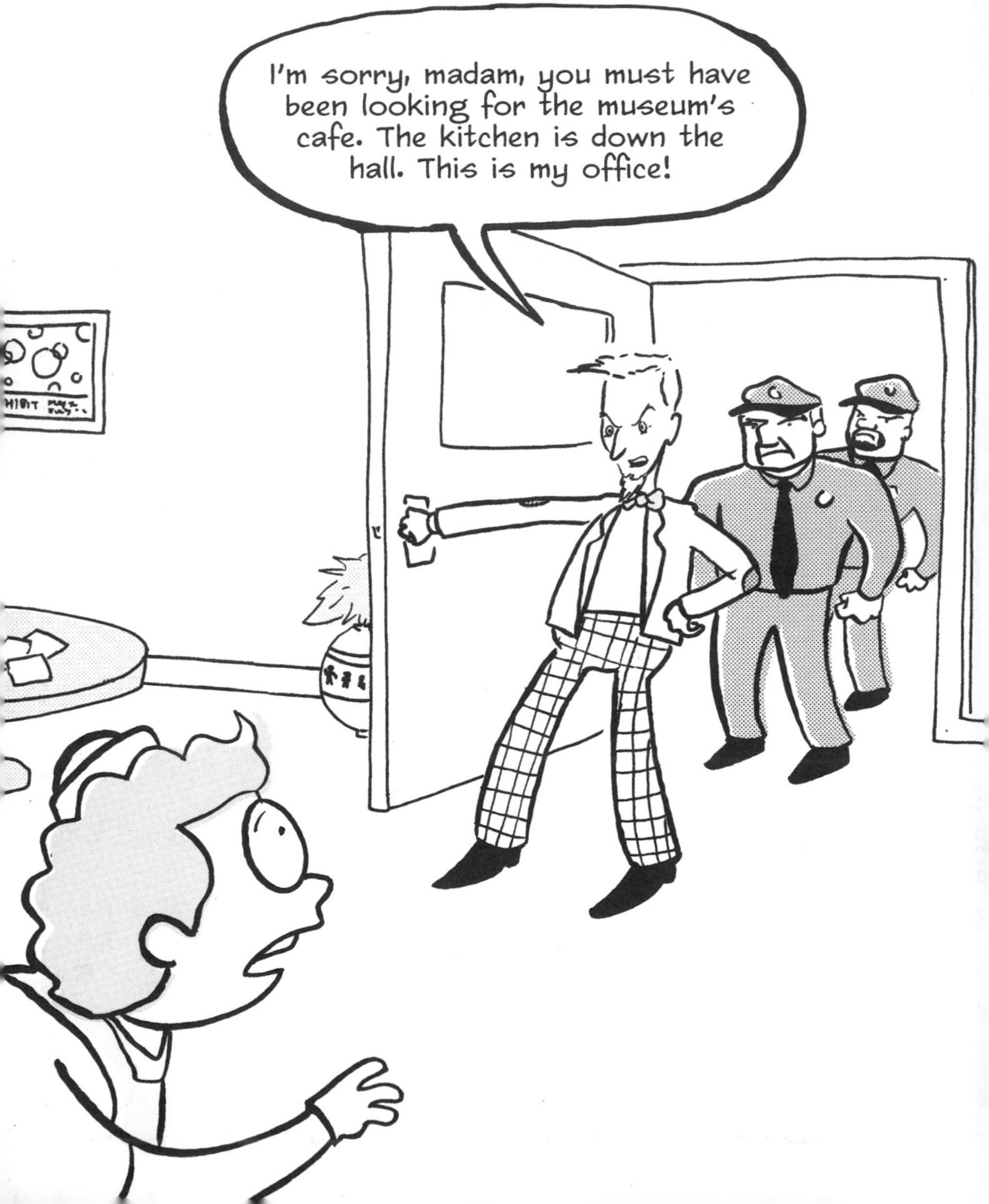
I'm sorry, madam, you must have been looking for the museum's cafe. The kitchen is down the hall. This is my office!

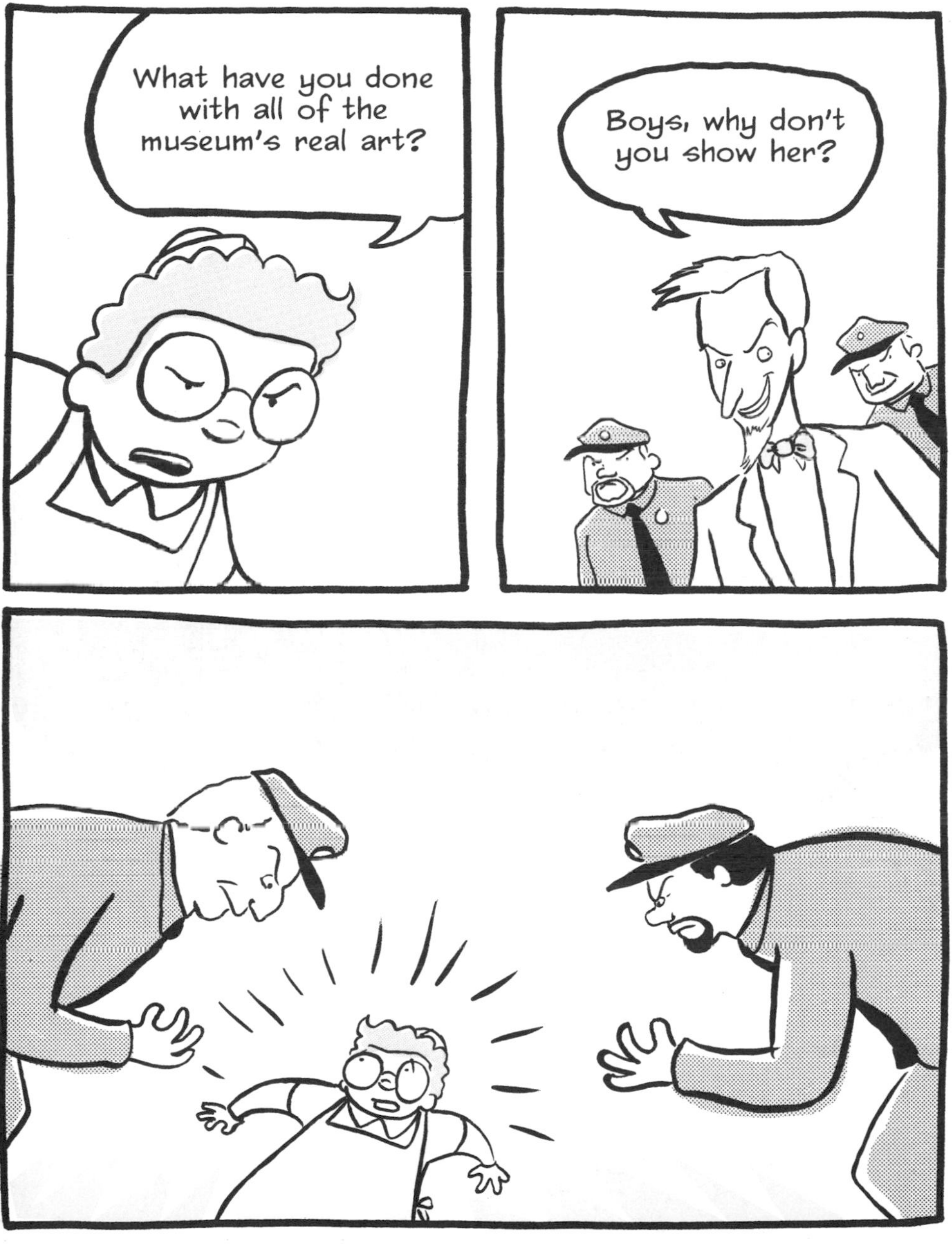
What have you done with all of the museum's real art?
Boys, why don't you show her?

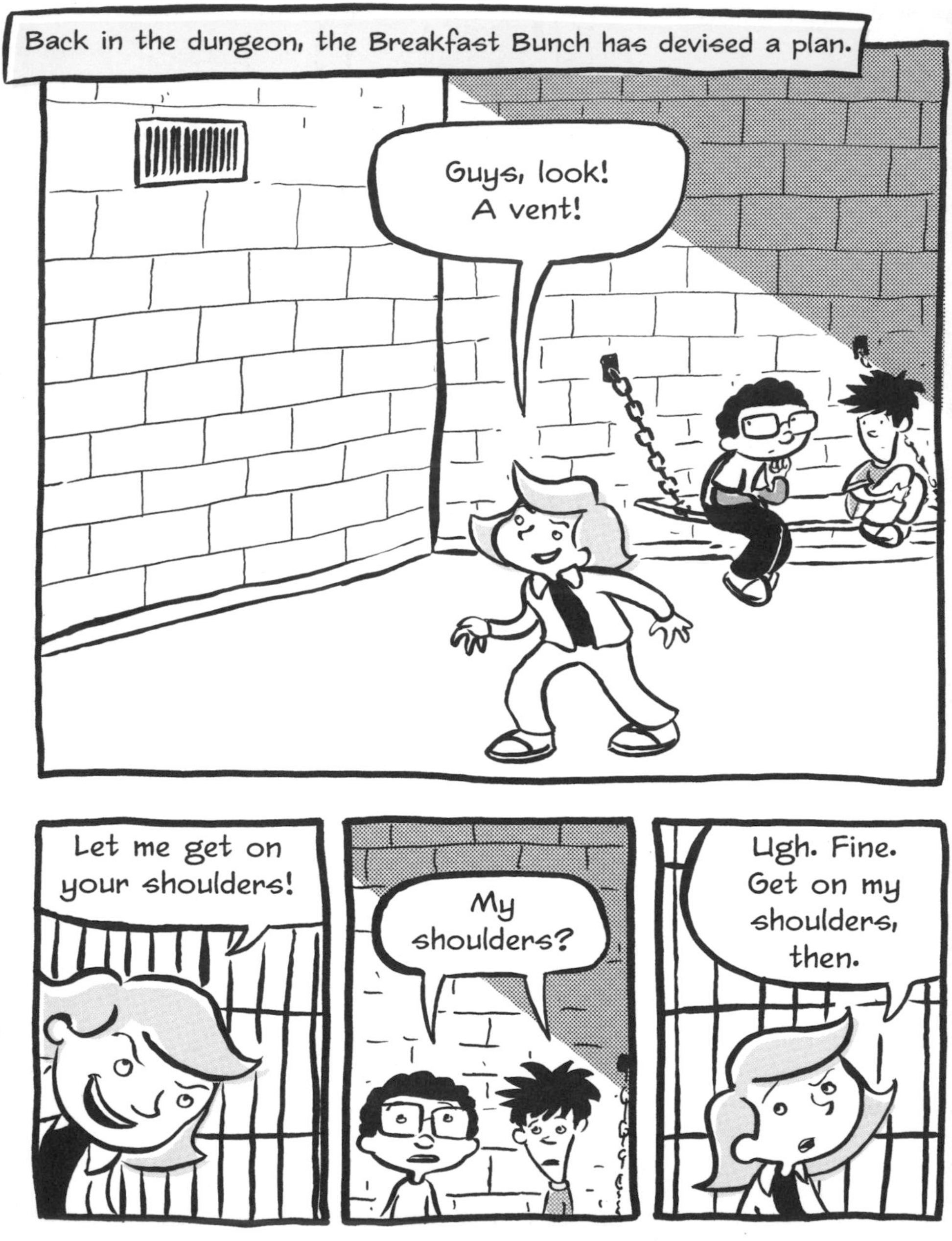
Back in the dungeon, the Breakfast Bunch has devised a plan.
Guys, look! A vent!
Let me get on your shoulders!
My shoulders?
Ugh. Fine. Get on my shoulders, then.

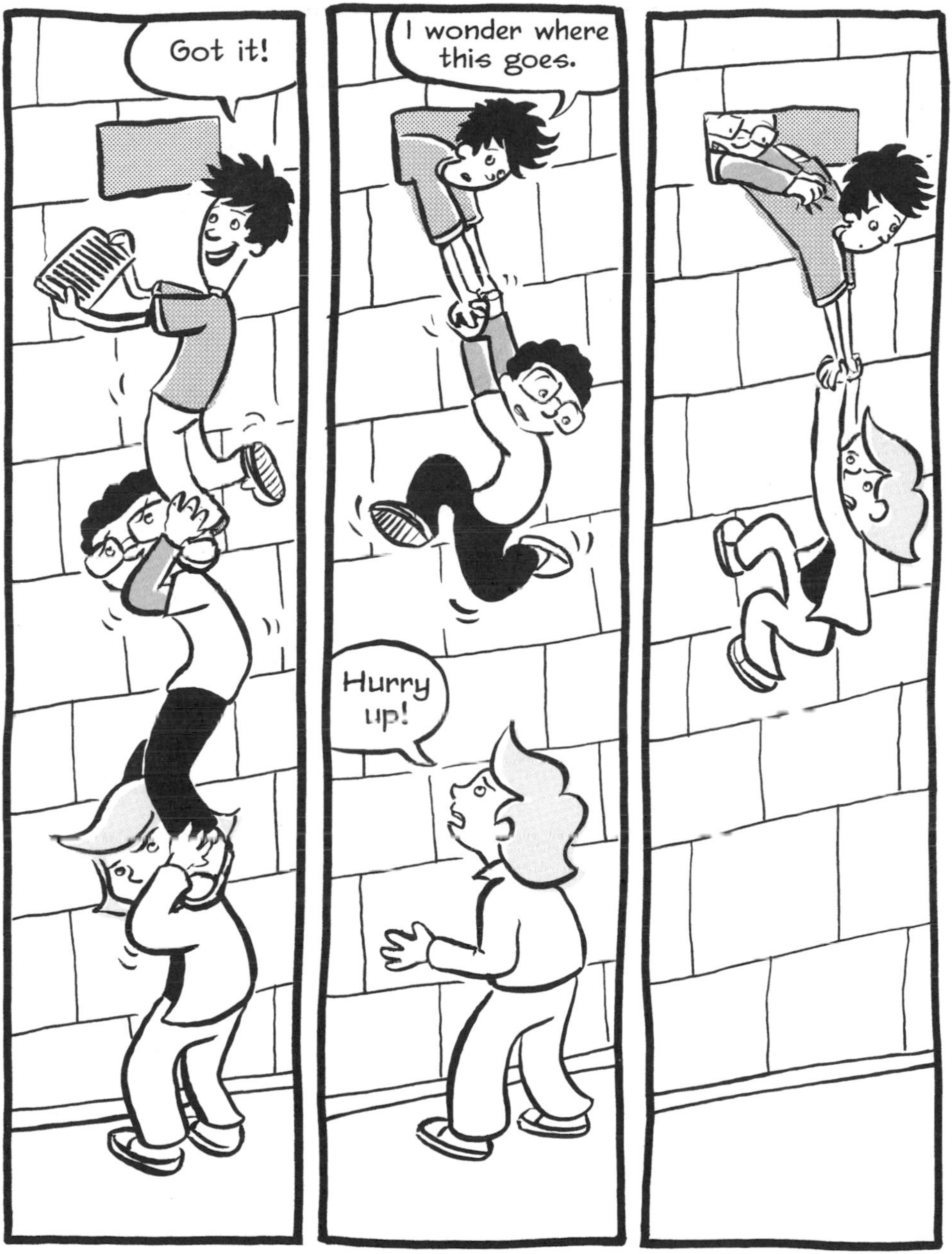
Got it!
I wonder where this goes.
Hurry up!

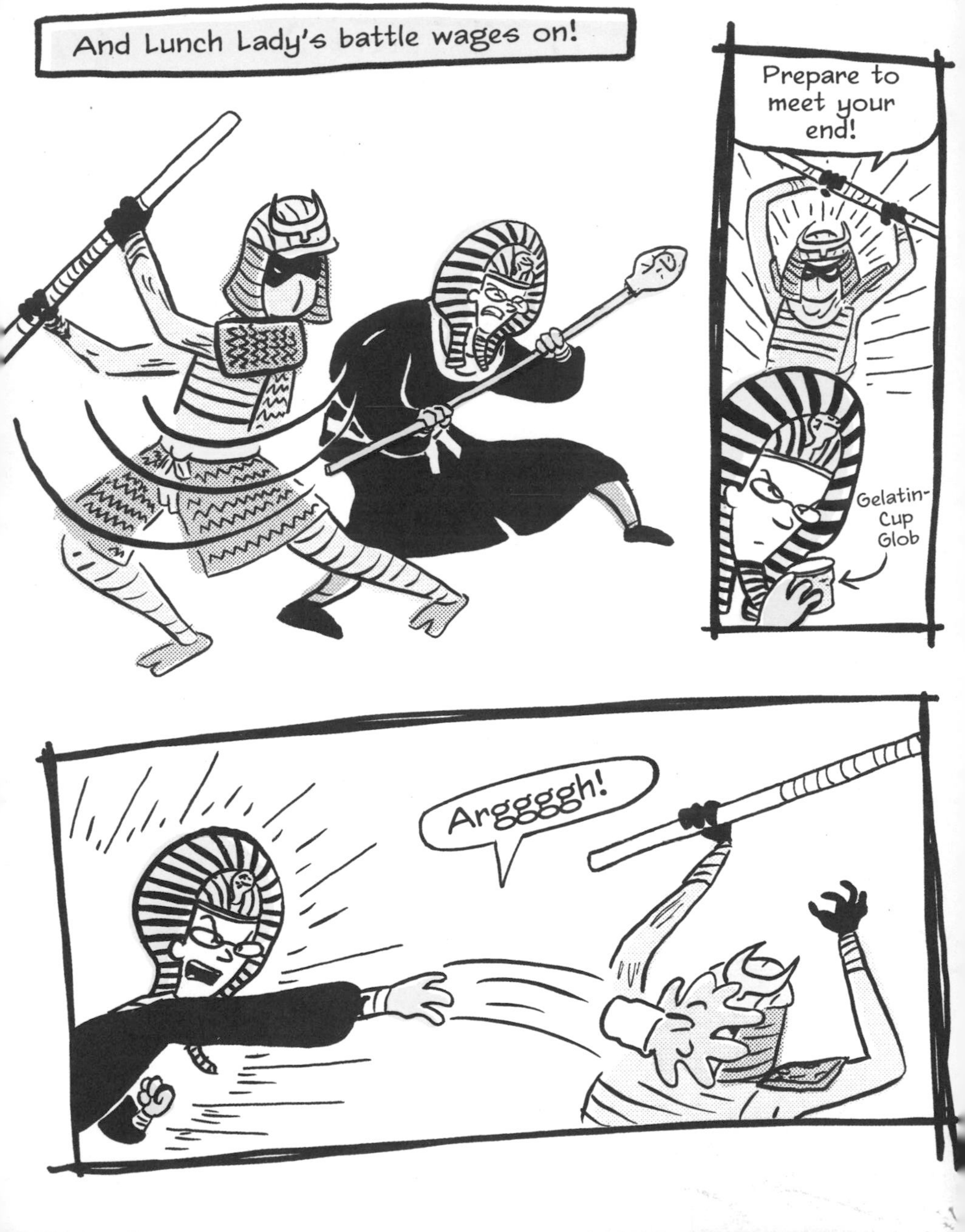
And Lunch Lady's battle wages on!
Prepare to meet your end!
Gelatin-Cup Glob
Argggggh!

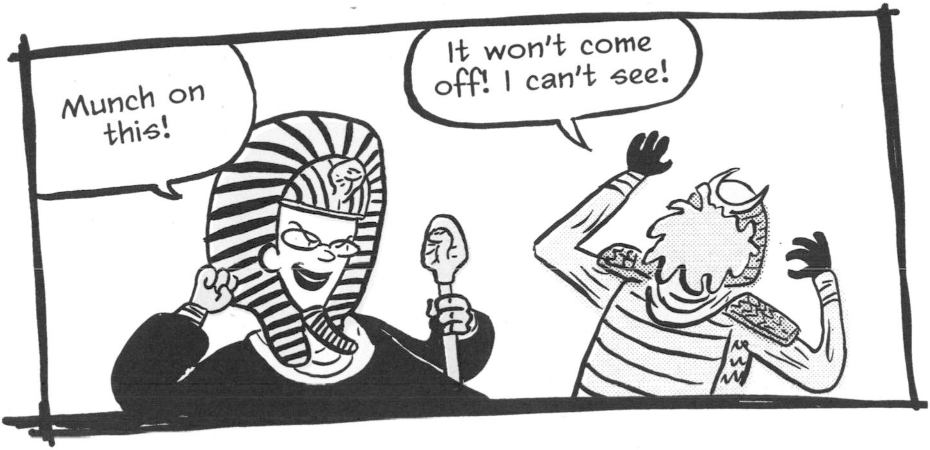
Munch on this!
It won't come off! I can't see!

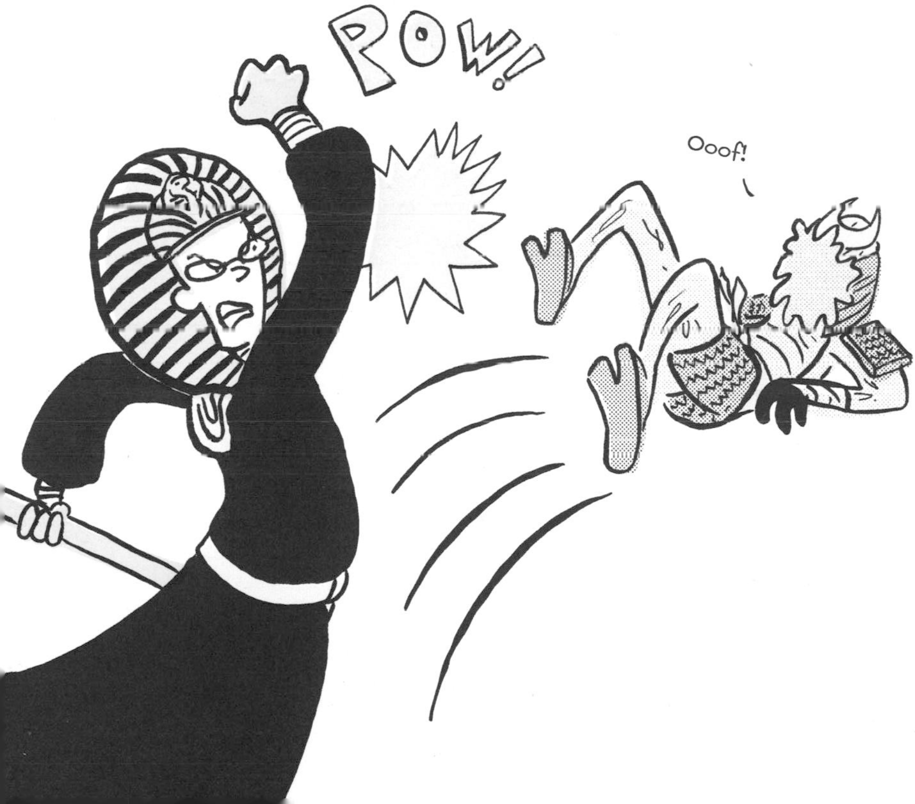
POW!
Ooof!

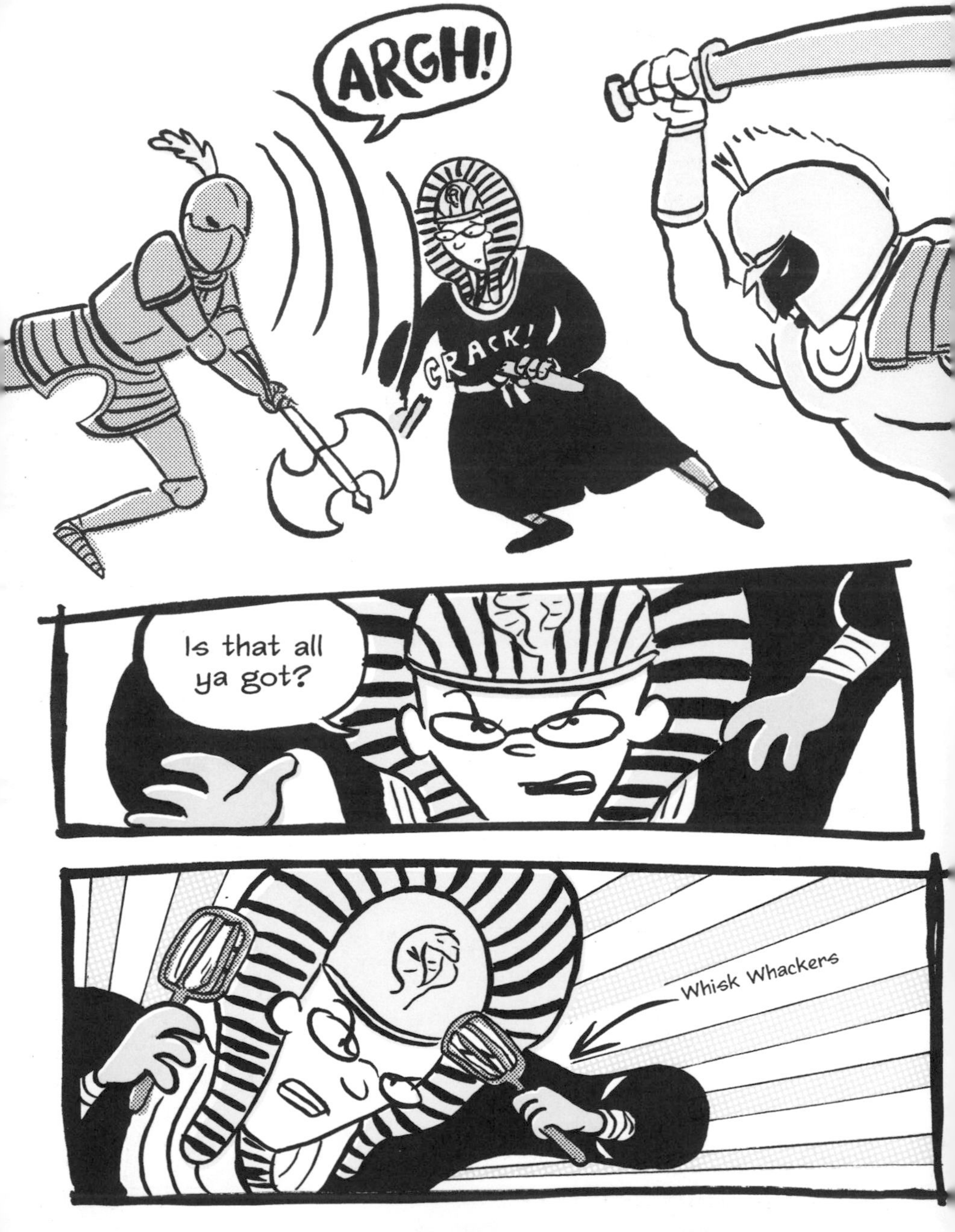
ARGH!
CRACK!
Is that all ya got?
Whisk Whackers

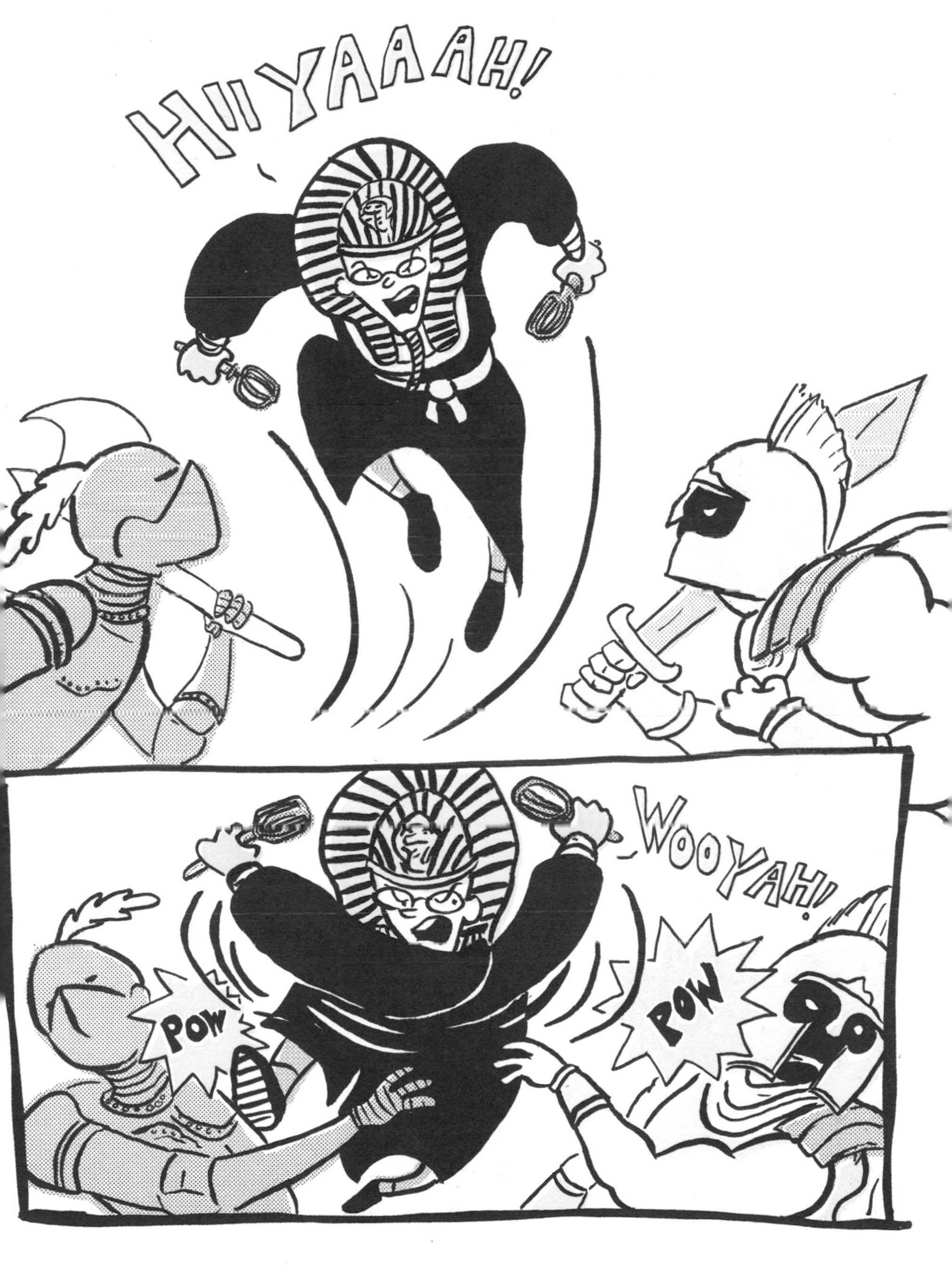
HIIYAAAAH!
WOOYAH!
POW
POW

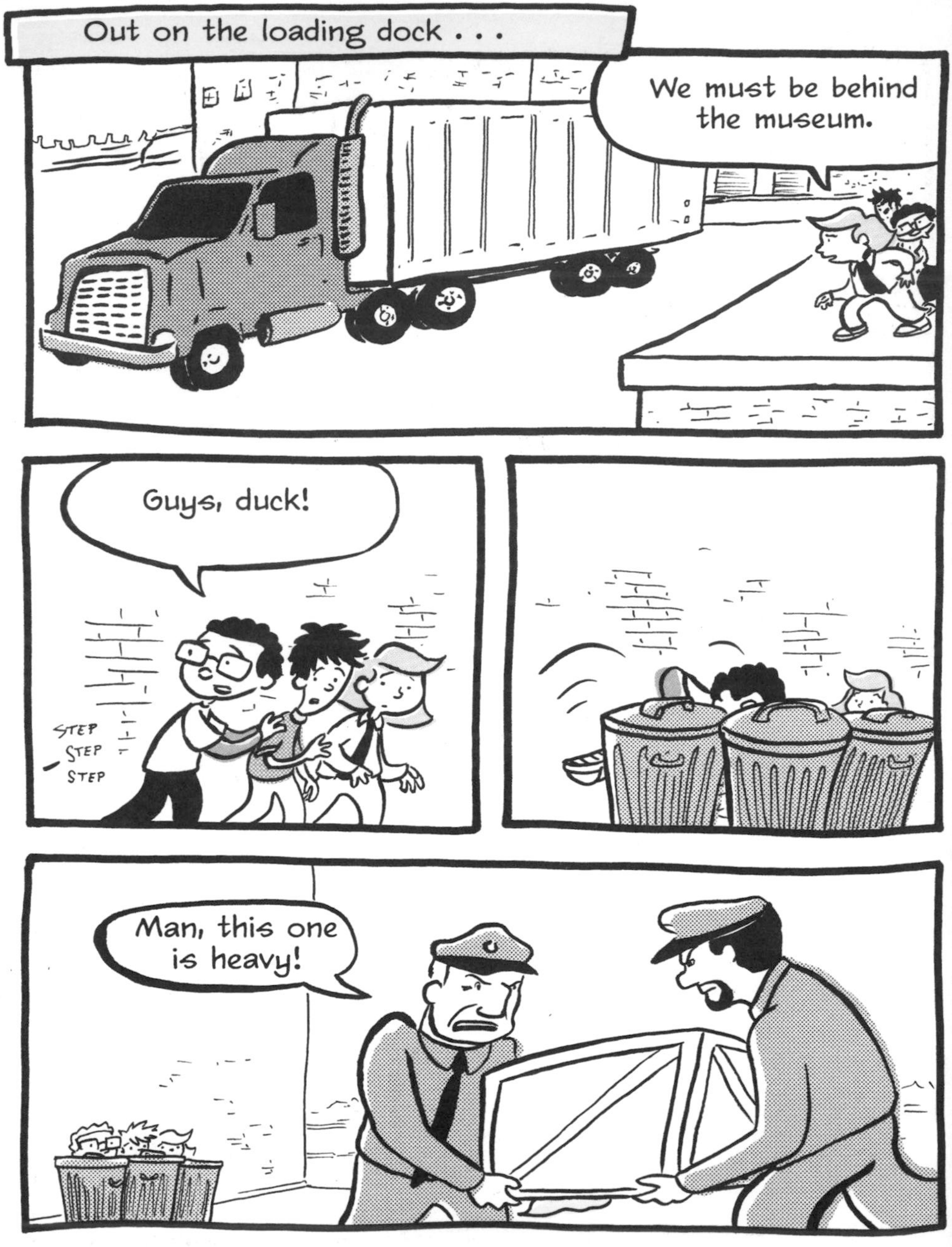
Out on the loading dock . . .
We must be behind the museum.
Guys, duck!
STEP
STEP
STEP
Man, this one is heavy!

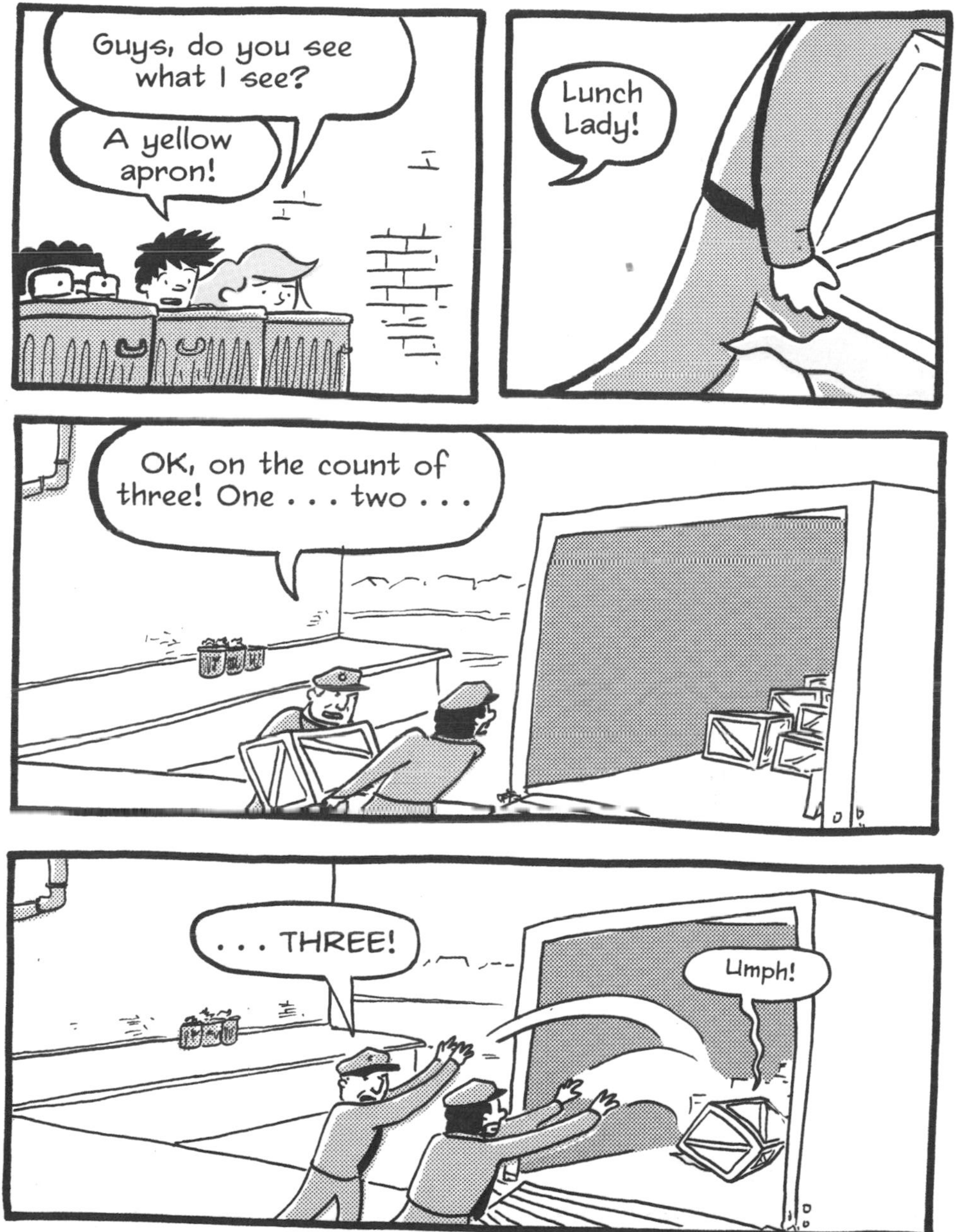
Guys, do you see what I see?
A yellow apron!
Lunch Lady!
OK, on the count of three! One . . . two . . .
. . . THREE!
Umph!

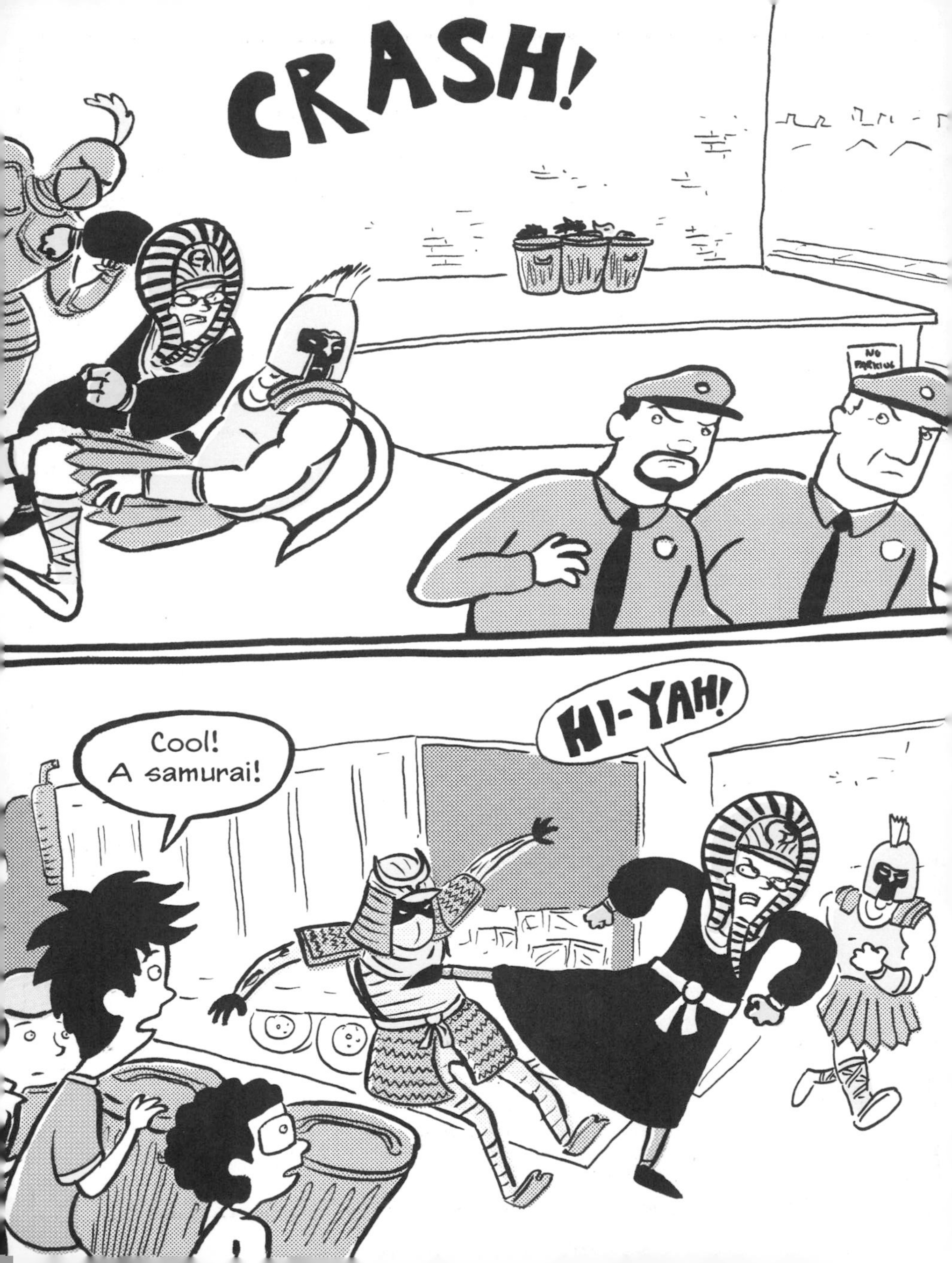
CRASH!
NO PARKING
Cool! A samurai!
HI-YAH!

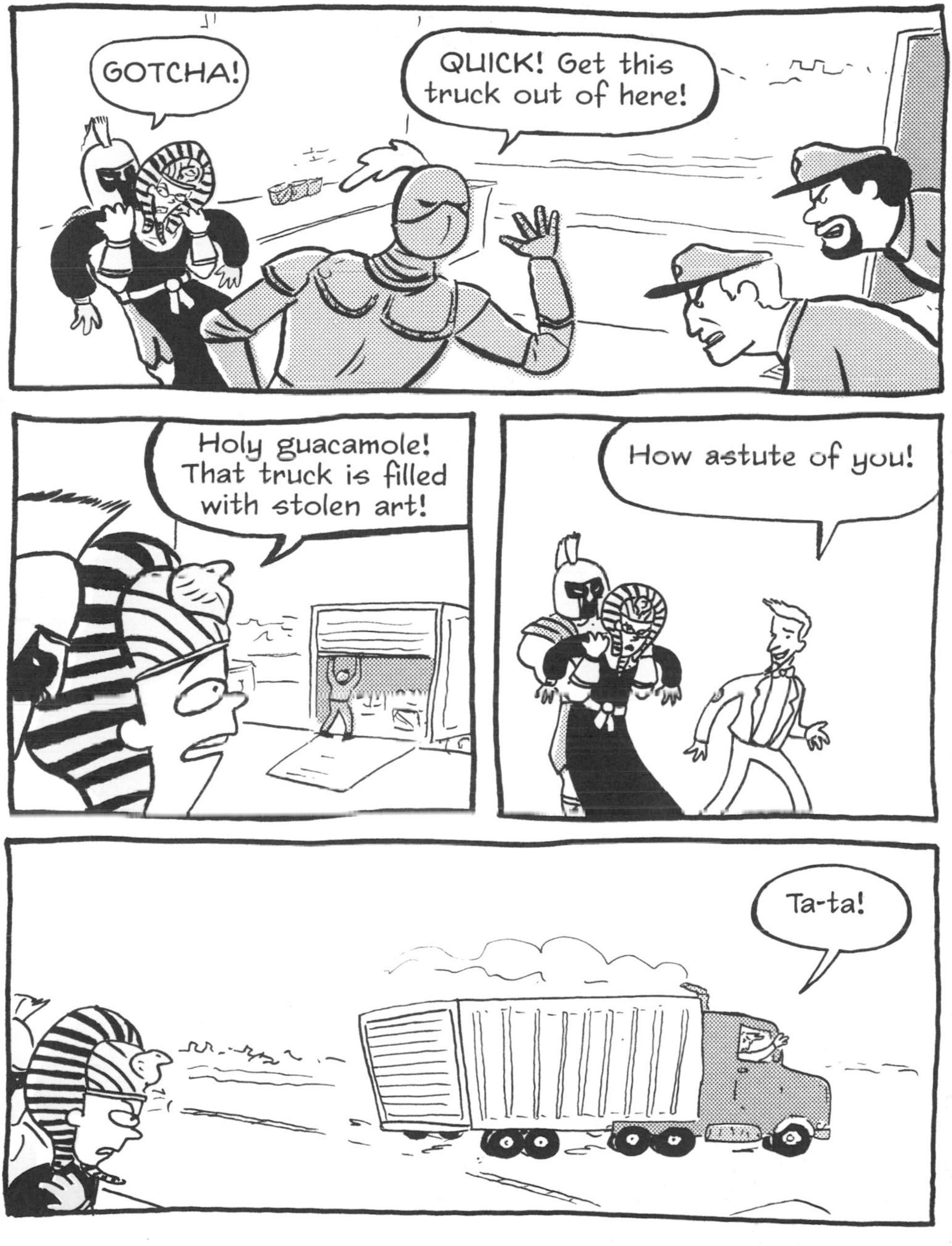
GOTCHA!
QUICK! Get this truck out of here!
Holy guacamole! That truck is filled with stolen art!
How astute of you!
Ta-ta!

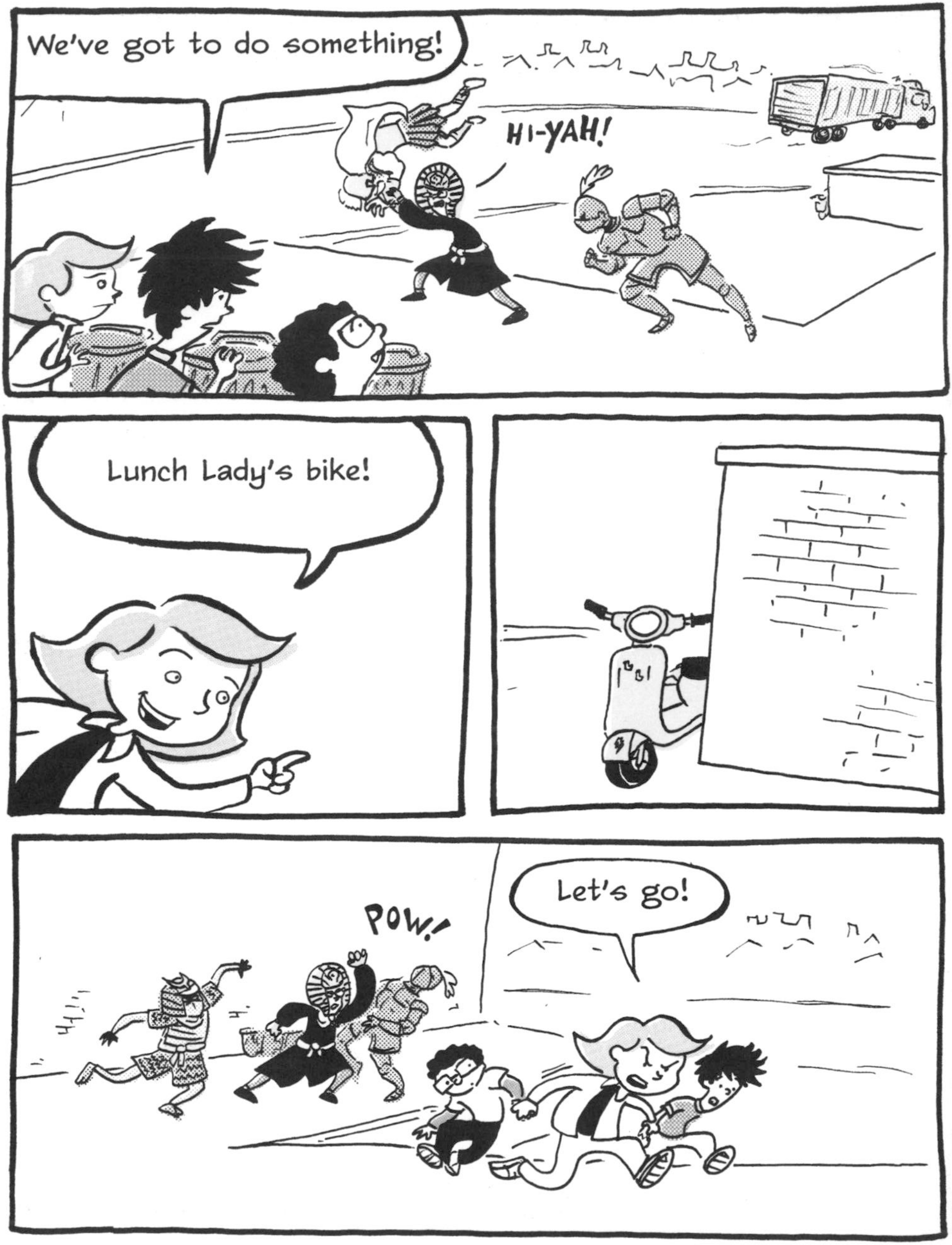
We've got to do something!
HI-YAH!
Lunch Lady's bike!
POW!
Let's go!

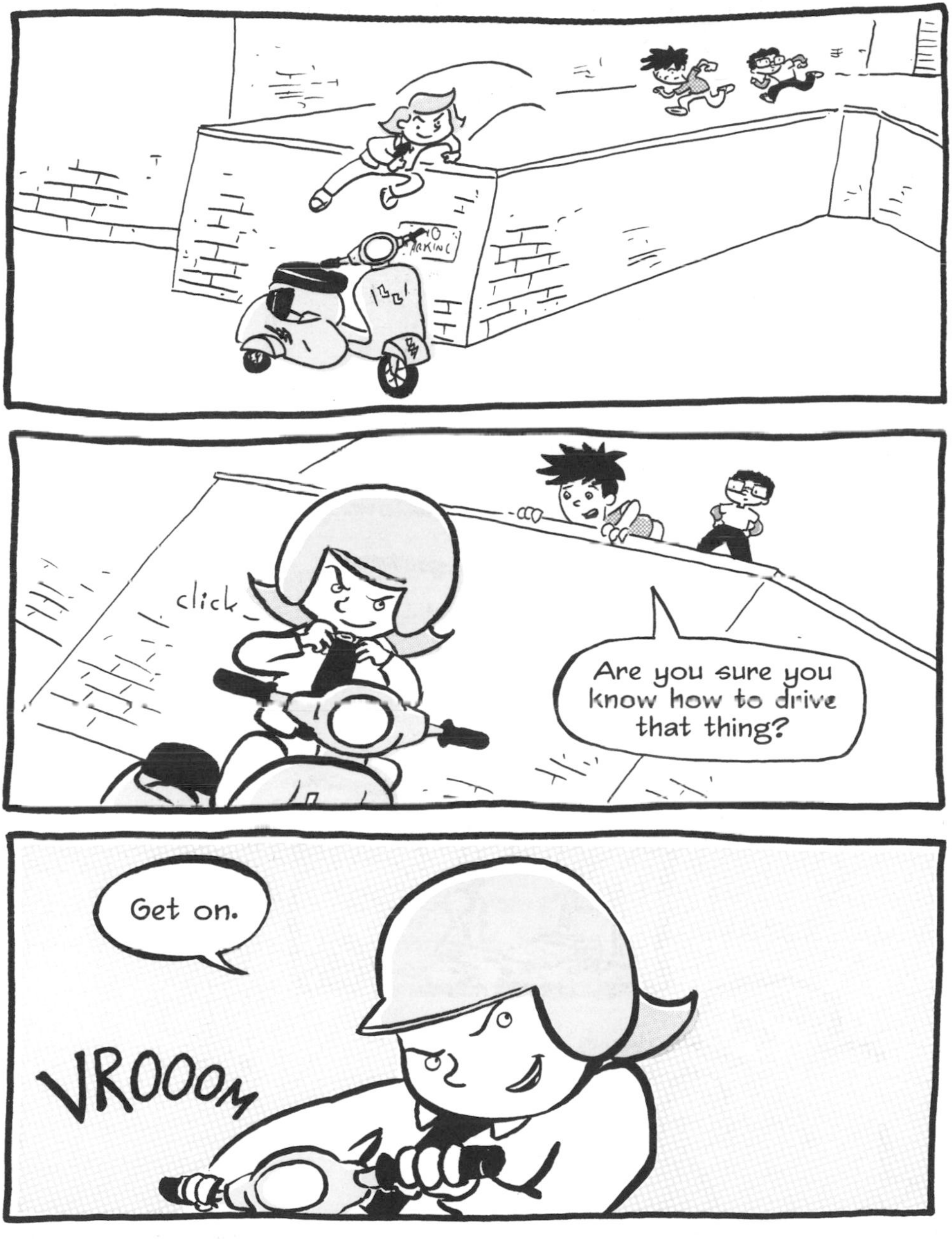
NO PARKING
click
Are you sure you know how to drive that thing?
Get on.
VROOOM

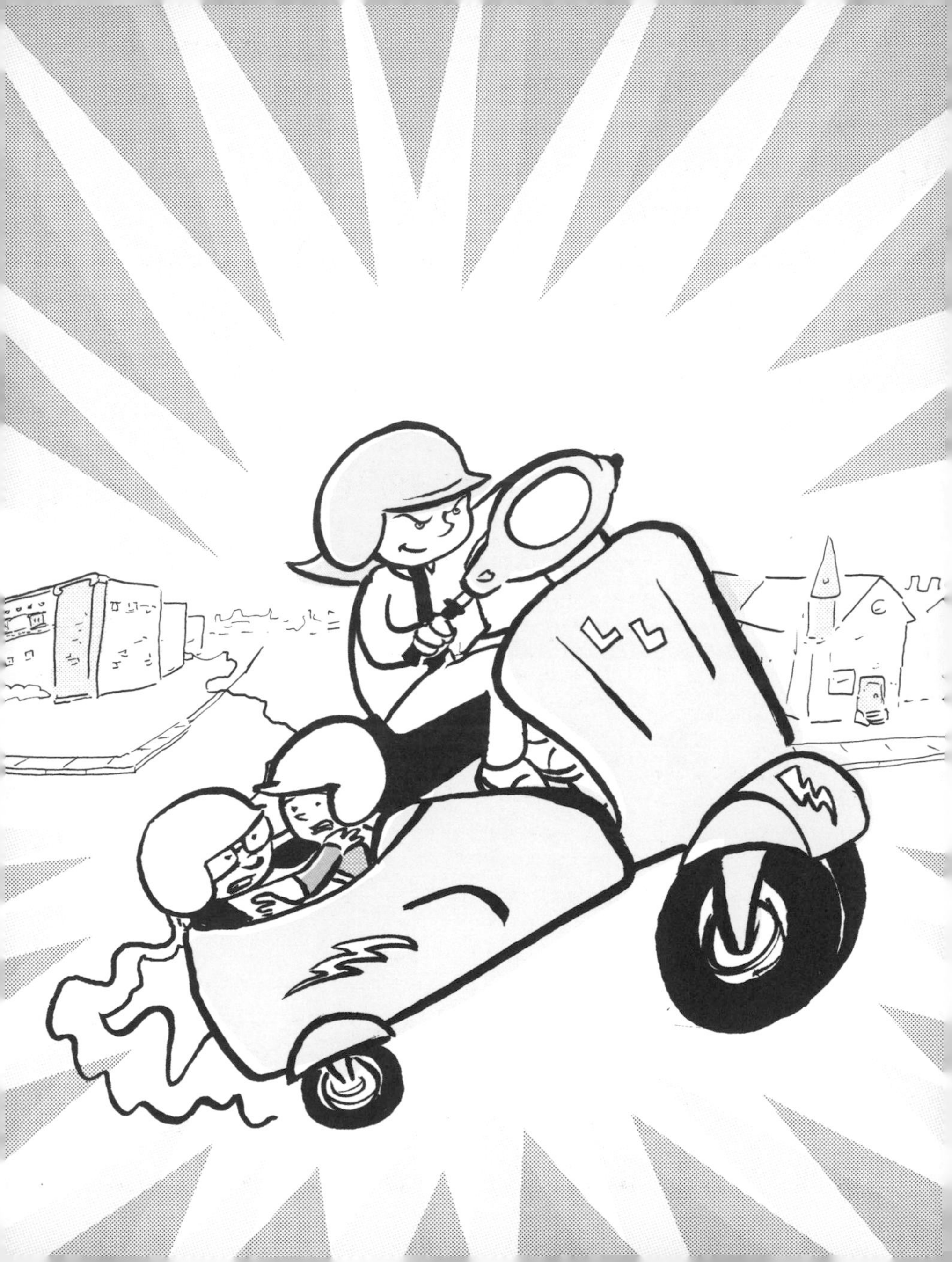

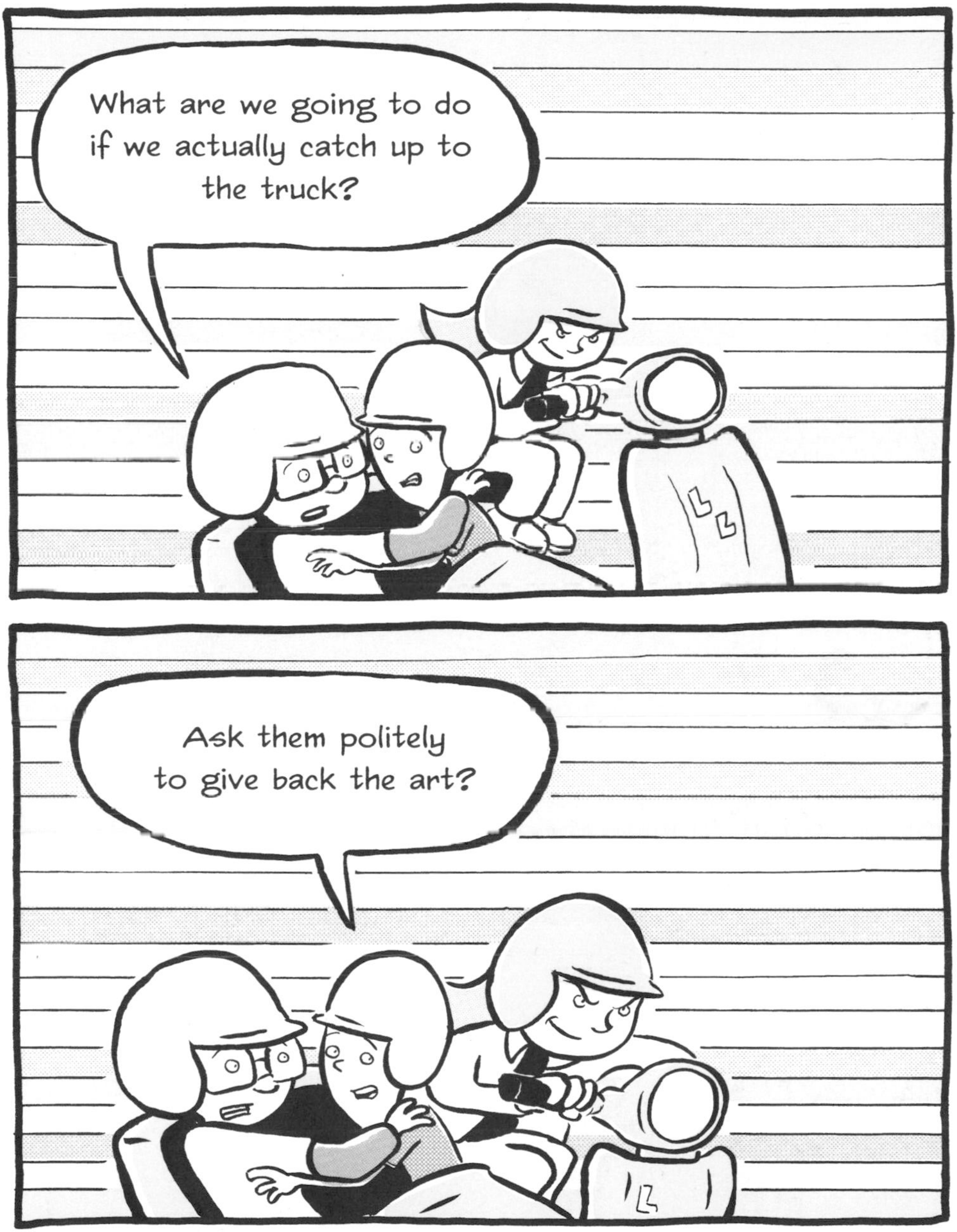
What are we going to do if we actually catch up to the truck?
Ask them politely to give back the art?

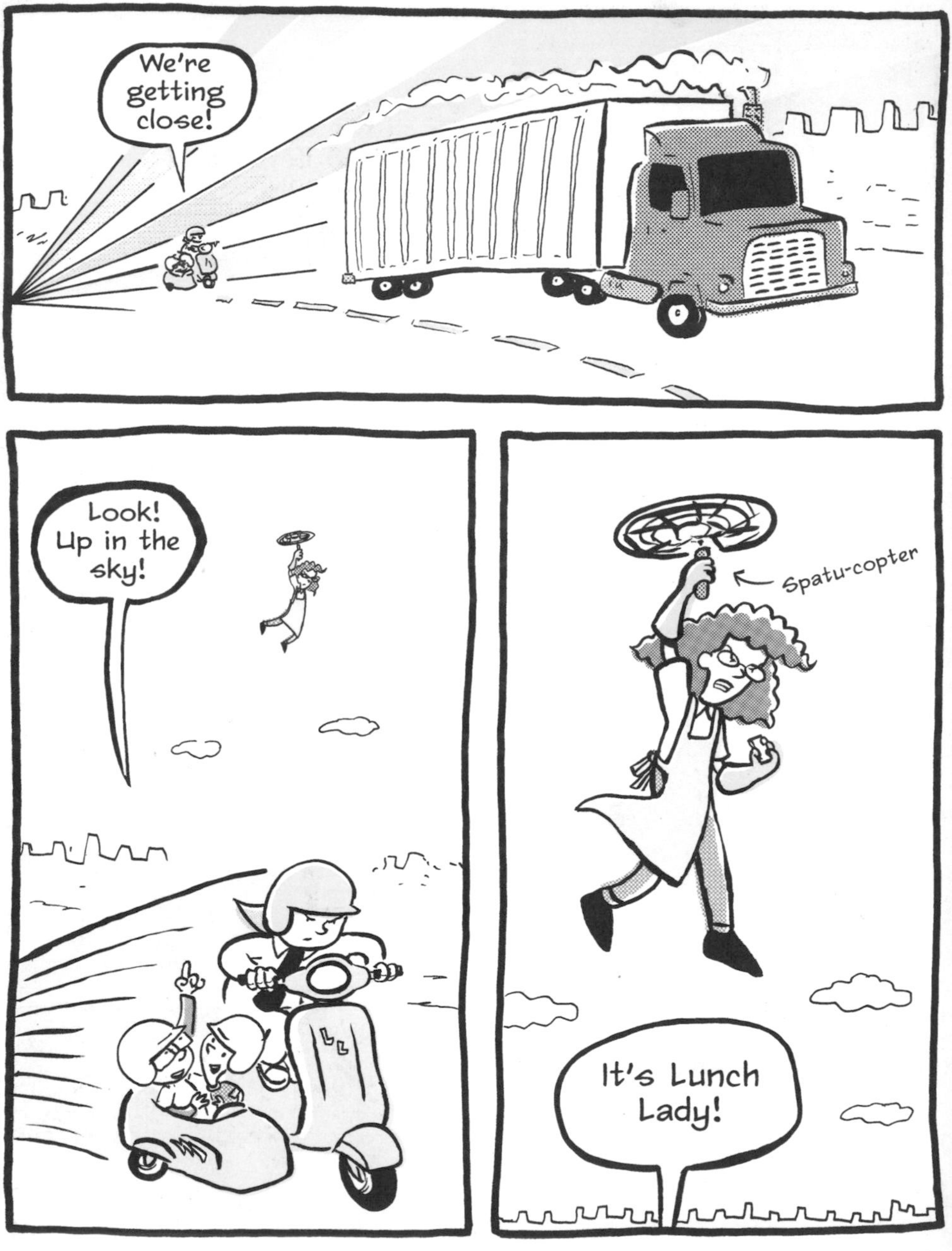
We're getting close!
Look! Up in the sky!
Spatu-copter
It's Lunch Lady!

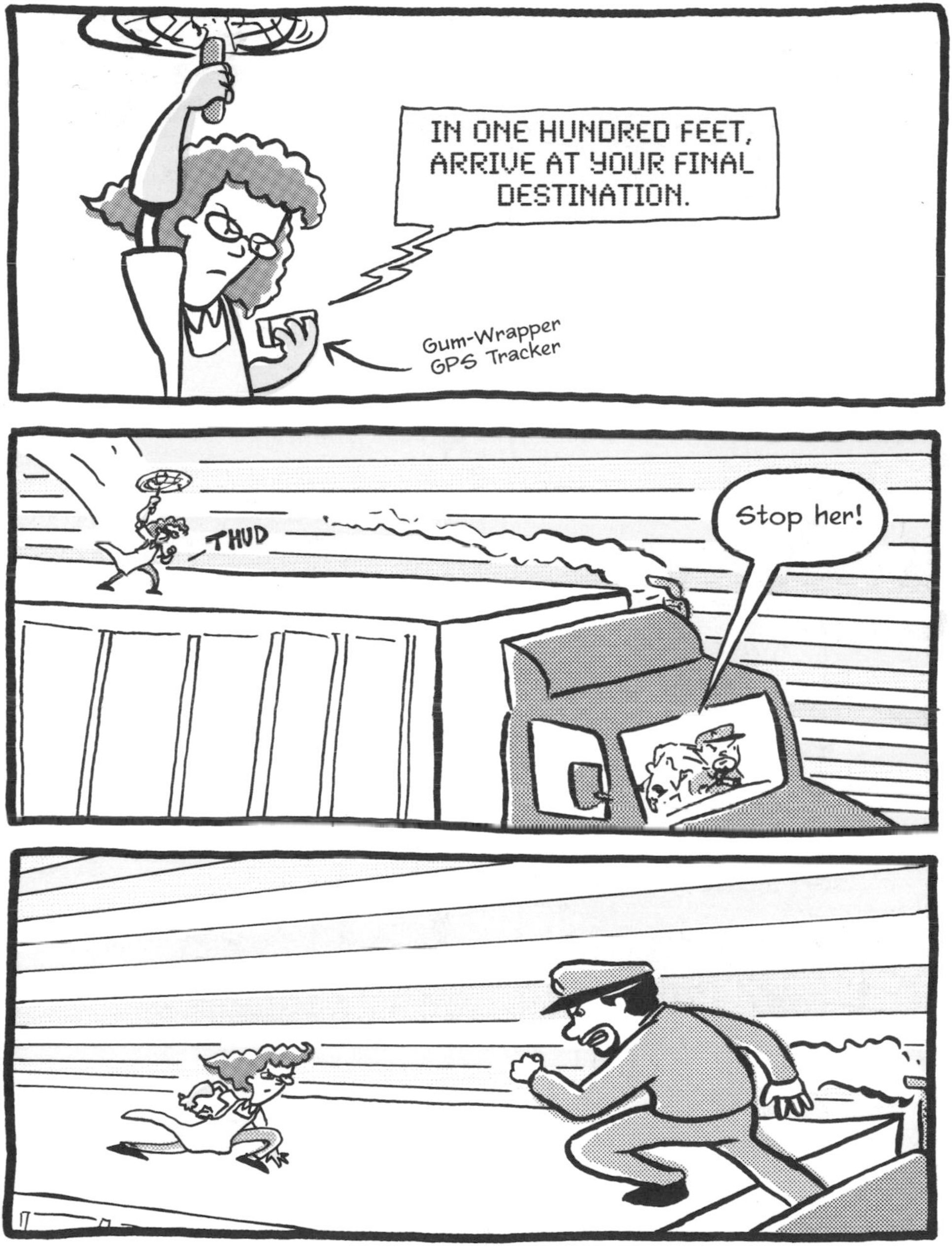
IN ONE HUNDRED FEET, ARRIVE AT YOUR FINAL DESTINATION.
Gum-Wrapper GPS Tracker
THUD
Stop her!

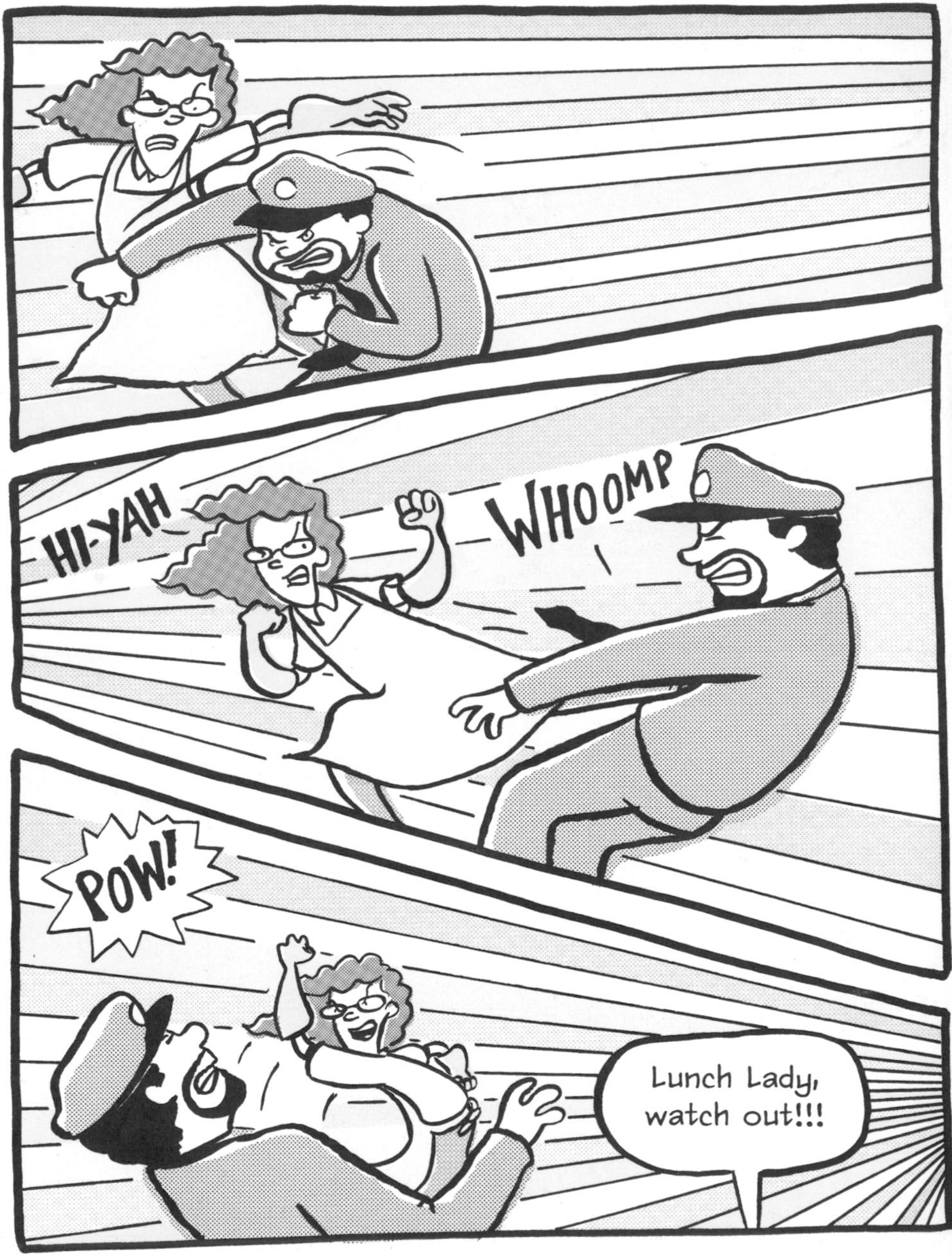
HI-YAH
WHOOMP
POW!
Lunch Lady, watch out!!!

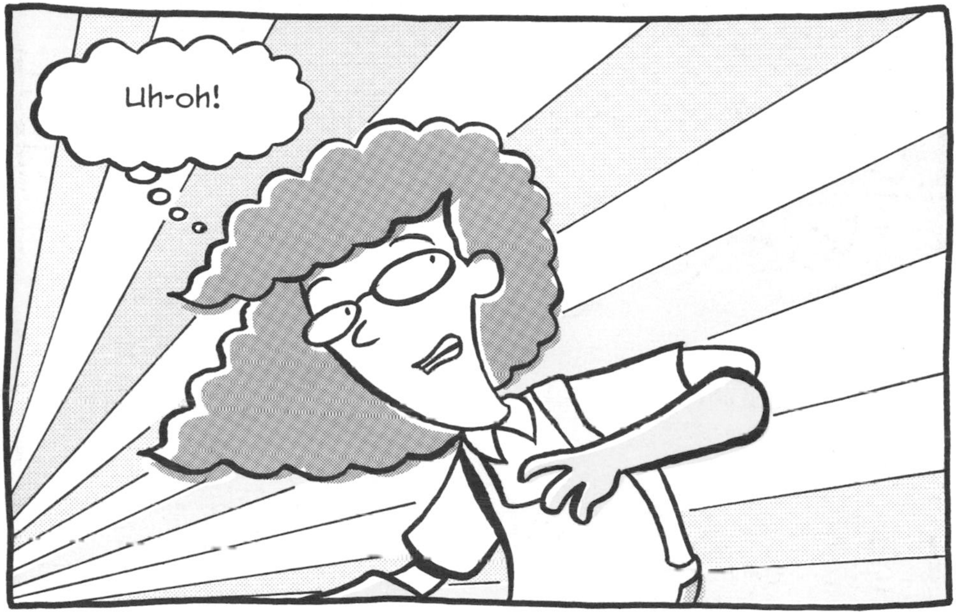
Uh-oh!

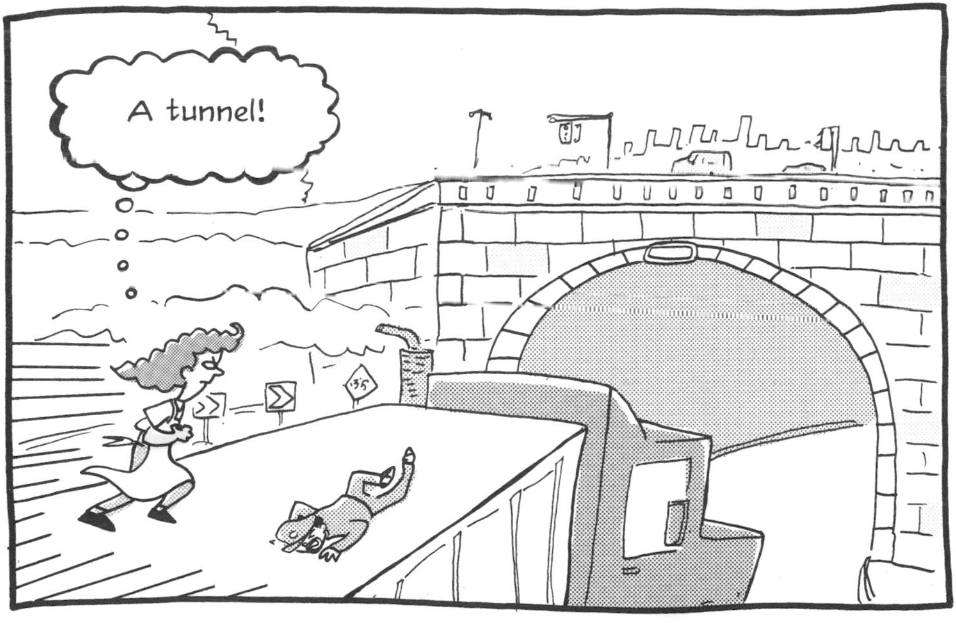
A tunnel!

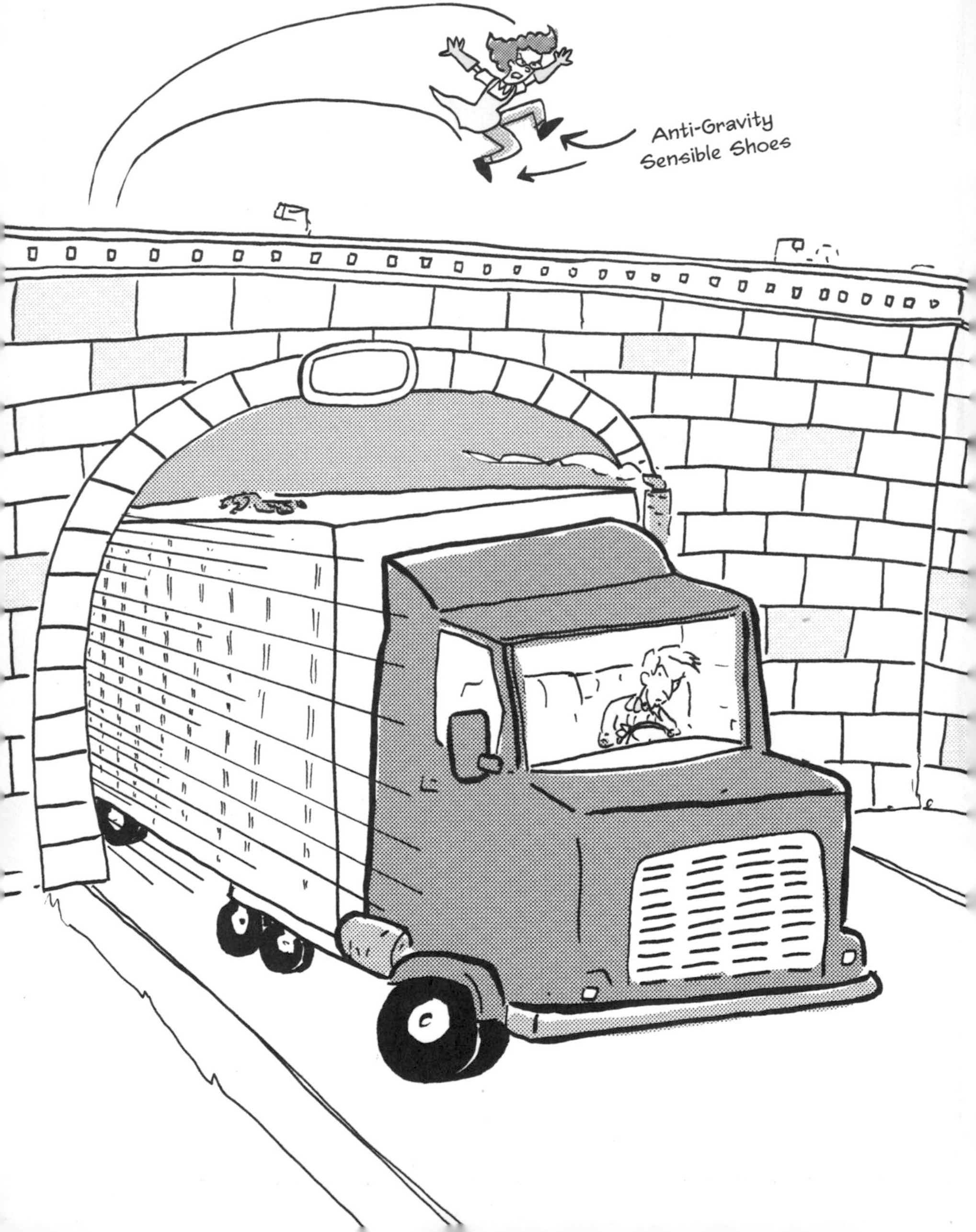
Anti-Gravity
Sensible Shoes

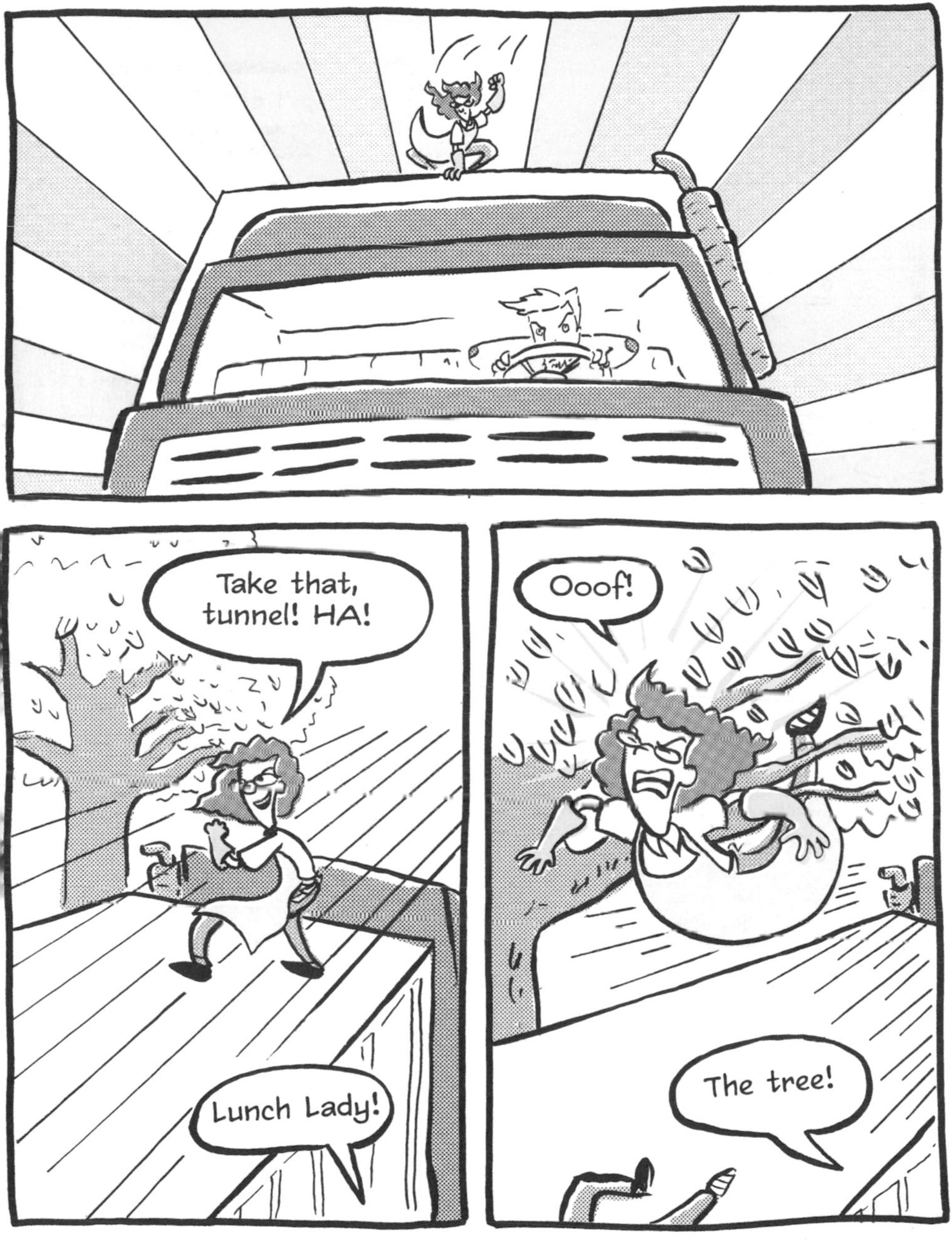
Take that, tunnel! HA!
Lunch Lady!
Ooof!
The tree!

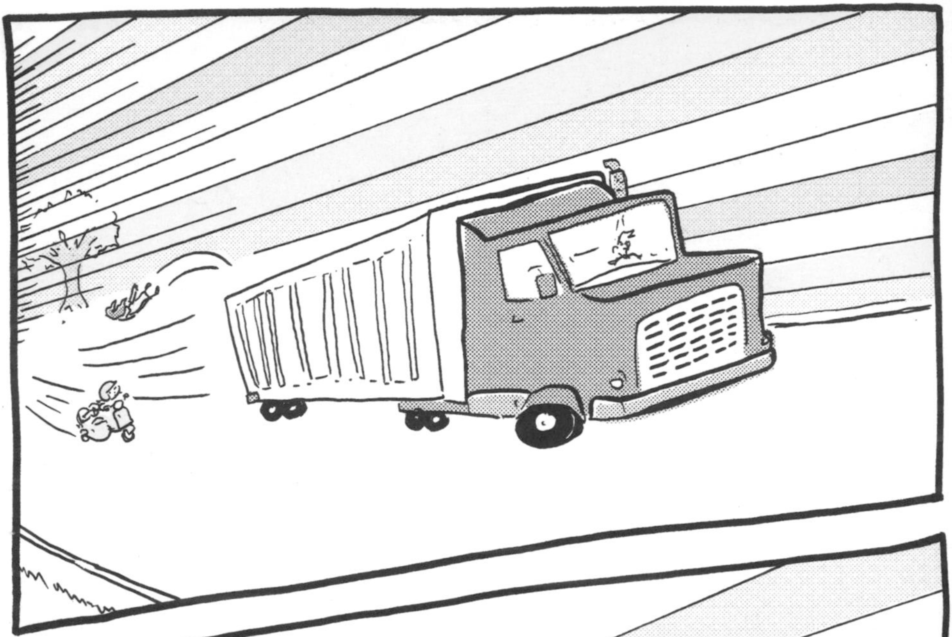

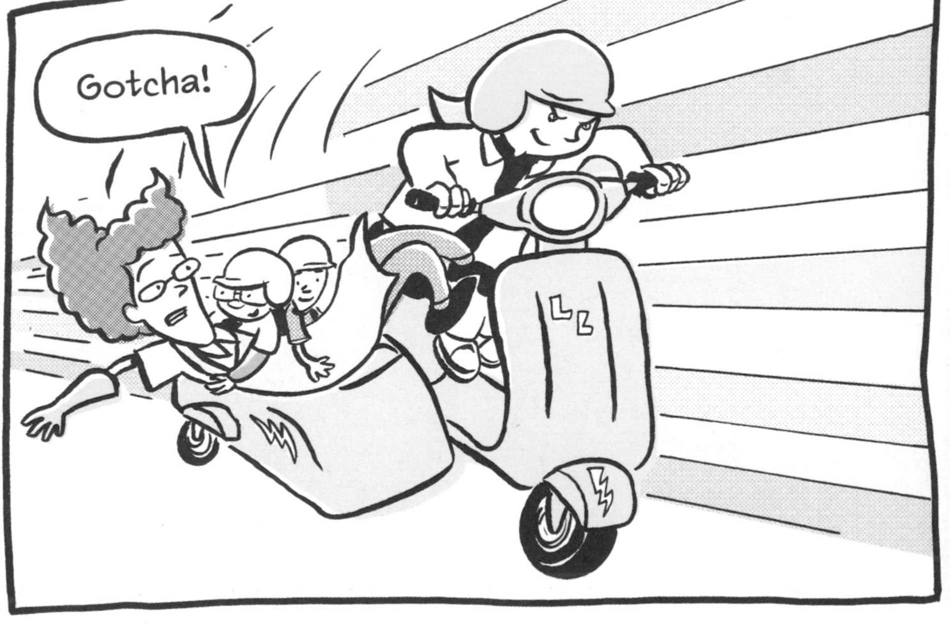
Gotcha!

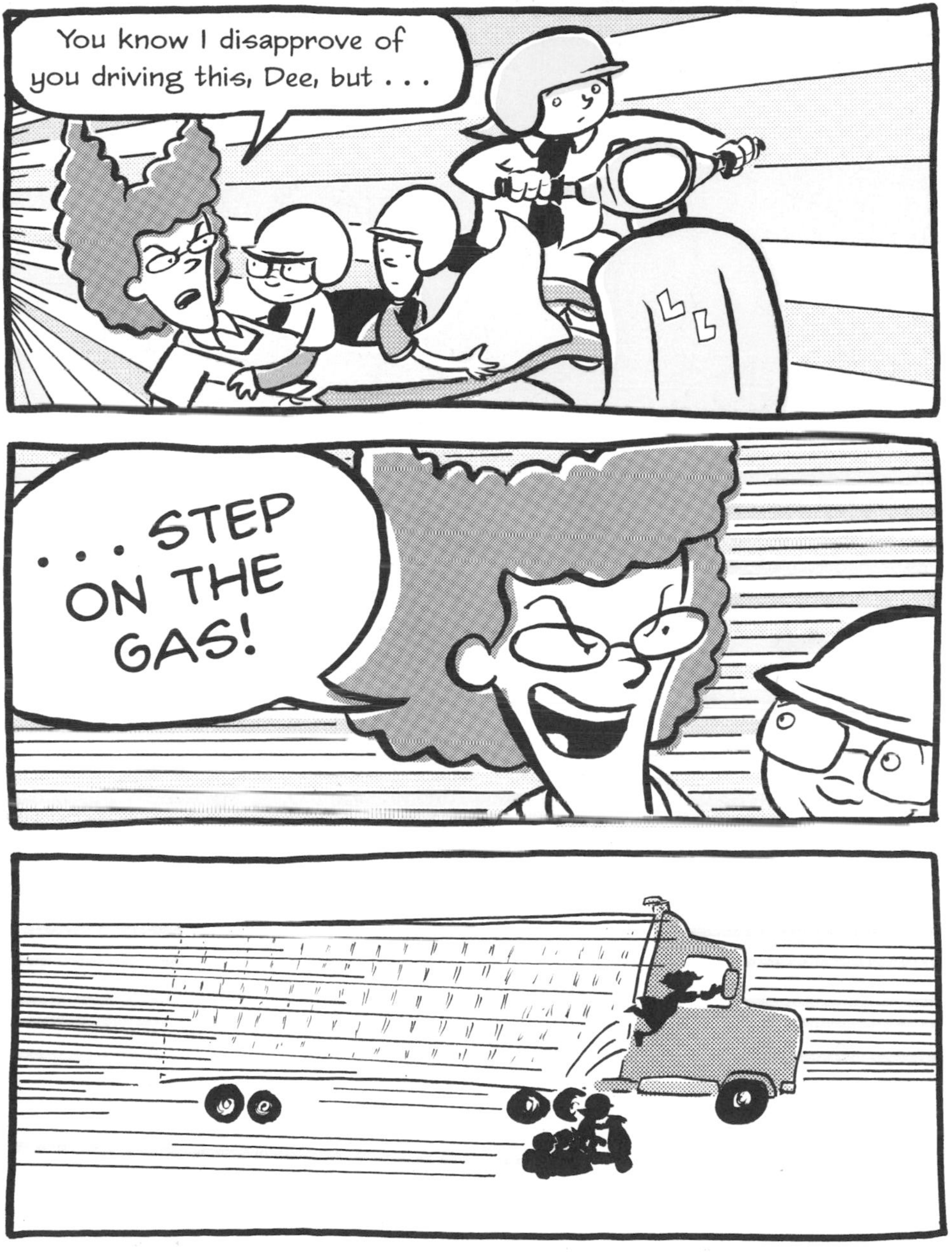
You know I disapprove of you driving this, Dee, but . . .
. . . STEP ON THE GAS!

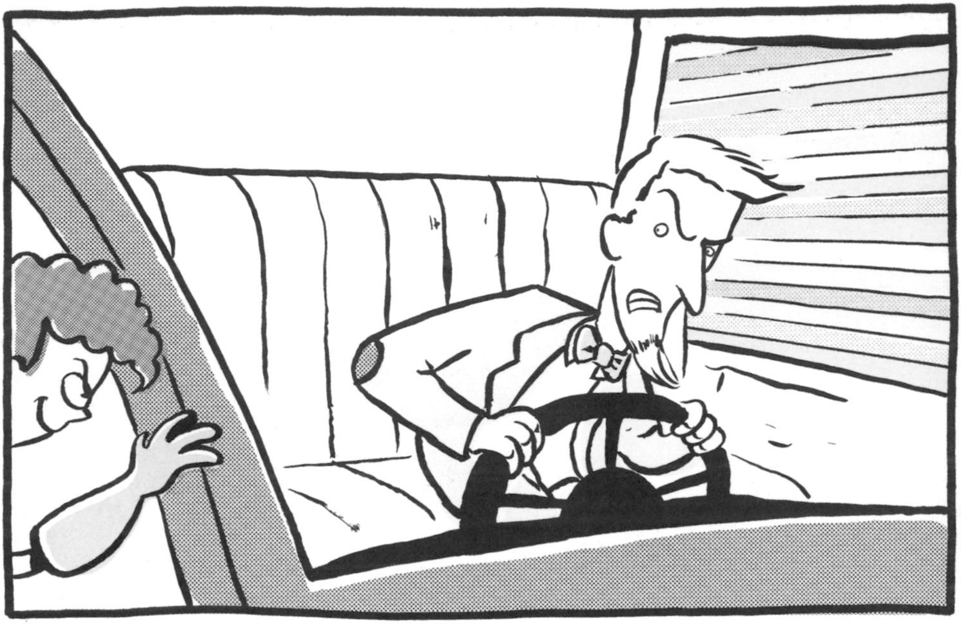

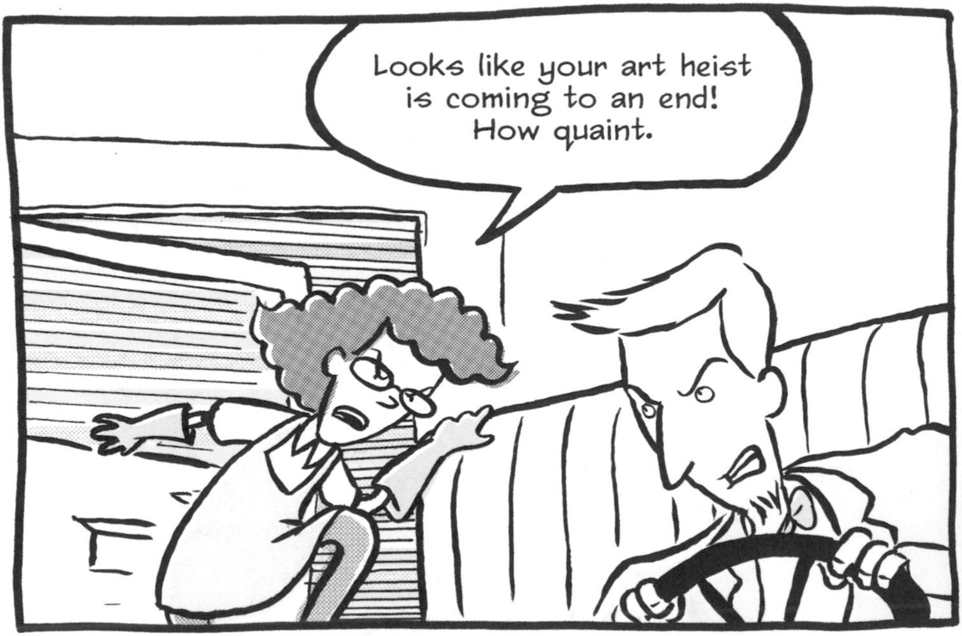
Looks like your art heist is coming to an end! How quaint.

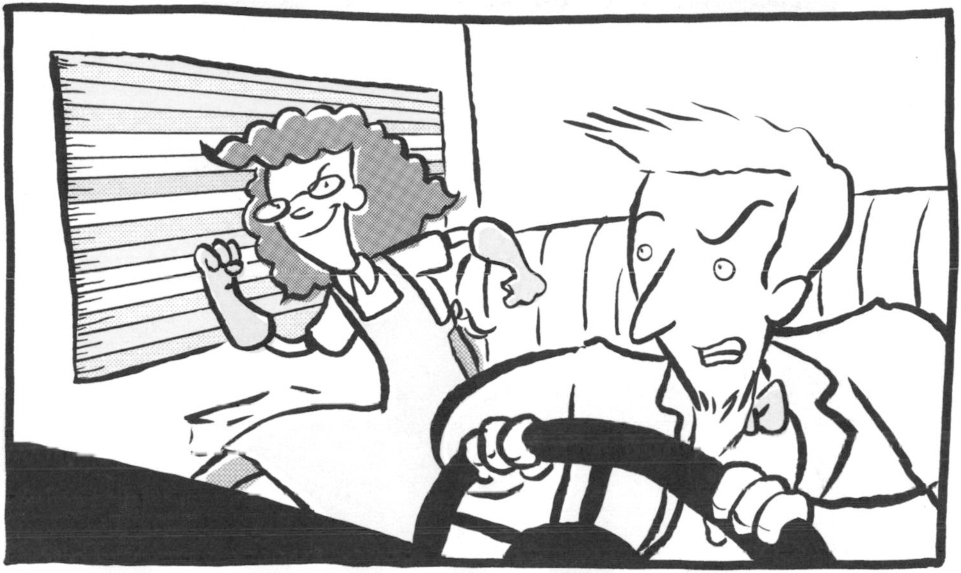

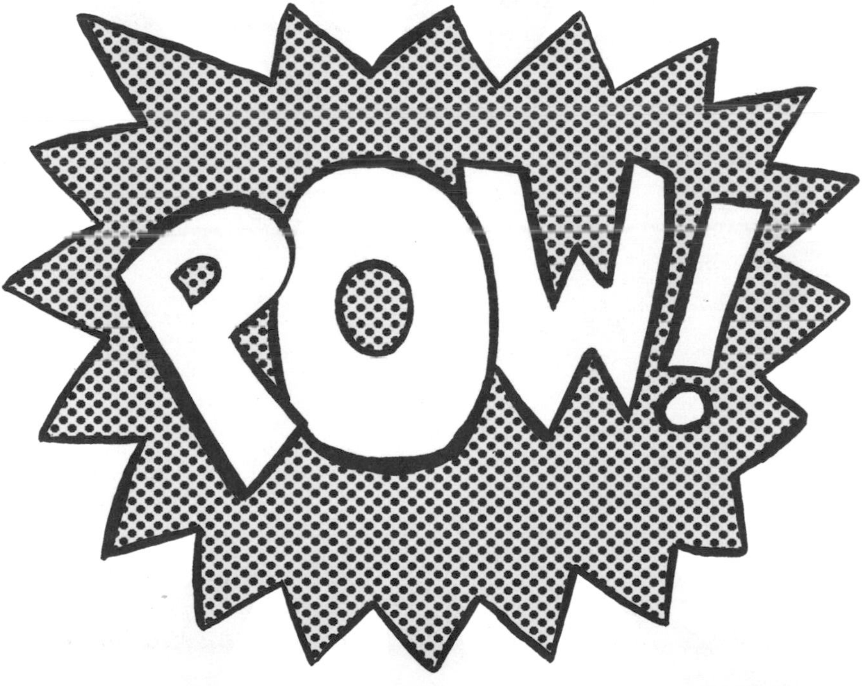
POW!

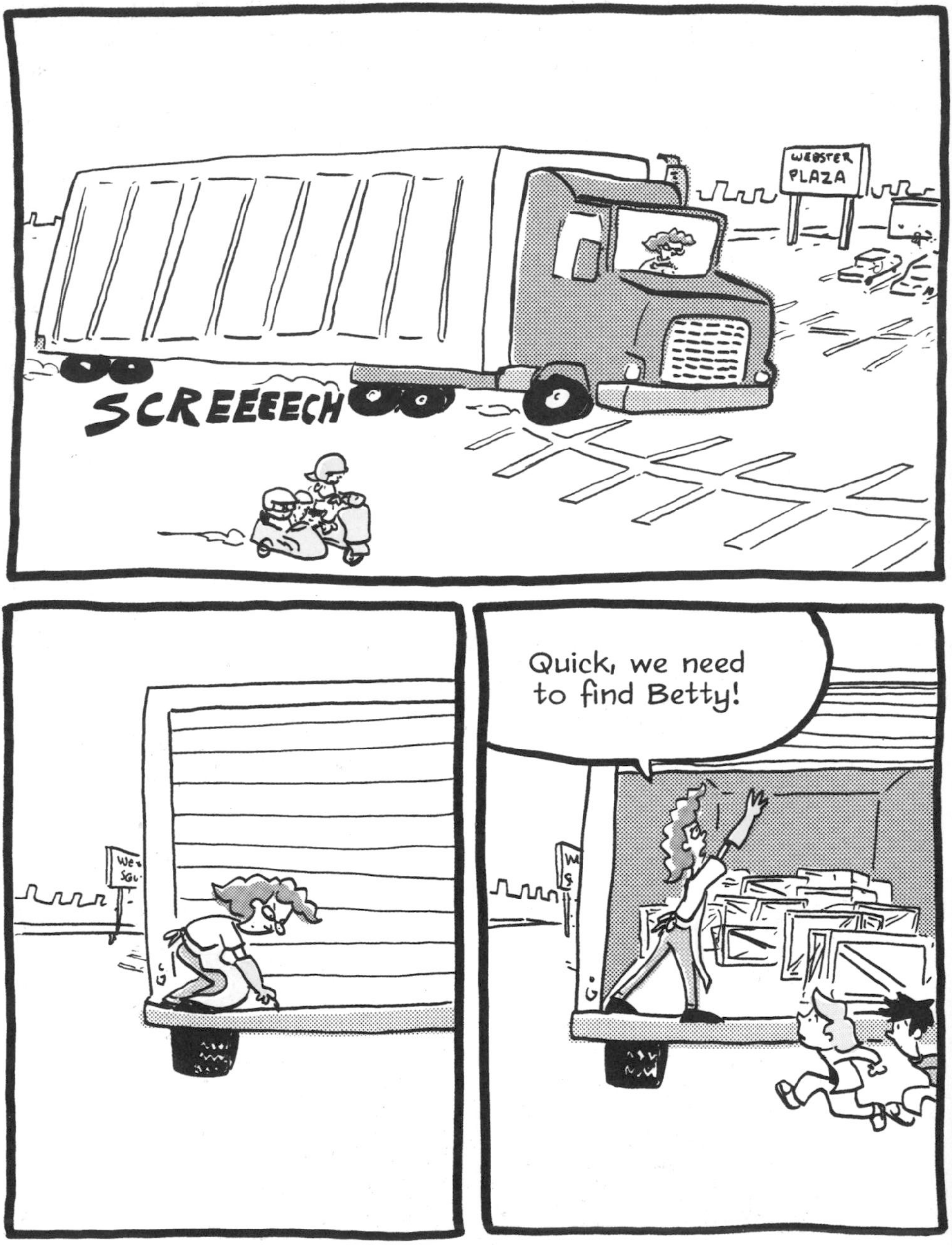
WEBSTER
PLAZA
SCREEEECH
Quick, we need to find Betty!

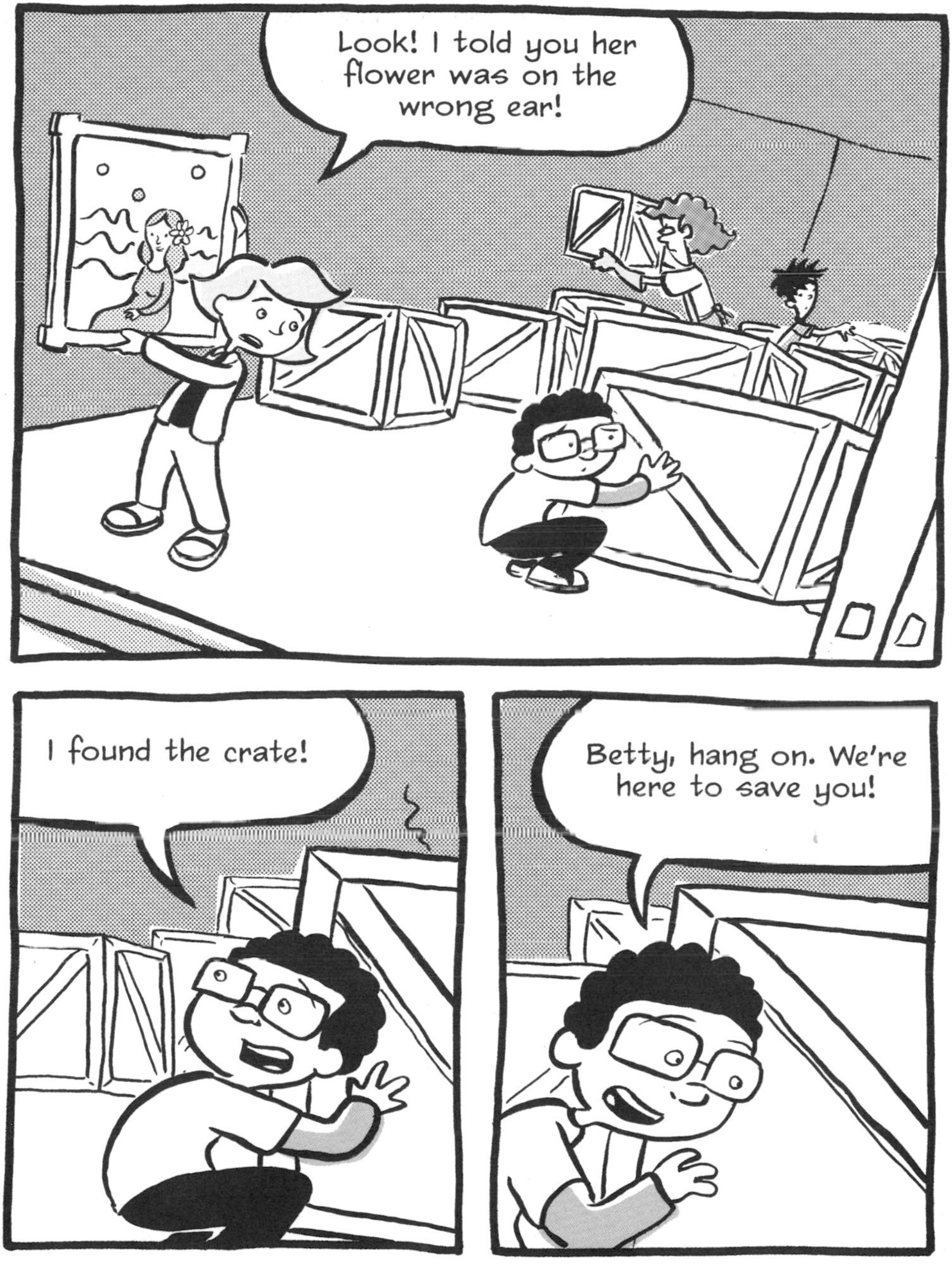
Look! I told you her flower was on the wrong ear!
I found the crate!
Betty, hang on. We're here to save you!

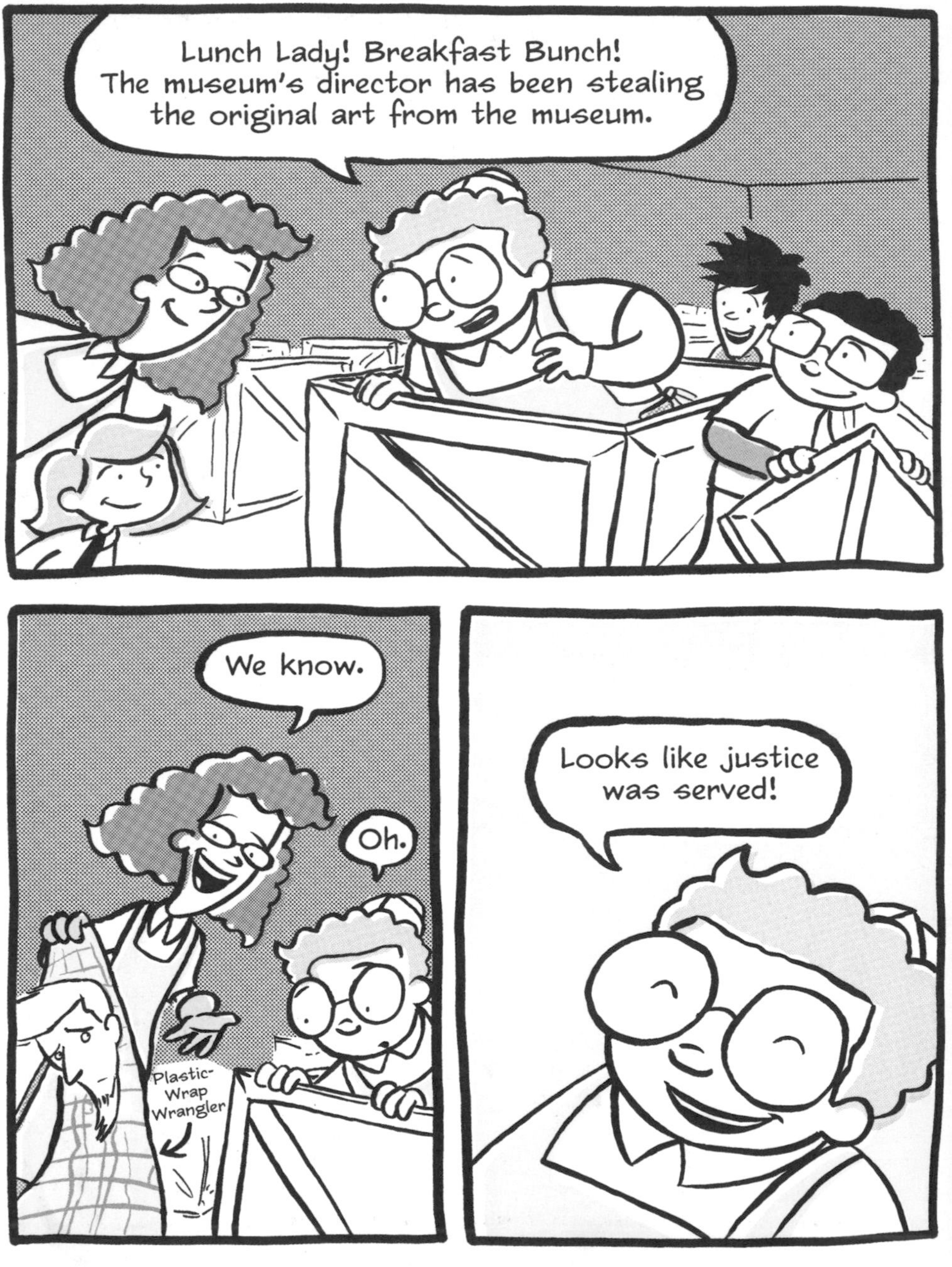
Lunch Lady! Breakfast Bunch! The museum's director has been stealing the original art from the museum.
We know.
Oh.
Plastic-Wrap Wrangler
Looks like justice was served!

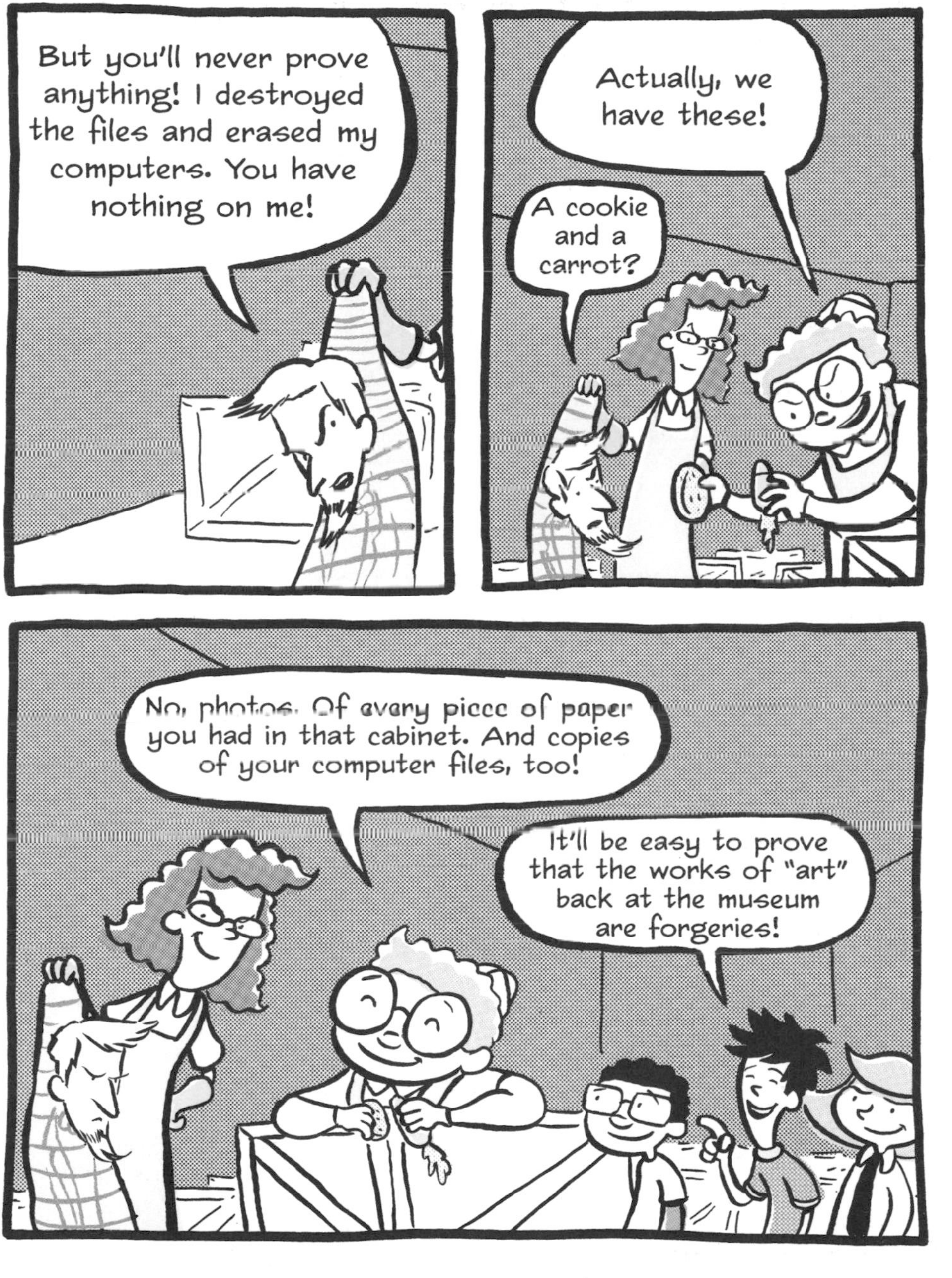
But you'll never prove anything! I destroyed the files and erased my computers. You have nothing on me!
Actually, we have these!
A cookie and a carrot?
No, photos. Of every piece of paper you had in that cabinet. And copies of your computer files, too!
It'll be easy to prove that the works of "art" back at the museum are forgeries!

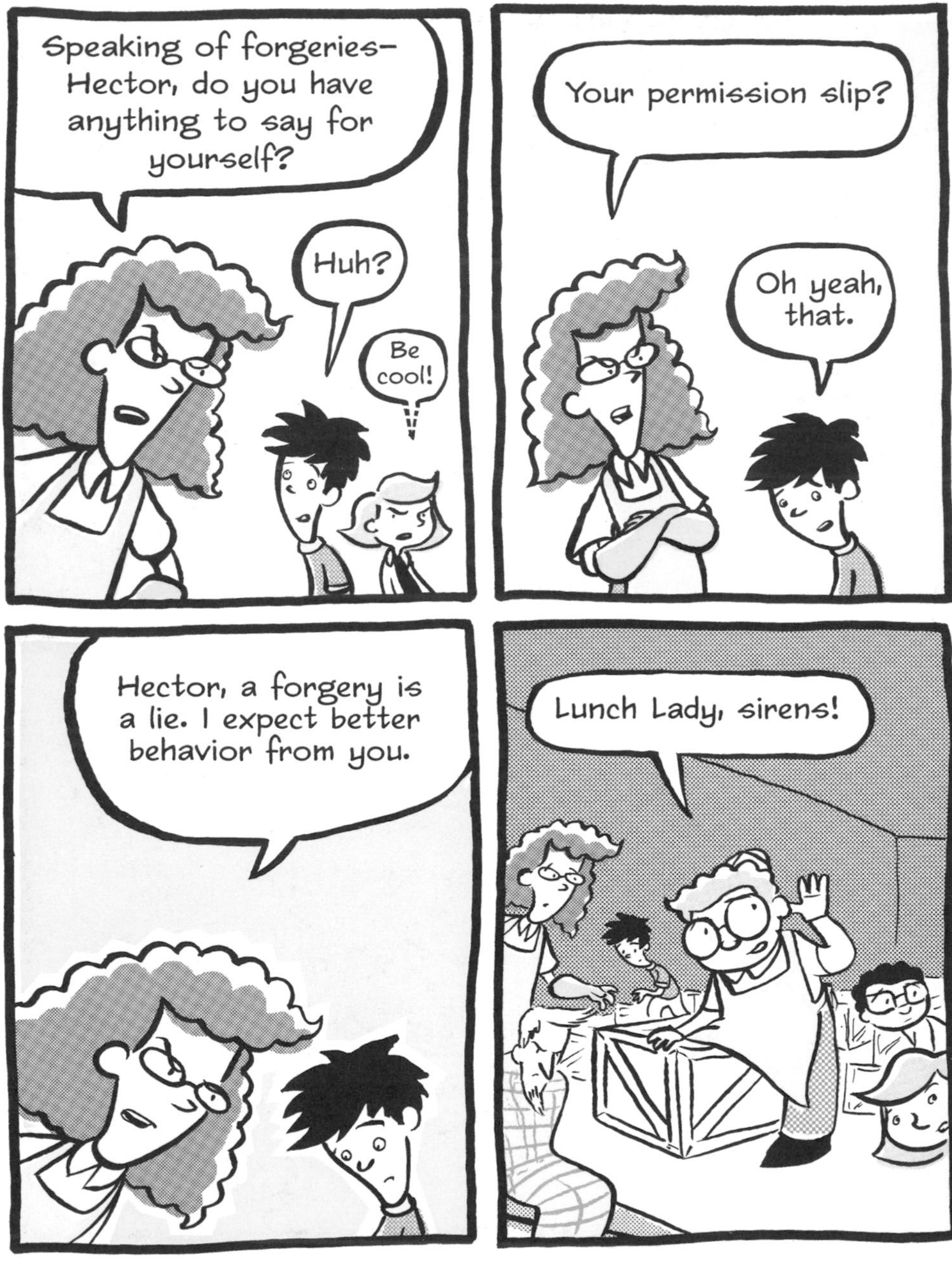
Speaking of forgeries- Hector, do you have anything to say for yourself?
Huh?
Be cool!
Your permission slip?
Oh yeah, that.
Hector, a forgery is a lie. I expect better behavior from you.
Lunch Lady, sirens!

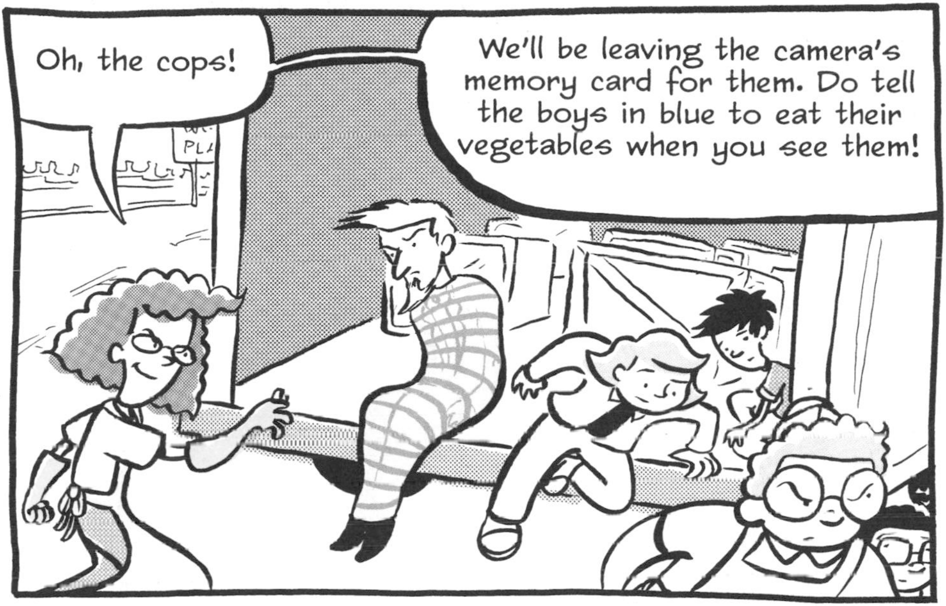
Oh, the cops!
We'll be leaving the camera's memory card for them. Do tell the boys in blue to eat their vegetables when you see them!

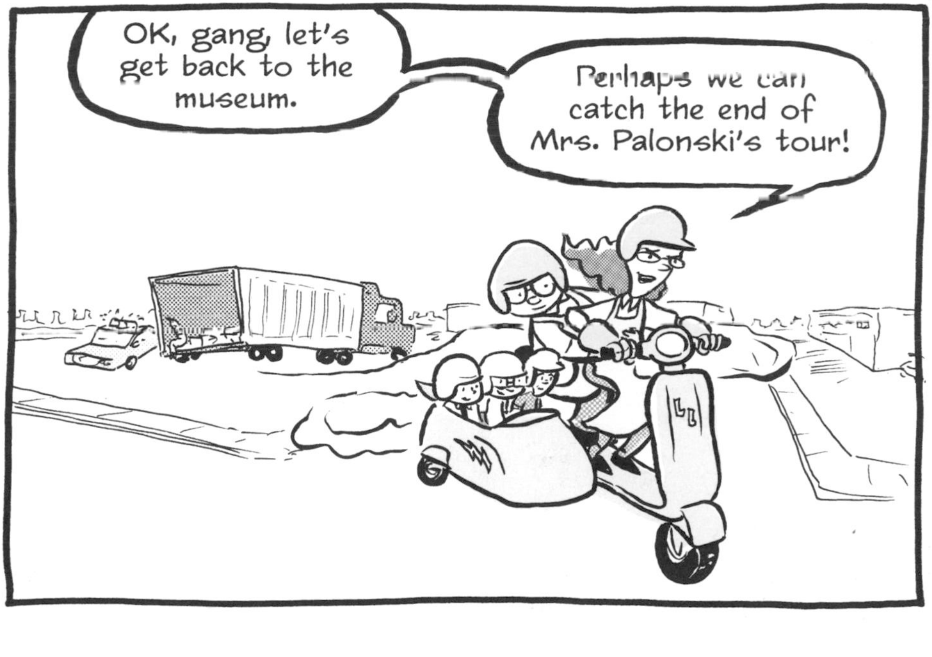
OK, gang, let's get back to the museum.
Perhaps we can catch the end of Mrs. Palonski's tour!

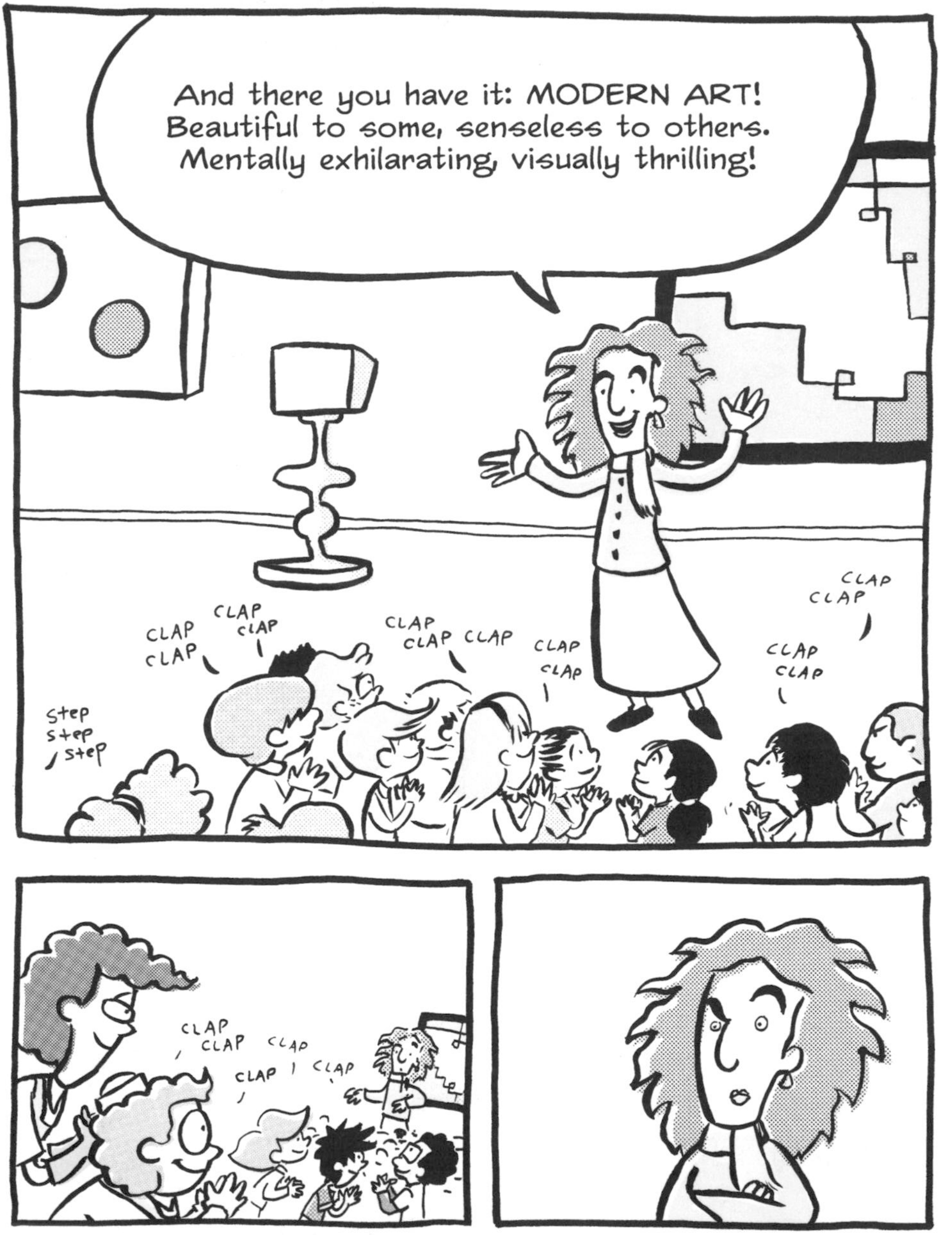
And there you have it: MODERN ART! Beautiful to some, senseless to others. Mentally exhilarating, visually thrilling!
CLAP CLAP
CLAP CLAP
CLAP CLAP CLAP
CLAP CLAP
CLAP CLAP
CLAP CLAP
step step step
CLAP CLAP CLAP
CLAP CLAP

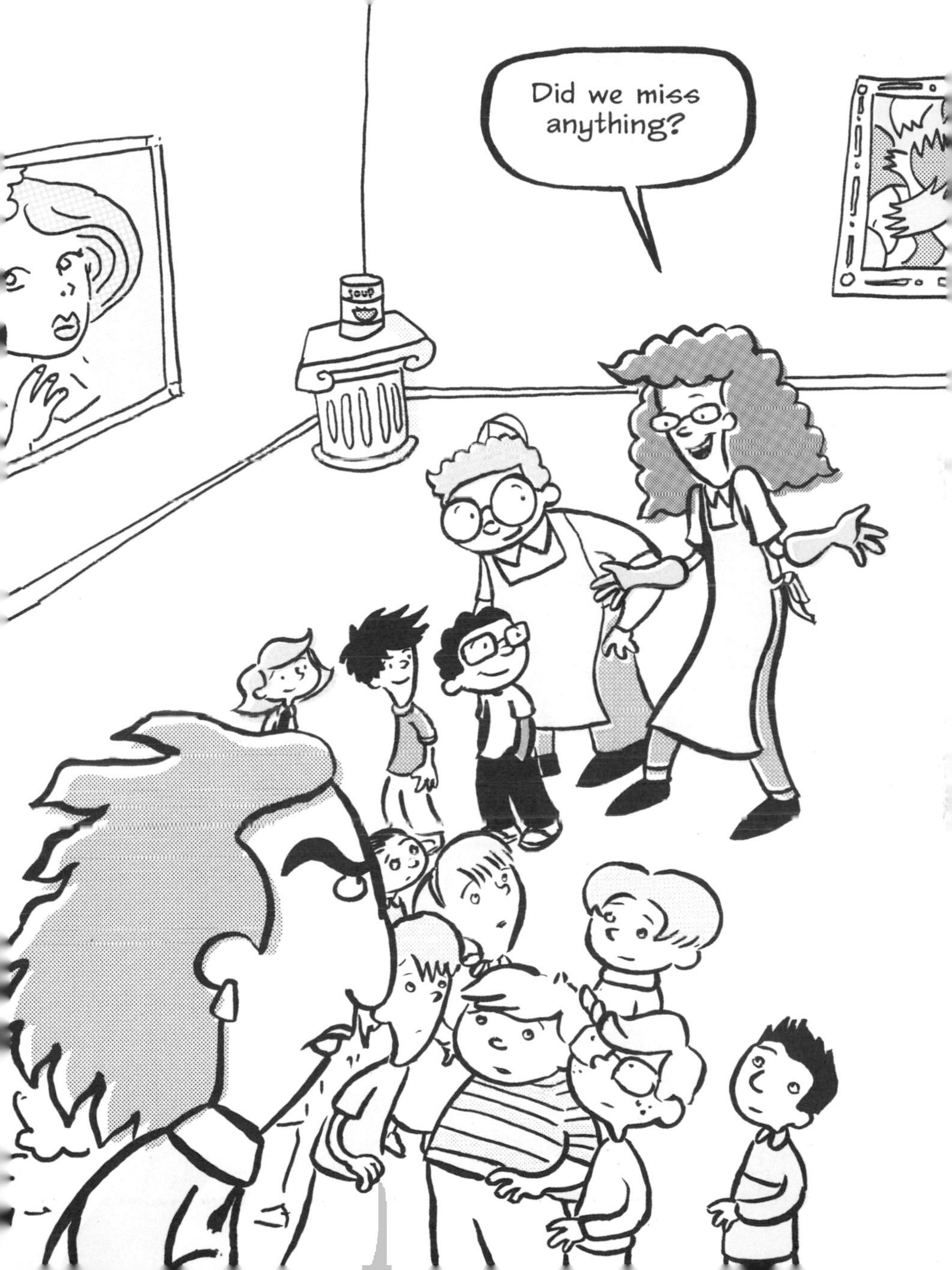
Did we miss anything?

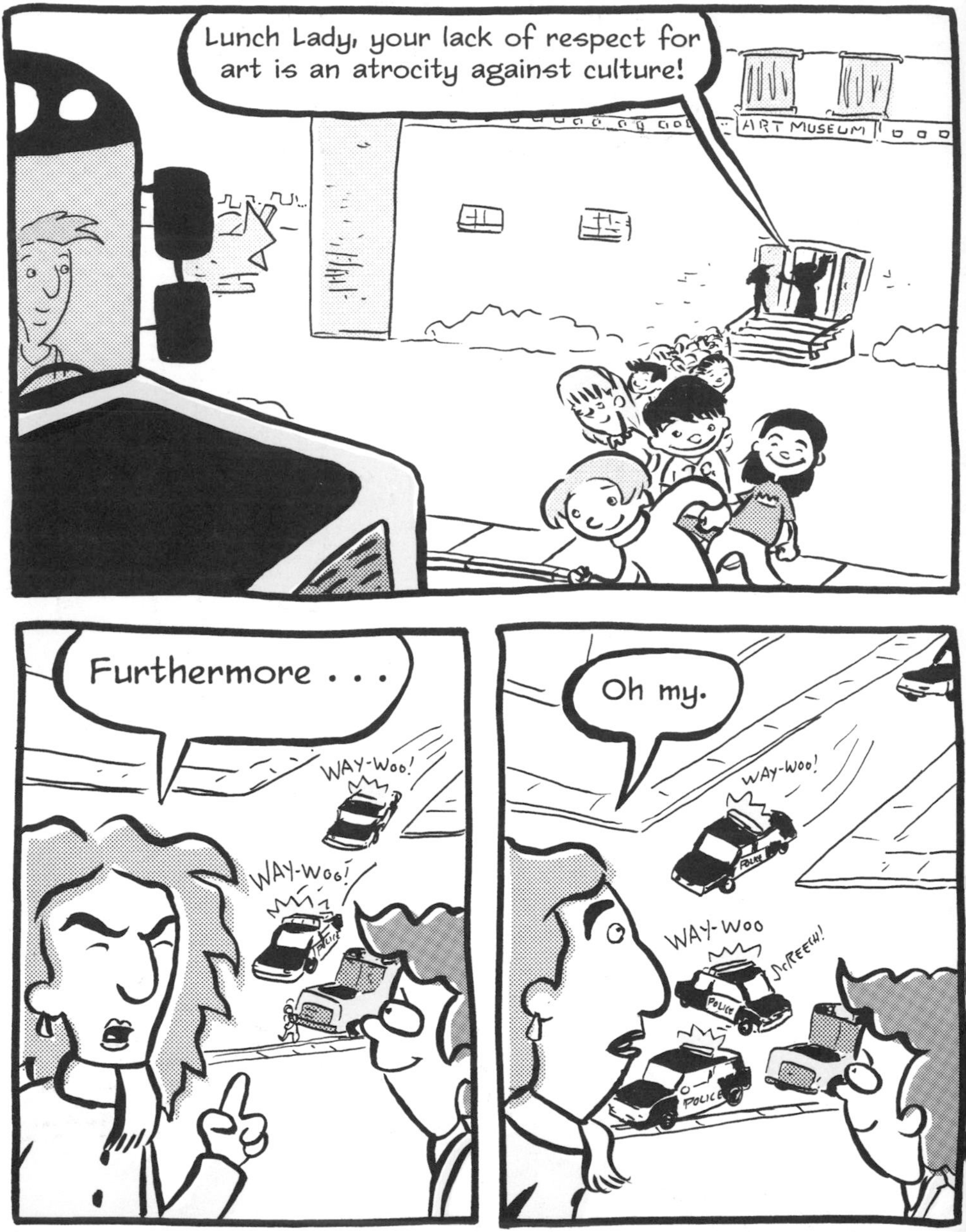
Lunch Lady, your lack of respect for art is an atrocity against culture!
ART MUSEUM
Furthermore . . .
WAY-WOO!
WAY-WOO!
POLICE
Oh my.
WAY-WOO!
POLICE
WAY-WOO
SCREECH!
POLICE
POLICE

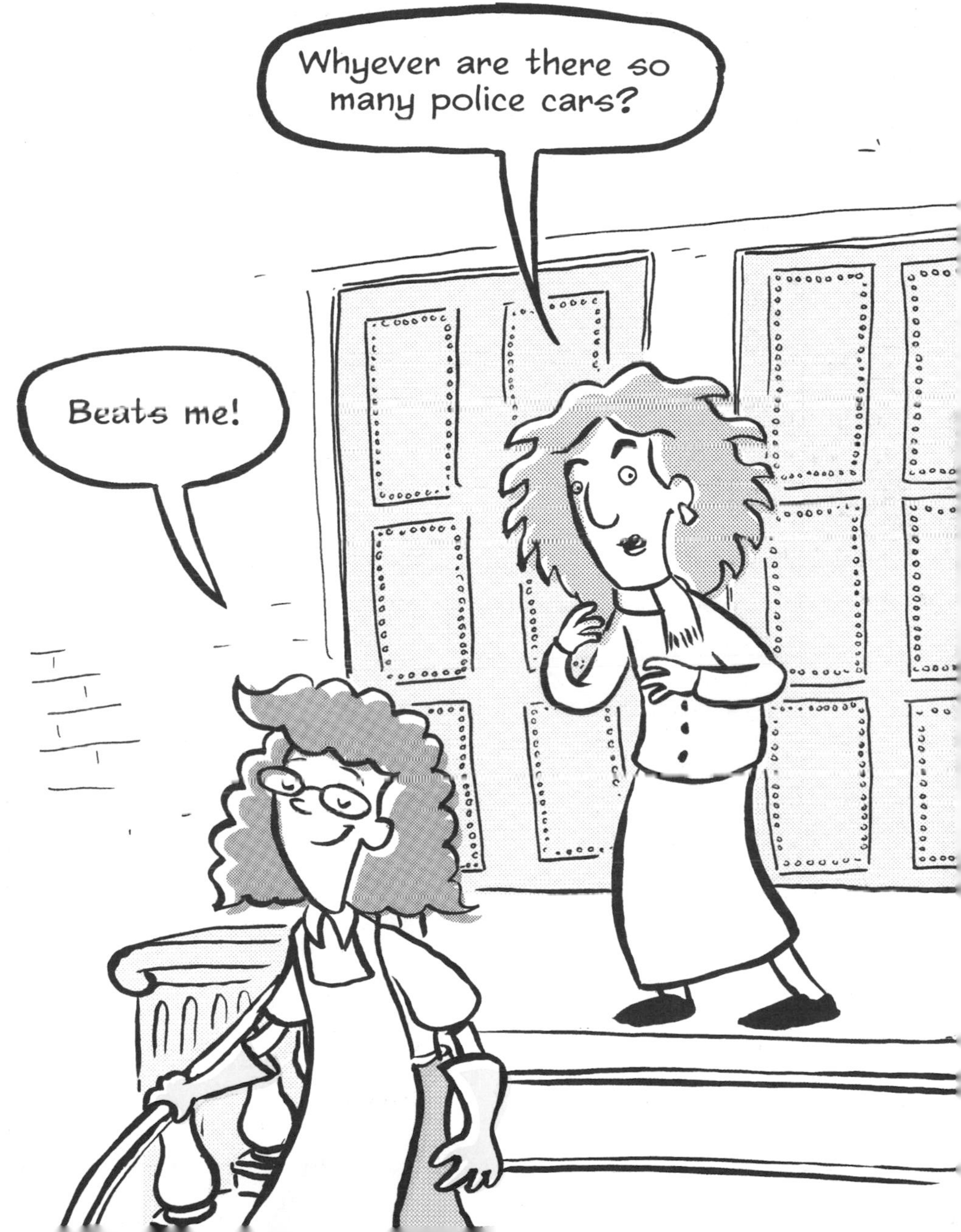
Whyever are there so many police cars?
Beats me!

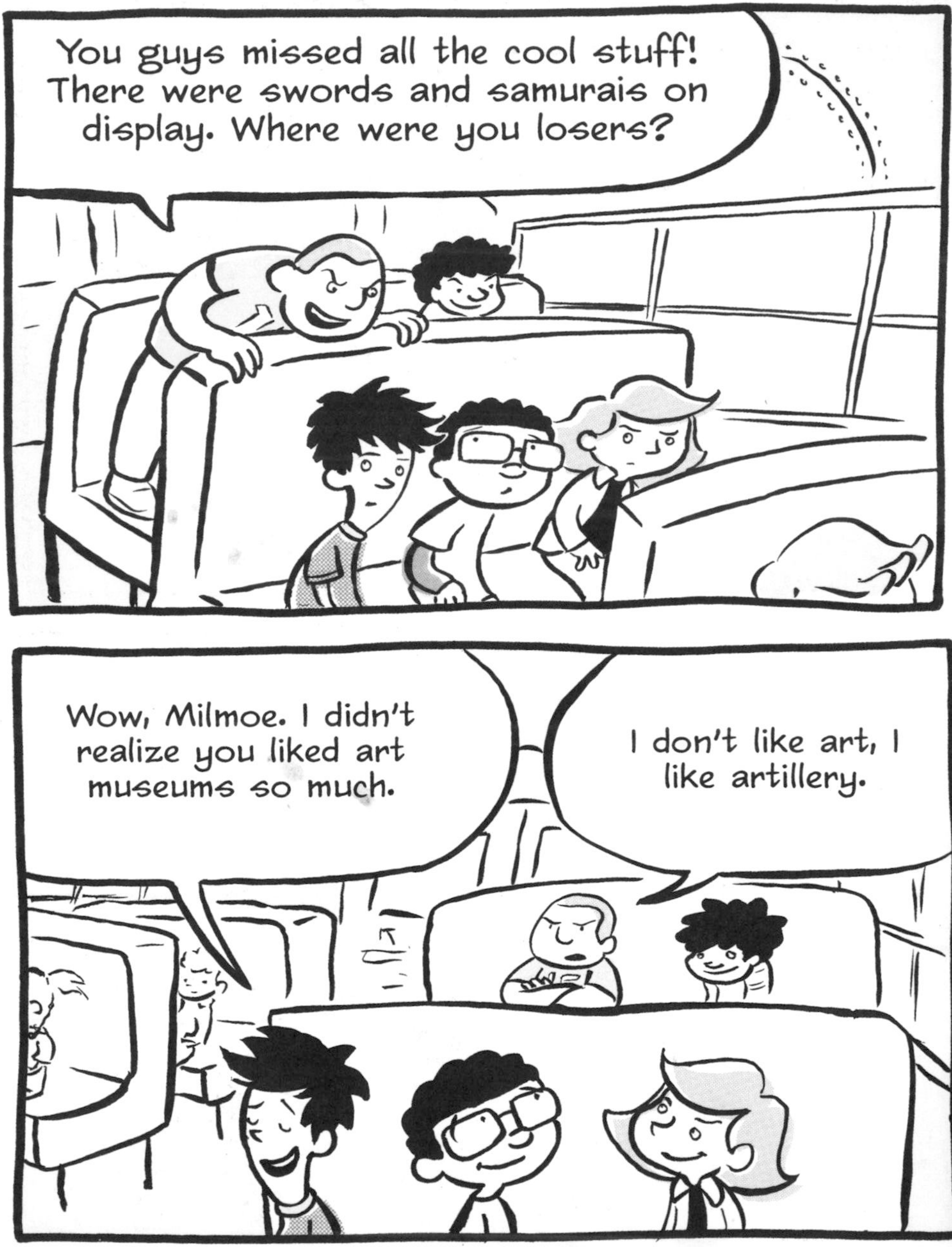
You guys missed all the cool stuff! There were swords and samurais on display. Where were you losers?
Wow, Milmoe. I didn't realize you liked art museums so much.
I don't like art, I like artillery.

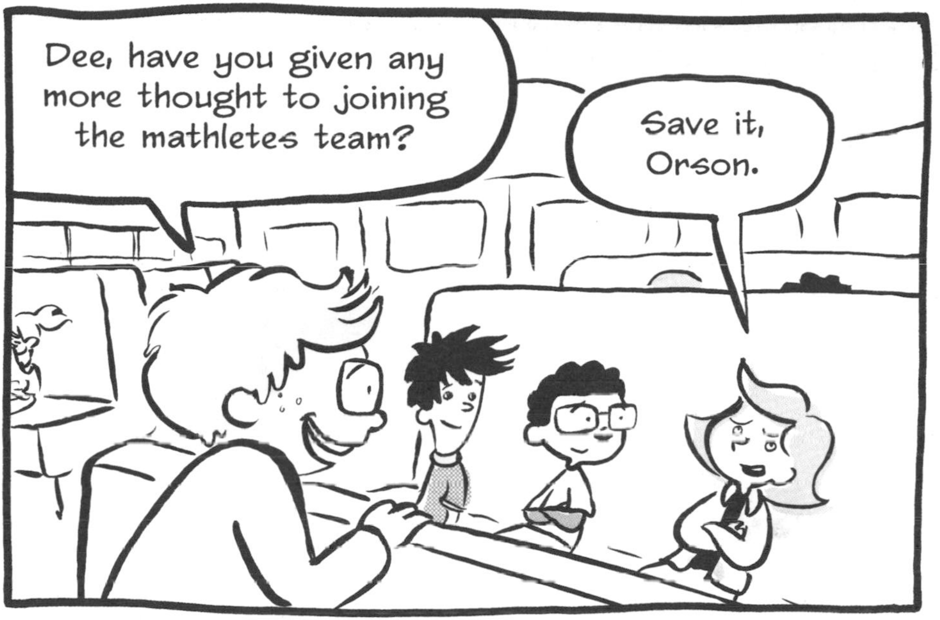
Dee, have you given any more thought to joining the mathletes team?
Save it, Orson.

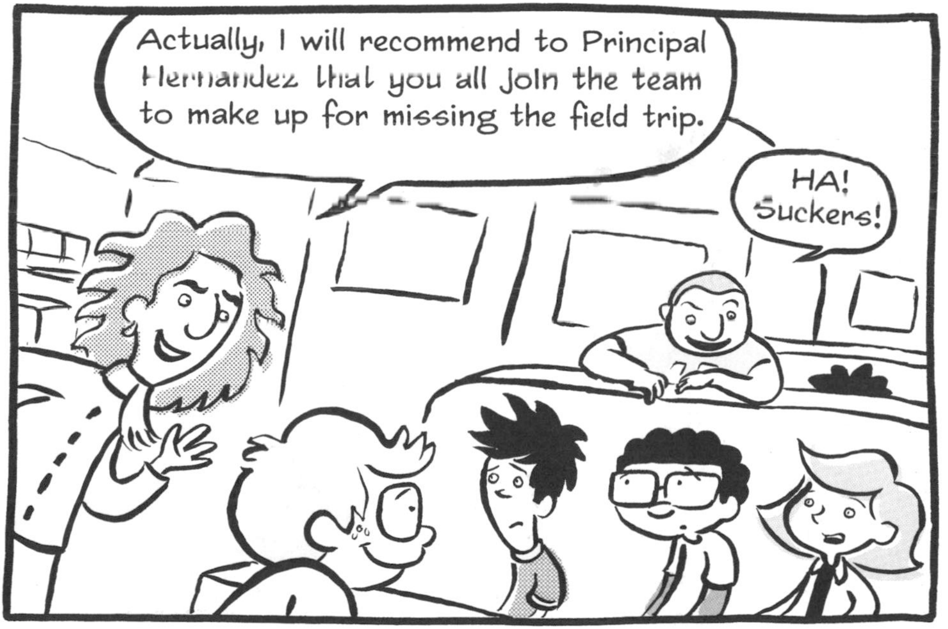
Actually, I will recommend to Principal Hernandez that you all join the team to make up for missing the field trip.
HA! Suckers!

FOR MARK LYNCH

The author would like to acknowledge the color assist in this book by Joey Weiser and Michele Chidester.

THIS IS A BORZOI BOOK PUBLISHED BY ALFRED A. KNOPF

Visit us on the Web! www.randomhouse.com/kids

Educators and librarians, for a variety of teaching tools,
visit us at www.randomhouse.com/teachers

Library of Congress Cataloging-in-Publication Data
Krosoczka, Jarrett.
Lunch Lady and the field trip fiasco / Jarrett J. Krosoczka.
p. cm.
Summary: Lunch Lady, a secret crime fighter, accompanies the Breakfast Bunch on
a class trip to an art museum, but when Dee, Hector, and Terrence begin to think
there is something strange afoot, she suspects nothing.
ISBN 978-0-375-86730-9 (tr. pbk.) — ISBN 978-0-375-96730-6 (lib. bdg.)
1. Graphic novels. [1. Graphic novels. 2. School field trips—Fiction. 3. Art—Forgeries—Fiction.
4. Mystery and detective stories.] I. Title.
PZ7.7.K76Luf 2011
741.5'973—dc22
2011005907

The text of this book is set in Hedge Backwards.
The illustrations in this book were created using ink on paper and digital coloring.

MANUFACTURED IN MALAYSIA
September 2011
10 9 8

First Edition